IF YOU
DARE

HARMONY WEST

ISBN (paperback): 979-8-9881181-3-8

For the readers whose favorite hockey men are masked

AUTHOR'S NOTE

Wes Novak would like me to warn you that his hockey team is called the Devils for a reason. There are few lines they won't cross for revenge. Proceed with caution. For more detailed warnings, visit www.harmonywestbooks.com.

This book includes graphic content. Whether you'd like to skip over or skip to the steamy chapters in this book, you can find these scenes in Chapters 11, 13, 18, 19, 21, 23, 24, 25, 28, 29, 30, and 41.

Chapter 1

After

Violet

I KILLED MY BEST FRIEND.

I didn't mean to. I'd do anything to take it back. But that doesn't matter.

I killed my best friend.

"*Not guilty.*" Outside the courthouse, my mother suppresses her sob with fingers covering her mouth.

Before Chloe, Mom was my best friend. But she hasn't been able to look at me since she heard the news at the beginning of summer.

That her daughter is a killer.

I shade my eyes against the sunlight. No part of this world should be shining anymore without Chloe.

Mom and I make our way to the parking lot in silence.

Not guilty. I'm not guilty, at least according to a judge. But that doesn't make me innocent.

The reckless endangerment charges carried a maximum penalty of two years in prison and a five-thousand-dollar fine. Even with a state-appointed attorney by my side, the judge decided to let me go. We were drunk; it was an accident.

From the courthouse, the Novaks emerge. What once was the perfect foursome, a family I loved and longed to belong to, is now a lonely threesome in semi-formal attire. Two parents who've lost a child and a brother who's lost a sister.

All because of me.

Mr. Novak keeps his arm around his wife's waist. She clutches her purse, nose red-tipped. They both flash me small smiles as they head for their SUV. Somehow, they don't hate me for killing their daughter, even if I hate me.

Wes is another story.

From the shoulders down, he's undeniably perfect. He always has been. Wes Novak, the most gorgeous hockey player at Diamond University. Hell, the most gorgeous guy on the entire campus. The last time I saw him in his black suit and gray button-down was at her funeral. He wore it again today hoping he'd be attending my funeral.

By the look on his face, he's not at all happy to see I'm still alive.

His thick brows pull together, the square edge of his jaw hard as steel. He could crack a nut with those clenched teeth. His previously tamed-for-the-courtroom brown hair is now unruly where he dragged his hands through it after learning my fate. I can't count how many times I've imagined running my hands through that hair.

His normally bright, mischievous blue eyes sear through me. Blazing with white-hot fury.

His parents may have forgiven me for the mistake I made that night.

But Wes hasn't.

Chapter 2

Before

Violet

THERE's a half-naked man in my dorm room. He pushes off the bed with neatly made pink sheets when he spots me, nothing but a white towel wrapped around his waist. I nearly drop the heavy box of books in my hands. We stare at each other in silence, both of us at a loss for words. He's the most gorgeous guy I've ever seen in person. The kind of beauty that only seems to exist on magazine covers. The kind of beauty that embarrasses you just by noticing it because you know you'll never be able to look away. Dark, wet hair that drips onto his bare shoulders, bulging biceps that make my mouth go dry, tanned stomach lined with a six-pack, and startling blue eyes that are like magnets, pulling me in.

He must be my roommate's boyfriend. Good for her, though I'll probably die of jealousy.

"You the new roommate?" He flashes a lopsided smile like he can read my thoughts.

"Yeah," I squeak, immediately hating myself. "I'm Violet."

Guys this gorgeous don't know I exist, let alone talk to me. I'm completely out of my element. I have no idea what to say, where to look, how to stand. I'm starting to forget how to breathe.

"Don't worry, I won't make it a habit of walking around your dorm in a towel." His low baritone sends tingles all the way to my toes. "I helped my sister move her stuff in, and I needed a shower. I'm just waiting for her because she has my student ID."

Brother.

My heart practically dances before I remember that he could still have a girlfriend. A guy this gorgeous can't walk around in girls' dorms half-naked and not have a million of them lining up to date him.

He strides toward me, planting his hands on the box. My heart stops at his nearness. He's a giant in front of me, his eyes a darker shade of blue the closer he gets. I pray he can't hear me swallow.

"I'm Wes." He takes the box and places it on the empty bed. To my horror, he pries it open.

"Wait, don't—"

But he's already picking up a book and examining the cover, then the blurb on the back. I want to melt into a puddle and not be conscious anymore. A romcom with a cutesy illustrated cover and a blurb about two coworkers who can't stand working together until an assignment forces them to collaborate and they fall in love.

I cannot let my new roommate's *brother* read my stash of alpha male romance novels.

"Wow, you read a lot of books. You must be smart."

Some small ember deep in my chest flickers at the compliment.

Other than my mom—who heaps praise on me to counteract my nonexistent self-esteem—no one has ever said something positive about my book collection. Usually, I only get questions about why my nose is always in a book and why I'd rather be reading than just about anything else.

A slender girl glides into the room, her curtain of blonde hair trailing behind her. She grimaces when she spots Wes. "Ew, put some clothes on. You're scarring my new roommate." She flashes a megawatt smile and wraps me in a hug that has a lot more strength behind it than I'd suspect from someone so petite. "Hey, roomie!"

Chloe and I have been texting for a few weeks since we got the notice we'd be roommates, coordinating what each of us would bring and ensuring the other isn't a serial killer. Like her brother, Chloe is absolutely stunning. Bright blue eyes, pearly white teeth, pert button nose. Angelic and lithe in a way that makes you want to poke her to make sure she's real.

"You need help moving your stuff in?" Wes asks me.

"My mom's helping me." I glance over my shoulder, but she must still be chatting with the RA about how they need to keep an eye on me since I've never been away from home before. Naive and completely unprepared for the real world. For navigating conversations with beautiful half-naked men in my room.

"I'll help," he says simply.

My heart beats faster, already imagining our forced proximity for the next hour, getting to breathe in his cologne and watch him lift my heaviest belongings with those biceps that could crush my skull. "That's okay. You just got a shower. I don't have that much stuff."

"It's no big deal—"

"Stop talking to us while you're *naked!*" Chloe shields her eyes and holds out his student ID. "Put some damn clothes on. You're grossing us out."

Wes flashes a cocky grin and gestures to his abs. "What do you think, Violet? Is my body gross?"

God no.

"Out!" Chloe commands and Wes finally listens, snatching his card and chuckling while he heads out the door.

As soon as he's gone, Chloe glides across the room like a wraith and flops onto her bed, propping her head up in her hand. Her side of the dorm is already fully decorated with fairy lights, paper lanterns, a desk organizer, a photo rack full of pictures, and wall art of her skating across ice with a foot in the air.

She's got that unobtainable, cool-girl aura. The type of girl who would've overlooked me in high school, surrounded by friends who were way more fun and exciting and bold like her. Nothing like me.

"You think my brother's cute," she accuses.

My eyes practically bug out of my head. If I was still holding my box of books, I'd definitely drop them. "What? No!"

She sighs. "It's fine. Everyone does. But I'm going to tell you this now: my brother doesn't date."

"Hon, that RA is a cutie! If you don't ask him out, I will." Mom bursts into the dorm, dragging my suitcase behind her. She ditches it in the doorway when she spots Chloe and flings her arms out. "You must be the famous Chloe!"

My roommate hops off the bed to meet Mom's hug like they're old friends reuniting and not total strangers. "About time I got famous."

"You're a figure skater, right?" I ask.

"Future Olympian," a deep voice cuts in.

Wes leans against the doorway, now completely clothed in long shorts and a white T-shirt. Even with clothes on, I still struggle to make eye contact with him.

"Says the future NHL player," Chloe says. "Mrs. Harris, this is my annoying big brother, Wes."

Mom takes Wes in before whipping her head around to me and whisper-yelling, "Forget the RA."

Oh my god. I'm going to kill her.

Wes's brows furrow. "What?"

Chloe loops her arm through Mom's like they're already besties. "Don't worry about it. Come on. You said you'd move all of Violet's stuff into our dorm."

"I said I'd help," he corrects, even as an amused smile pulls at his lips.

"I heard *all*." Over her shoulder, Chloe winks at me.

I already have a good feeling about her. About both of them. Except I think I actually stand a chance at becoming Chloe's friend.

But the gorgeous, totally unattainable hockey player? I don't stand a chance with him.

Chapter 3

Before

Wes

I DON'T HAVE time to be a stalker.

Between morning classes, training on the ice or in the gym by afternoon, followed by practice, an hour of lectures from Coach, and studying before bed, my schedule's fully booked.

Yet here I am. Here I've been since she showed up on campus. Following Violet Harris.

She's oblivious to the shadow at her back. But in the few days since I met her, I've memorized her daily routine and her coffee order. I know the snacks she prefers from the vending machine. I know the smile she uses when she's genuinely happy to see someone and the one she uses when she's being polite.

Stalking isn't in my blood. Girls chase me, not the other way around. Which makes my obsession with Violet Harris a total fucking enigma.

"Are you going to ask her out?" A bubbly voice half-shouts.

Chloe climbs onto a stool at my table. Violet's ordering a sub twenty feet ahead of us.

Everything about her screams that she's a girl who either

doesn't know how to stand out or doesn't want to. Long, brown hair swept up in a ponytail, a gray shirt that's way too big on her, and round hazel eyes like a scared bunny. Her thighs are incredible in those shorts. All I can think about is how they'd feel wrapped around my back while I'm driving my cock inside her.

"Keep your voice down," I hiss. "And no. I don't date."

Chloe knows that, but she likes to pretend I'll come around someday. "Good."

I lift a brow. "Why's that good?"

"Because Violet's my roommate, and if you start dating her and break up, I'm stuck in the middle."

I give her a sardonic smile. "On second thought, maybe I'll make an exception for her."

"Too bad, she's forbidden."

I don't really give a shit who Chloe does and doesn't want me to be with. I'll never be interested in that shit again after what Britt did. I'm focusing on college, hockey, friends, family, and fucking. That's it. Messing around with relationships and feelings and all that bullshit is the fastest way to fuck with your head and screw everything up. Not making that mistake again.

"Why would you think I'd be into her anyway? I just met the girl."

"So why are you following her around like a stalker?" Chloe waves over her head, catching Violet's eye.

She smiles and heads our way. My stupid heart stutters. "Making sure she's not some psycho who will kill you in your sleep."

Chloe side-eyes me. "I know you, Wes. You've never looked at a girl like that."

Chapter 4

After

Violet

RETURNING to Diamond University was not in my plans. But Mom paid my legal fees and this is where she said I'm going, so I'm here.

"Don't forget your box of books." Mom doesn't look at me when she says it. I can't remember the last time she made eye contact with me.

My only friends in the world now exist inside these books.

Chloe should be here. We should be starting our sophomore year of college together and sharing a dorm room.

But I ruined that. I took away her future. Her life.

We'll never have boyfriends together like we vowed to at the end of last semester. She'll never get to read that book I keep saying I'm going to write. We'll never giggle over our favorite smutty scenes again or fangirl over our latest celebrity crush.

This year, my roommate is a stranger. Probably a freshman from the looks of her side of the dorm. She's already decorated her bed, desk, and wall with bright colors and soccer memorabilia. So bright and cheery, it makes me want to puke.

I begged Mom to let me go anywhere other than Diamond and tried to convince her that I can be an English major anywhere, but she doesn't want to deal with the hassle of me transferring. I chose Diamond University—or, more accurately, Diamond chose me for a full-ride—and according to her, I need to stick it out. Since I'm destitute without her, I don't have a choice.

While families in other dorms chat and laugh and cry, Mom and I stay silent while we move my boxes and bags into the room. Last year, Chloe and Wes helped us move my stuff in. I was so nervous, a doe-eyed freshman with no idea what the next year held in store for her.

I'd give anything to go back to that time. To try to undo the timeline of events that got me here, without Chloe.

As soon as all my stuff is in the dorm, Mom hovers awkwardly in the middle of the room while digging through her purse.

"Thanks for helping me move in," I manage.

Someone outside the room squeals and a tall girl breezes in.

My roommate is absolutely stunning. Beautiful, flowing black hair and radiant skin, outshone only by her bright smile. Last year, her beauty would've stirred envy in my stomach. Now I can't bring myself to feel anything at all.

"Hey! I'm Aneesa." I expect her to jut her hand out for a shake, but she wraps me in a hug instead, her flowery perfume suffocating.

Last time someone hugged me, I was in the hospital and shivering with a towel wrapped around my shoulders, still in nothing but my wet swimsuit. Mom was crying with me in her arms. I couldn't bring myself to shed tears for Chloe yet. Her death still hadn't hit me.

Sometimes, it still hasn't.

Aneesa pulls back but keeps her hands on my shoulders. "You're a sophomore, right? English major? I looked you up."

I manage a weak smile. "Right." The reminder stings. An English major who hasn't written a word or cracked open a book in months. My two greatest passions for my entire life, and I haven't felt a pull toward either of them since she died.

Aneesa releases me. "I'm a freshman. Bio major, pre-med." She flashes a smile at Mom. A beautiful genius who's accustomed to validation from adults for being the smartest, most accomplished girl in the room.

"Nice to meet you, Aneesa. Good luck with your freshman year." Mom clears her throat. "I'm going to head out, Violet. Let me know if you need anything."

She manages a small smile and a brief flash of eye contact before she leaves the room. She doesn't hug me or dissolve into tears like she did last year. I am her only child and her greatest disappointment.

Aneesa frowns out the door after her. "Everything okay with your mom?"

Maybe she somehow doesn't know about the accident. Diamond University is a sprawling campus that draws plenty of international and transfer students, but Diamond is still a small college town. There's nothing they love more than gossip or a murder mystery.

Except there's no mystery with this one. My best friend died. I'm the one responsible. Case closed.

The only mystery is how I got away with it.

"Yeah. Fine," I tell Aneesa, busying myself with making my bed. "Just family stuff."

Aneesa is on her feet in seconds, helping me. A lump forms in my throat at the small kindness. "Is she still upset with you over . . . what happened?"

I should've known there was no way anyone on this campus

might not have heard about the worst moment of my life. About the worst thing I've ever done. I was an idiot for hoping I might be able to start fresh with someone. That I might at least have a few hours feeling normal before somebody told her the truth about me.

That she better watch her back because apparently I like killing my roommates.

"Yeah. She pretty much hates me," I tell her, pushing the emotion back down before it can bubble up and explode.

I know, deep down, that my mother doesn't actually hate me. She loves me unconditionally. But she hasn't looked at me the same since that night. She probably never will.

"I'm sure she doesn't hate you," Aneesa insists. "It was an accident."

"It was stupid. I was drunk. I wasn't thinking straight, and someone died because of me. I ruined the lives of so many people. Her family, my family. I don't blame any of them for hating me. They should."

Chloe's blood is on my hands, and I still haven't figured out how to wash it off. My skin will be stained with it for the rest of my life.

Aneesa drops the bedsheet and faces me. "I can't even imagine what you're going through," she says, voice gentle. "But . . . you can't punish yourself forever. That won't do you or anyone any good. It won't bring your friend back."

Tears prick my eyes, and I can't bring myself to say anything because if I try to talk, I'll sob, and I am not sobbing in front of my roommate during our first time meeting each other. I focus on making my bed, and Aneesa lets silence fall between us.

When I'm finished, she grabs her lanyard. "I was just about to go get lunch. Do you want to come with me?"

She knows the worst thing about me and she's still willing

to be seen with me in public. I don't even want to be seen with me.

"Sure. Thanks," I tell her.

She'll come to her senses soon. When she notices the stares as everyone's eyes follow me across campus. When she hears all the whispers and finally gets sick of being friends with the murderer.

But for now, I give her a grateful smile for the kindness I don't deserve.

Wes

"Wes, that's your fourth plate of pancakes this morning."

"I'm in training, Mom." I shovel in another bite even though I haven't been hungry since my sister died.

Across the table, Mom shakes her head. She could always see right through my bullshit. She slips on her jacket over her blouse. She can't stay here any longer dealing with my mopey ass—that bank's not gonna manage itself. "You're lingering so you don't have to leave for campus. You can't avoid Violet forever."

I stiffen. I fucking hate hearing her name.

From his spot in front of the stove, Dad flips the last of the pancakes. He's still got his pajama bottoms on. A retired NHL player who coaches in the afternoons. "You know she's just as upset about Chloe's death as we are. You need to figure out a way to forgive her, son."

I don't know how the fuck either of them can say that. *Forgiveness.* The last thing Violet Harris deserves. She killed my sister. She ruined our lives. They knew Violet less than a year. Welcomed her into our home and our family with open arms. Now their daughter is dead because of her, and they've just . . . forgiven her.

I'm the only one in this house whose fists clench at her name. She deserves to die for what she did. At the very least, she deserves prison time. Lots of it. But she didn't even get that.

Reckless endangerment. That's all they charged her with. Not fucking murder, even though that's exactly what it was. She should be locked up.

Instead, she got to walk.

Now she doesn't even have the decency to transfer to a different school. Doesn't give a single shit about what seeing my sister's killer every day on campus will do to me.

"She killed Chloe." I grip the fork so hard, the metal bends. "She's a murderer, and she got away with it. I'll never forgive her for taking Chloe away from us."

Mom's blue eyes, the same as my sister's, turn soft. Pitying. That only makes me clutch the fork harder. "Your lack of forgiveness won't hurt Violet, Wes. It'll only hurt you."

Don't worry, Mom. I'll make sure it hurts Violet too.

BLADES SLICE THROUGH ICE, the puck smacking against the net. Shouts barely break through the buzzing in my ears. A couple guys slam into me chest-first. The winning goal and I'm not even celebrating.

"Dude," Trey shouts, "I get that hockey is a violent sport, but do you really have to take it out on your teammates? It's just practice."

I got stuck with Trey as a roommate again this year. He doesn't suck too bad to live with, but he doesn't shower enough and he's never washed a dish in his life. When he's not on the ice or in the gym, he's getting blitzed at frat parties. I'm amazed he's made it to his senior year. He's just pissy because I slammed him to the ice ten minutes after Coach blew the whistle. He's not a bad defenseman, but he's not good enough either. Not if we want to win, and winning's all I've got now.

"What do you think practices are for, Trey?" I ask. "Boston isn't going to take it easy on your ass, so why should I?"

Trey shakes his head. "Whatever, man. You need to get laid."

He's not wrong about that.

Luke, my goalie, leans on his stick. "She's back today, isn't she?"

All the guys near us wait to gauge my reaction. They know exactly how I feel about Violet Harris. "Yeah," I grit out. "She is."

But not for long. I plan on doing whatever it takes to get her off this campus.

Chapter 5

Before

Violet

"Now you'll get to meet the hockey team." Chloe loops her arm through mine, leading me to the Village, one of Diamond's most popular dining halls. "Some of them, anyway."

In the cafeteria, I'm hit with the mouthwatering aroma of tortellini. The room is brightly lit with stacks of colorful plates. Chloe leads the way along the pasta bar, and I grab everything she does, too exhausted and overwhelmed by my first week of classes to put any thought into what I want to eat.

The dining hall nearly takes my breath away. A towering ceiling with massive windows bordered by stone walls. Stately chandeliers hang down above dozens of long, mahogany tables filled with students and faculty, everyone buzzing. This entire week, I've been filled with a mix of nerves and excitement. This feeling of possibility like I've never had before. That maybe this is a new start for me.

Chloe leads the way to a table in the middle of the dining hall, and I instantly know where she's guiding us. Three hulking hockey players who are nearly the same size as Wes dwarf their seats.

The Diamond University hockey team.

The Devils.

"They're all very attractive," she whispers to me like a warning. "But don't bother getting your hopes up if you want a relationship. They have too many puck bunnies waiting in the wings to settle down with one girl. Except for Luke, he's sweet. But I've already called dibs."

"How do you know all of them?"

"I've been to Wes's games. Under the guise of being a supportive sister, but really, I'm there to check out the rest of the players." She stops at the end of the table, beaming. "Guys, this is my roommate, Violet." They all turn to stare at me, and I want to melt. "Violet, this is Luke, Brody, and Trey."

Chloe was right. They're all attractive. Luke instantly reminds me of a golden retriever—dark blonde hair, square jaw, and a bright, friendly smile. His eyes light up when they land on Chloe, and I have a feeling Luke has called dibs on her too. Brody is more like an ornery cat with tousled brown hair, a Roman nose, and distrusting dark eyes. Trey stares at me like a hyena who just spotted a wounded gazelle. Chin in his hand, amusement in his green eyes, and a crooked smile that makes me feel like I've been dipped in oil.

"Tell me, Violet." Trey's singsong voice sends a shiver down my spine. "Have you been deflowered?"

Brody is the only one who laughs. Chloe rounds the table and smacks Trey just before a looming, solid figure steps up beside me.

My breath catches in my lungs.

Wes.

How is he always this beautiful? His water-blue eyes take us in, hair just as dark dry as it was wet, full lips neutral and giving nothing away.

"Your sister's assaulting me," Trey tells him.

"Maybe you should learn to keep your mouth shut and she wouldn't have to."

Trey scowls, but everyone else laughs.

Wes glances down at me, a smile on his face that makes my legs wobble. Not warm or friendly, exactly. Almost . . . possessive. Like he already knows he makes my limbs weak. "You joining us, Violet?"

God, the way he says my name . . . a crazy part of me wants to drop to my knees in worship. Do whatever I need to do to keep him saying my name over and over.

All I can do is nod and sit beside Chloe. When Wes takes the other seat beside me, my stomach twists. He's so close, his knee nearly brushing mine under the table. I can barely swallow my food.

I'm quickly realizing that being Chloe's roommate means spending a lot of time holding my breath around Wes Novak.

Wes

VIOLET'S INTO ME, but by the way she gets tongue-tied and avoids eye contact, she has no clue the attraction's mutual.

Something about her fascinates me. Every little movement, every time color rushes to her cheeks, every time she looks at me before quickly glancing away. She's never been with a guy before, that much is obvious. The thought of being the first man to get her in bed, the first man to make her come, the first cock she has inside her, makes me hard.

Chloe gets the guys talking about hockey, and I smirk. She thinks she can keep me from Violet, but I'm not going to stop this girl if she offers herself up to me on a silver platter.

"So what's your major?" I ask her.

She struggles to swallow before answering. "Um. English."

"Cool. You want to be an English teacher?" I bet she'd be a popular teacher. At least among the male students. Especially if she starts wearing clothes that show off that tight little body instead of hiding it.

Her nose scrunches adorably. "No. Actually . . . I want to be a writer." There's that blush again.

"What do you write?"

"Um." She bites her lip, pushing the pasta around on her plate like she's searching for an answer.

"What? Do you write erotica or something?" When her eyes widen, my mouth falls open before I laugh. "*Do* you? I've gotta read it."

She's full-on cherry red now. "No! Just . . . romance."

"Romance, huh?"

I wonder what kind of dudes she writes about falling in love with. Not guys like me, that's for sure. Probably sweet, spineless princes who say whatever she wants to hear. Not the kind of guy who will wrap his belt around her throat and fuck her so hard, her nails tear into the mattress.

I lean toward her to whisper in her ear, staring down at her arms as my voice gives her goosebumps. "I still want to read it, even if I can't get off to it."

She coughs, rushing for a sip of her water. "*Oh*. Uh, well, I haven't written a book yet, so I don't have anything to really read anyway."

"You should. I bet you'd be good at it."

For the first time since I met her, she smiles at me. A bashful little smile that tells me I said the right thing. God, she's already putty in my hands. I bet if I called her beautiful, she'd be begging for a spot in my bed tonight.

"Your turn to ask me a question," I tell her.

"Um. How old are you?"

"Twenty. I'm a junior."

"What's your major?"

"Finance. I'm hoping for the NHL, but if that doesn't pan out, I guess I'll become one of those obnoxious finance bros."

She giggles and *fuck*. The sound is fucking magical. Soft and delicate just like her. "In that case, I hope the NHL works out for you."

She's got a sense of humor. I like that. "That's what my dad did. Now he's retired and coaching, but I'd like a backup plan. Something to keep me busy when I'm forced into retirement at thirty."

"That's smart."

Even though I barely know the girl, her validation sparks a flicker of pride in my chest. I shake it off. She doesn't have to think I'm smart to want to fuck me. "I have my moments. I'm not the meathead jock you probably thought I was."

What most girls think I am. The guy with the big muscles and the tiny brain who's only good for fighting and fucking.

Violet shakes her head, eyes on her plate. "I didn't think that."

They shouldn't, but her words make me smile.

Chloe stands, chair squealing. "You ready to head back to the dorm, Violet? We have a *lot* of gossiping to do. Did you see Trey's hair?"

Trey shakes his head, but I chuckle. He's an asshole who likes to give everyone shit but doesn't know how to take it. I love watching my sister give it right back to him.

Even though Violet's barely eaten half the food on her plate, she nods quickly and stands, eager to get away from me and the effect I have on her panties. God, I'd love to know how fucking wet she is for me.

"I'll walk you back," I tell them.

Chloe rolls her eyes. "It's literally a five-minute walk and it's not even dark."

I point at Trey. "You think he's the only creep on this campus?"

She glances down at Trey, who's ignoring us now. "You're right. You better come with us."

On our way out of the dining hall, I hold the door open for them. Chloe knows exactly what I'm up to, but Violet flashes me a little smile and murmurs a *thank you* while I watch her ass shake as she passes me. What I wouldn't give to grab it right now and squeeze.

Not yet. She's the kind of girl who scares easy. Who will want to see the first kiss, the first ass-grab, the first fuck, coming.

Chloe nudges her. "What do you think, Violet? They're cute, right? Wes, you should set us up with a couple of your teammates so we can go on a double date."

My shoulders stiffen. She knows exactly what she's doing. "Hell no. You stay away from those assholes."

"*Trey* is an asshole. But Luke is sweet. And that adorable Southern accent." She presses a hand to her chest and swoons like a Southern belle. Jesus.

"You're not allowed to date until you're thirty."

Chloe rolls her eyes. "What about Violet?"

Violet nearly stops breathing when my gaze lands on her. "No hockey players for her. She needs to meet a nice nerd in the library."

She doesn't like that answer. She fixes her gorgeous hazel eyes on the sidewalk ahead of us, clutching her arms over her chest. Good. Maybe that means she's not looking to get fucked by a nice guy.

Chloe groans. "No fair, I want a hot nerd."

That manages to pull a laugh out of Violet. Despite myself,

the beautiful sound inflates something in my chest like a balloon.

When we reach their dorm, Chloe stands with her hand on the knob while I hover in the doorway. "Okay, we made it to our room in one piece. You can go now."

"Wait." I plant a hand on the door to stop her from closing it in my face. "These are the rules. One, you're too young for parties." Chloe rolls her eyes dramatically. "And two, you're too young to drink."

She sighs. "Oh my g—"

"But if you do," I continue, "and you end up in a bad situation, you call me. Both of you."

Violet smiles. The thought of any guy touching her while she's drunk—touching her at all—makes my blood boil, even if it shouldn't. Even if I should care less about a girl I just met. But there's something about her. Something that's already dug its claws in and won't let go.

She has no idea what I'm capable of making her feel. What I'm capable of doing to her.

Chapter 6

After

Violet

EVEN THOUGH I don't meet anyone's gazes, I can feel the eyes of each of my classmates on me as I shuffle into my Advanced Fiction Writing class. I was so excited when I registered for this class last semester, determined that I would finally figure out how to write my first book.

Now, all I want to do is bolt.

I can't remember the last time I put pen to paper or typed a single letter in a word processor.

The chair beside me screeches. "Hey, Violet."

A familiar thin voice and red hair. Maxwell. Relief rushes through me. He gives me a small smile, the one person in this room who doesn't hate me.

Last year, Chloe dared me to flirt with Maxwell at a party. At first, it was completely humiliating, but we ended up having a nice conversation. Other than Aneesa, he's my only remaining ally.

"Hey, how was your summer?" I manage.

"Good."

He doesn't bother asking about my summer. He knows exactly how it went.

Professor Tate breezes into the room, either completely oblivious to the attention on me or actively choosing to ignore it. Either way, I'm grateful. She was my favorite professor last year, and I'm relieved to have another class with her. She taught my Intro to Fiction Writing course, and I've liked her since the first day. She's casual, always has an easy smile, and lets us write whatever genre we prefer.

Thank god she doesn't force us to introduce ourselves to the rest of the class like other professors do on the first day. She spends most of our class time explaining the syllabus and what we'll be learning this semester.

When we have ten minutes remaining, she instructs us to find something to write with. "You're going to do a freewrite. I want you to freewrite every day at the start of class to get your creative juices flowing. Consider it like stretching and warming up before a run. For this freewrite, I want you to reflect on your strongest memory and write about it. No stopping. You must continue writing for the full five minutes. I don't care if it's *I don't know what to write* until the next thought pops in your head. But your pen—or fingers—cannot stop moving. Now write!"

I hurry to grab my pen and start scribbling about the strongest memory that flashes through my mind.

The night Chloe died

My hand freezes next to the letters scrawled in ink, already bleeding through the page.

"No stopping, Violet," Professor Tate calls.

But my stomach churns, beads of sweat prickling up along my neck as the room grows hotter. A buzzing fills my ears, drowning out the sounds of my classmates scribbling across their notebook pages or typing on their laptops.

Professor Tate's voice breaks through the buzzing, muffled. "Violet?"

Now everyone's eyes are on me again.

I can't let my mind go back to that night. I won't.

Bile rises in my throat.

Hand over my mouth, I race out of the room.

EVEN THOUGH ALL I want to do is go back to my dorm room, bury my head under the comforter, and cry, I can't skip my first day of work.

Work-study is part of my full-ride to Diamond. If I don't work, I don't get to remain a student. Luckily, the library was hiring.

Reading and writing have been my solace my entire life. My dad died when I was four, so it's almost always just been me and Mom. Being a single parent meant she had to bust her ass working two or three jobs, so I spent most of my time at home alone. No one at school ever understood why reading and writing became the only things I wanted to do. Mom's supportive, but even she doesn't fully understand the obsession. Why I'd want to go to college for an English degree that will offer few job opportunities when I've watched her struggle my whole life. But writing and books are all I've ever known.

Chloe would be so happy for me if she knew I landed a job at the library. Too bad this place is so quiet, I can't keep my thoughts off her.

"Should be an easy job for you. Students normally come to the library to study or find a book for class." Edith is an older librarian with white, cropped hair, thin-framed glasses, and an appetite for steamy romance.

I already like her.

"Your job is to make sure I don't have to do mine." She's perched on a chair low to the ground. So low you almost can't see her behind the circulation desk. She pats her legs. "These old things aren't what they used to be. Your job is stacking books and keeping my nose in my latest novel. If you can do that, I don't care what you do in your downtime. Study, do homework, read a book, text your boyfriend, scroll on the TikToks, whatever it is you kids do these days."

I grin. "I think I can manage that."

She guides me through how to use the computer and the library system before I push the full cart of books back to the shelves. Edith disappears into the back office to read undisturbed.

While I'm stacking, the door to the library opens. Someone dings the bell at the desk.

"I'll be right there!" I call.

I hope Edith is right about this being a lowkey job that involves blessedly minimal interaction with my fellow students. But I can't pretend to ignore the looks. It's been even worse being back on campus than I thought it would be.

But that's what I deserve.

A pair of heavy boots approaches. I keep my eyes on the stack of books in front of me until the footsteps get unnervingly close. The hairs on the back of my neck stand up.

Whoever they are, they're getting closer and closer. At the last second, I realize they don't intend to pass me.

When I finally turn, there's a flash of movement before I'm shoved up against the bookshelf. My spine slams into the wood, a gasp escaping my lips.

He pins me by the shoulders, looming over me with fire raging in his blue eyes.

Wes Novak.

When I imagined our reunion after Chloe's death, I thought Wes would wrap me in a warm, tight hug. That he'd sob in my arms while I attempted to comfort him. That we'd cry together, finding solace in each other in the darkest moment of our lives.

But there is nothing warm or comforting about him now.

The scent of his cedarwood cologne wafts up my nose. Gone is the guy who used to wear long shorts, a simple T-shirt, and old sneakers. The hockey player with the boyish smile and rugged good looks. Startling blue eyes, six-foot-four frame, sex-addled brown hair, and arms that looked like they could pick me up and throw me.

This man in front of me is in dark jeans, a button-up with sleeves rolled to the elbows, and a pair of black combat boots I've never seen before. Boots he wore to stomp me into the earth.

This man wants me dead.

"Why the fuck are you here?" he growls. His sharp, square jaw flexes. The muscles bulging on his biceps are rock-hard on either side of me. Before Chloe died, I would've given anything to be in this position with Wes.

Now, it's terrifying.

This is the first time he's spoken to me since that night. Since he told me to shut the fuck up because I was screaming over the dead body of his little sister.

I dare a glance away from him, desperate to make eye contact with anybody who might be able to save me. But there's no one around.

I am all alone with Wes Novak, the captain of the Devils.

"I . . . I work here," I stutter, legs trembling.

His scowl deepens, and he moves just a centimeter closer, but the walls are closing in on me. I am a mouse caught in a trap and the snake is preparing to strike.

"Not in the library." His growl grates its way down my spine. "On this campus. My campus. *Her* campus. You don't belong here anymore."

He's right. I don't belong here. And right now, I wish to god I was anywhere else. My knees wobble. "My mom made me come back. Believe me," I whisper, "this wasn't my choice."

How could Mom not think this would happen? There's no way she could've missed the way Wes glared at me when we left the courthouse. She must know he's out for blood. Maybe at this point, she doesn't care what happens to me.

That muscle in his jaw feathers. Like he doesn't believe I'm here against my will. As if I want to be reminded of all my memories with Chloe. Of all the memories she and I will never make together. Reminded of what I did.

"You should be in jail."

"I know," I whisper.

Wes leans closer. So close, someone watching might think he's leaning in to kiss me. I almost brace for him to reach out and skim a finger down my cheek. To brush his lips against mine.

But the fury in his eyes tells me if he touches me, it won't be gentle. He'll make it hurt.

"The judge may have let you off easy, but I won't make the same mistake." His voice is low, reverberating down to my toes. Before, I heard his voice in my dreams. Now, it'll echo in my nightmares. "If you don't leave this campus, I'll make your life a living hell. I'll make you pay for what you did. Make you suffer worse than you made her suffer. You'll be begging for a prison cell when I'm through with you."

I swallow, hardly able to get any words out. He hates me.

I've never been hated before, but it's no less than I deserve. "I promise you won't ever see me," I plead. "I'll stay out of your way."

He's so busy with his classes and hockey, our paths shouldn't cross. We can avoid each other with minimal effort. I'll stay away from any corner of the campus he wants, avoid all the buildings and dining halls he frequents. He'll forget I exist.

Wes pushes off the shelf and away from me. I suck in air like a fish stranded ashore.

"Not good enough." His voice is flat, lifeless. More terrifying than his fury. "I want you gone."

I can't look away from the fierceness in his eyes, no matter how much I long to. A deer unable to do anything more than stare at the blinding headlights, at death barreling toward her.

Diamond was the only university to offer me a full-ride. The prestigious creative writing program is one of the best in the country. My only hope of finishing the book I promised Chloe I would write for her. I get why Wes doesn't want me here, but my heart aches painfully at the thought of leaving.

Disgust curls his lip when I remain silent, distorting his beautiful face. He shakes his head, forced to look away from me and clench his fists at his sides before he strangles me right here in this library.

Please just walk away.

Instead, his piercing blue eyes slice into me again. And this time, I won't recover. "I'm telling you now, Violet. If you don't get the fuck off this campus, I'll kill you myself."

Chapter 7

After

Wes

MY LEG BOUNCES while I wait outside the office for the Dean of Student Affairs, fists clenched in my lap. This has to be a goddamn joke. An oversight. Who lets a fucking murderer return to a college campus? These people can't be that fucking stupid.

When the door finally opens, my hands reflexively jump to adjust my collar. Now that I'm a senior, all my professors have advised that we dress for college fairs to impress the recruiters. Just so happens that my button-up works well for an official meeting with the dean too.

"Mr. Novak!" Dean Forrester calls. "Great to see you. Please come in."

I put an extra ounce of squeeze into the handshake so he knows I mean business. By the time he offers me a seat, my ass is already in the chair. "I won't take up too much of your time, sir. I'll get straight to the point. I want Violet Harris off campus."

Dean Forrester takes a seat behind his desk and that easygoing smile is already replaced with a frown. "I'm afraid we can't accomplish that, Mr. Novak."

I nearly spit, *why the hell not?* But I manage to bite my tongue. I'm not going to get what I want by giving in to my temper. "I don't think it's in the student body's best interest to have a murderer walking around campus."

Dean Forrester folds his hands together on his desk. "Therein lies the issue. Miss Harris wasn't charged or convicted of murder, and she was acquitted of her reckless endangerment charges."

Acquitted. The word swirls in my mind like a raging storm. The same way that bogus judge's verdict did. *Not guilty.*

How? How is that fucking possible?

"She *killed* somebody." I can't keep the edge of fury out of my voice now. "Isn't that enough?"

How can they just let her keep walking around and going on with her life like she didn't do anything wrong? Where the hell are the consequences? My sister is in the *ground.* And no one's doing a damn thing about it.

Dean Forrester leans back with a sigh. "I understand this is a difficult time for you and your family—"

"You *understand?*" I snort. The words are flying out of my mouth now, and fuck it. I've never been good at playing nice guy. "No, you don't understand at all. If you did, that bitch wouldn't be on this campus right now."

Dean Forrester's face pinches. His patience with me is thinning. "I'm sorry we're unable to do more for you at this time, Mr. Novak. What I can suggest is avoiding Miss Harris as much as possible. From what I understand, she's a sophomore and an English major. As a finance major, you shouldn't have any issues with running into her on campus or in any of your classes. I expect as captain of the hockey team, you'll be especially busy this year."

If it were as simple as avoiding and ignoring her, I wouldn't be here right now. But the reality is, I can't get my mind off her. My thoughts always drift to my sister, and when I think of Chloe, I think of Violet. I fucking hate that my memories of my sister are now tainted with the image of her killer.

The injustice makes my blood boil. And no one else seems to give a shit. Not my parents, not the administration, and certainly not that fucking idiot judge. No one wants to do what needs to be done.

So I guess that leaves me.

Maybe there's a reason she's here. Even if she transferred, even if she moved to another state, I still wouldn't be able to get her out of my head. I'd still be out for blood, no matter where she was, so maybe it's actually better she's stuck here with me.

I stand and hold out my hand to the dean. "Thank you for your time, sir."

His brows lift as he shakes my hand and stands to walk me out, but I'm already through the door.

I will be judge, jury, and executioner.

I'll get the justice my sister deserves.

Chapter 8

After

Violet

As soon as my shift is over, I beeline for my dorm room and toss clothes at random into my suitcase.

Aneesa, who is at her desk video chatting with a couple of friends, tells them she has to go and closes her laptop. She rushes to my side, still in her grass-stained soccer uniform. "What's going on?"

"I'm leaving." Mom will understand when I explain the situation. She may be disappointed in me right now, but she won't want to see me tortured by the vengeful brother of my dead best friend.

"What, why? Did I do something?" Aneesa's eyes are round. I almost feel bad for her, but I'm too preoccupied with being terrified for myself.

"No, it has nothing to do with you." My hands tremble when I yank a pair of shorts from my dresser.

"So why are you leaving?"

"Because no one wants me here." Tears prick my eyes. One day, and being back on this campus has already been absolute hell. I can't believe I ever thought there was a chance I might survive this day, let alone this year.

Aneesa rushes to my side and grabs my hand. "I want you here."

I brush away the tears. "Thank you, but there are some very dangerous people who don't."

She frowns. "Like who?"

I shake off her hand and return to packing my bag. "Like the brother of my dead best friend."

Since he confronted me in the library, I haven't been able to get his face out of my head. The snarl to his lips, the fury in his eyes that seared through me. He said he would kill me.

And I believe him.

Aneesa's lips purse. "I'm sure he's not exactly happy to see you, but he'll get over it. If he really hates you being here that much, he can leave."

"He's a senior. And he's the hockey captain. He's definitely not going anywhere." And if Wes did leave because of me, that would just be another way I ruined his life. More guilt weighing on me.

"That sounds like his problem," Aneesa insists. "You have just as much right to be here as he does, Violet."

"I don't have a right to anything." I appreciate what she's trying to do, but she has no clue what she's talking about, so I keep my voice firm. Conversation over. "I need to call my mom and tell her to come get me."

Aneesa nods and returns to her laptop to read her email. At least, she pretends to.

Mom answers on the third ring. "Violet?" she asks. She used to call me hon.

"I need to come home." My voice is already watery.

Silence. My first day of kindergarten, I cried so much that the teacher let me call Mom from the front office and she left work to pick me up early. My first day of college, I called her crying that I already missed her and she stayed up on the phone with me until I fell asleep.

A dull ache roots deep in my chest when she doesn't offer to come get me this time. "You knew this first day back wouldn't be easy. You can get through this."

"I will literally attend anywhere else," I plead. "Just please don't make me stay here." She can send me to a university in Alaska for all I care. At least there, no one will know who I am. What I've done.

"What happened?" Her tone is gentler now, full of concern.

My voice cracks. "Wes hates me."

"He doesn't hate you," she soothes. "He's hurting and angry, but that will pass when he realizes what happened was an accident. You've worked so hard for this opportunity, Violet. Few people are lucky enough to get a free education, let alone at their dream school. You've wanted to be a writer your whole life, and you can't flush away all your hard work for anyone. If you leave, you'd have to figure out a way to pay for a place to stay, a car, tuition. We don't have the money for that. Trust me, Wes will find it in his heart to forgive you, and you'll be so glad you decided to stay."

"What if I just take a gap year?" My heart is pounding in my chest now. I can't stay here. I can't. "I'll come back after he graduates."

"You'll forfeit your scholarship." A pregnant pause. "What happened with Wes, Violet? If something happened, I can talk to the Novaks."

That would only make Wes resent me more if he found out I ran to my mommy and got his parents involved. I have enough guilt weighing me down. I don't need more.

Mom is right. I'll never get a free ride anywhere else, and

this is what I've been working for my entire life. All I have left is my education, my career. My writing is the only remaining part of me that brings me any flicker of joy, of hope. I can't give that up.

Wes is pissed right now. He threatened to kill me in the heat of the moment. But he would never actually hurt me.

He'll be busy with his own classes and a hectic hockey schedule. Between working out, practice, games, and travel, he'll forget all about me.

All I need to do is survive until he graduates.

Chapter 9

Before

Violet

A MONTH INTO THE SEMESTER, Chloe and I already have a routine. She wakes up at the ass crack of dawn to train, and we meet up for lunch on Tuesdays and Thursdays when our schedules align. In the afternoons, she attends class, and in the evenings, she studies and watches Netflix on her phone or her laptop before bed while I read. Despite being one of the coolest, funniest girls I've ever met, the only friend she seems to have is me. Maybe that's why she hasn't said anything about me not having any other friends either.

"You should write a book," she says.

I'm halfway through the one I'm currently reading—a romantic fantasy—and I had no idea this one was explicit. I blush when I get to the first use of *cock*.

"I've always wanted to write one," I admit.

"So why haven't you?" Chloe sits up to face me.

Even though I call myself a writer and I'm in college to get a creative writing degree, I've always told myself that writing books is something I would do as an adult when I finally had stories to tell. Someday, somehow, I'd wake up and know that this was the time to write a book and become an author.

Plus, the thought of sitting down to write a whole book is so daunting. I've always let the fear stop me. The fear that I won't come up with any ideas that are worthy of a book. The fear that I've spent my whole life loving books and dreaming about being an author, but when I finally put words on the page, I'll realize that I'm no good at this and I'll need to let go of the dream I've held onto my entire life. The fear that only the people who have lived a life worth writing about can write a book worth reading.

"I'm too boring to write a book," I tell Chloe.

She sits up and swings her legs over the bed. "That's nothing we can't fix. Let's start with tonight. Go with me to the hockey game."

"What?" My heart flutters in my chest at the thought of seeing Wes. "No. I hate sports."

"Come on. I dare you."

I laugh. "What are we, twelve?"

"You're never too old for a game of Dare." She closes the distance between us and squeezes my arm, puffing out her bottom lip. "*Please*, Violet? This is how you'll get inspiration for your novel. Think of how much story material you'll get by doing things you never would've done otherwise."

"Fine. Then I dare you to . . . flash someone. At the game." Surely that will get her to change her mind about playing Dare. This could get ugly.

She shrugs. "Deal."

I sit up, snapping my book shut. "What do you mean *deal*? You're going to *flash* someone?"

She grins. "If that's what will help you write your book, I'll flash the whole rink."

"Chloe, I love you, but I hate sports," I repeat. We're already searching the bleachers for the best seats, Chloe ignoring my protests the entire way as she pulls me behind her.

Sure, butterflies flutter in my stomach at the thought of watching Wes fly across the ice, of being near him. But another part of me knows being around him will only cause me more pain, wanting him and knowing I'll never have him.

When he said I should focus on finding a nerd in the library, the words were a sucker punch. I know I'm not good enough for a guy like Wes, but I didn't expect him to confirm it out loud.

That's how he sees me. Some forgettable nerd. Nothing at all like the fun, wild girls he's used to sleeping with.

"You can't go to Diamond and not go to the hockey games." Chloe nods to the bleachers above us. "That's our guy."

"What are you talking about?"

"The scrawny guy with the glasses. That's the guy I'm going to flash when we score."

I laugh. "That would make his day."

She leads me by the hand. "Let's go."

"Wait. You're not seriously going to flash him, are you?" I whisper.

"You dared me to. I don't back down from a dare." She peers at me over her shoulder, blue eyes mischievous. "Do you?"

I can't remember the last time anyone dared me to do anything. Maybe on the playground in fourth grade. But now, I don't want to back down from a dare either.

Chloe takes a seat right next to the guy with glasses and I sit beside her. She grins brightly at him and asks if he's excited about the game. I cover my mouth to suppress the giggle.

Once the game starts, Chloe attempts to explain everything to me, but most of it goes over my head. Apparently, Wes plays center, whatever that means. All I know is to watch for number three to dart by in the red and black jersey. Every time he does, my heart skips.

The whole game, I barely know what's going on, but Chloe's chants and jeers get me invested. The puck sails across the ice, followed shortly by the players. Insults are hurled, punches thrown, and whistles blown nearly nonstop. Maybe I like hockey after all.

Wes beelines for the edge of the rink, but a member of the opposing team cuts him off. They slam into the wall together and I flinch.

The rival rips off Wes's helmet, but before his fist can connect with Wes's nose, Wes bulldozes into him and knocks him down onto the ice.

I gasp, heart in my throat like I'm in the rink with them, waiting for a referee to tear them apart and send them both to the bench. But Wes simply slips his helmet back on and his rival returns to his feet, both of them rejoining the others darting back and forth across the ice.

"What the hell? They're just allowed to keep playing?" I shout to Chloe.

"Hockey is, like, sixty percent playing, forty percent fighting."

When our team scores the winning goal, Chloe jumps from her seat and yanks up her shirt in front of the guy beside her. His eyes practically bug out of his head, and Chloe and I burst into a fit of giggles.

"Oh my god!" I squeal. "I can't believe you did that!"

His face is bright red, but a tiny, shocked smile plays on his lips.

I'll never be as fun and bold as Chloe, but every part of me longs to try.

When she and I finally manage to pull ourselves together, she leads me down the bleachers. "Let's stick around with the puck bunnies to congratulate the guys. Especially Luke."

I don't bother asking what a puck bunny is. "When are you finally going to ask him out?"

"When you dare me to," she says simply before clutching my arm. "But please don't dare me to do it right now because I don't want to get rejected in front of the whole team."

"He would never reject you." I'm amazed she could even think that's a possibility. In just one month, Chloe has become my new favorite person. She's funny and lively and bubbly. I'm sure half the guys on this campus fantasize about dating her, Luke included.

Chloe beams at me, squeezing my hand. "Have I ever told you you're the best friend I've ever had?"

I mirror her grin. "You're mine too."

Once most of the crowd has disappeared from the stadium, we're the only ones left with a group of girls I assume must be the puck bunnies. They giggle and waggle their fingers at the players still on the ice until the guys skate over.

Wes is the only one who approaches us when he leaves the ice. Chloe's enthusiasm falters a little when Luke stays behind, chatting with their coach.

The instant Wes takes off his helmet, all the air leaves my lungs. His magnetic blue eyes land right on me.

I'm enchanted by the sweat dripping from his inky hair, and the huge, dazzling smile that seems to shine just for me.

"Great game!" Chloe says.

But Wes doesn't take his eyes off me. "What did you think, Violet?"

My stomach flips every time he says my name. "Yeah. Great game."

Jesus. I literally can't come up with an original thought.

"You into hockey?" he asks.

I am now. "A new fan," I manage.

His grin widens.

Holy shit. Maybe I was wrong about Wes. Maybe I haven't been imagining the way his eyes light up when they spot me or the way he seems drawn to me like a moth to flame. Like I am to him.

"Hey, we should—" Chloe starts.

Before she can finish, a redhead breaks free of the group of puck bunnies to cling onto Wes's enormous bicep. "Oh my gosh, *Wes!* You did *amazing.* I couldn't take my eyes off you the whole game."

She's beautiful and curvy, and I instantly shrivel, knowing there's no way I can compete with a girl like her.

Wes turns his whole body to face her, smiling flirtatiously, and my stomach drops. Chloe and I are forgotten.

Of course. I've known since I met him that Wes is out of my league, but I still keep trying to convince myself that maybe I've somehow stepped into an alternate dimension in which a guy like Wes could fall for a girl like me.

Chloe loops her arm through mine. "Let's go. Luke's busy."

For a split second, I almost wish she wasn't my roommate. Wish that being friends with Chloe didn't mean being forced to be around her brother.

I've never been in love before, and I know I'm not now. I barely know Wes. This is just a crush, nothing more.

But there's a reason it's called a *crush* and not something nicer. Because falling for someone you know will never want you back is crushing.

Chapter 10

After

Wes

THE LOCKER ROOM reeks of BO and ass. That's how you know we went hard at practice.

"So is that Violet Harris chick kicked off campus?" Trey asks me.

The hairs on the back of my neck rise at her name. I hate the effect she has on me, even when she's not around. The rest of the team listens in, and I slam my locker shut. "Nah, they're letting her stay."

Trey frowns, pulling his jeans up over his boxers. "That's bullshit, man."

"I thought so too. But now I've got new plans for Violet Harris."

Twisted delight swells in my chest. Since I left Dean Forrester's office, I've come up with a long list of ways I'm going to make Violet pay for what she did. Each bit of torment far more satisfying than getting her kicked off campus.

A wide grin spreads across Trey's face. "Yeah? I want in on this."

Of course he does. Trey is the most sadistic fuck on the

team. His goal on the ice isn't to stop the opposing team from scoring—it's to wipe out as many of their players as possible.

Which means he won't hesitate to follow whatever instructions I give him, no matter how fucked up.

Luke rounds the corner, leaning against the row of lockers with brows pulled together and mouth a thin line. "Let's hear these plans."

This time last year, he wouldn't have even entertained the idea of doing anything to hurt Violet. To hurt anyone. He's the goalie in a contact sport for a reason—he's big enough to sideline a guy if he has to, but he'd rather keep his hands clean.

Guess Violet is the exception. Maybe his feelings for Chloe went deeper than I realized. He hasn't been the same since we lost her.

I take in the faces of my teammates, my friends, all of them ready and willing to follow their captain's orders. Exactly as I expected.

The judge didn't serve justice. But the Devils will.

"I'm going to get the justice my sister deserves, no matter what it takes. We're going to make her life a living hell here. She's going to regret stepping a toe back on this campus."

Violet

If I'm not leaving campus, I'll just have to become invisible. Wes won't torture me if he forgets I exist.

Despite the heat, I wore a hoodie and sweatpants to class today. I pull my hood up when I head for my dorm to hide out until dinner with Aneesa. This is how I'll get through this semester and the next. Then Wes will graduate and I'll finally be free of him. No longer have to worry about what he has planned for me.

Chloe would be so disappointed to see how I've regressed. She's the one who pushed me to step out of my comfort zone freshman year, to help me stand out. But now that's the last thing I want to do.

I hike up the straps of my backpack, and the hairs on the back of my neck stand up like they do when someone's watching me. I'm always being watched on this campus, but I naively hoped my feeble disguise would stop the stares this time.

Carefully, I peer around to see who might be watching. But the small grassy lots in front of the brick buildings are vacant, everyone in class.

I dare a glance over my shoulder. A tall, broad figure with his hood pulled low to hide his face is trailing behind me, hands in his pockets.

Wait. No. That's not his face under the hood.

That's a mask.

An all-white mask with a cluster of pinprick holes at the mouth.

Shit. Who the hell wears a mask on campus in broad daylight? Is he following me or just headed in the same direction? His clothes don't give anything away. Inconspicuous, plain black shirt over a pair of dark jeans.

But the combat boots—

No. Not him.

Anyone but Wes.

Part of me wants to break into a run. But there's no way I could outrun Wes Novak. He's a hockey player in the best shape of his life. He practically sprints across ice—he could close the distance between us in seconds.

Fuck. *Fuck, fuck, fuck.* Wes can't be following me for any

good reason. He said he didn't want me on this campus, warned he'd do anything to make my life a living hell. He's going to hurt me, and there's nothing I can do to stop him.

Maybe somebody will spot us—a timid girl hurrying down the sidewalk and a suspicious masked man following her—and they'll intervene.

All I have to do is make it to my residence hall. Nobody can get into Nohren without a student ID registered to the building. Wes can't do anything to me once I'm inside anyway. Minus the stairwells, cameras monitor our movements in every corner. If he hurts me, I'll have evidence.

Not that they'll be able to identify him.

My heart's pumping wildly when I finally reach the door, but I breathe a little easier when I swipe my card and the automatic door swings open. I'm almost there. Almost away from him—

Feet rush toward me, thundering up so fast, I don't have time to move. All I can do is squeeze my eyes shut and brace myself.

The footsteps pass me with a small breeze. When I open my eyes, Wes is strolling through the door.

I let him right in.

The RA at the front desk glances up when we enter and an amused smirk pulls at her lips. "A little early for Halloween."

Wes shrugs off her comment, and she drops her eyes back to her computer. Of course. Students have worn stranger things on campus. He's not streaking, so why should she care? As far as she's concerned, he's probably going to surprise his girlfriend with a mask kink.

Besides, he's Wes Novak. The captain of the hockey team can wear wherever he wants.

Do whatever he wants.

I dart for the elevator, hoping he'll head for a friend's dorm and forget all about me. But when I step through the open elevator doors, he follows me inside.

My lungs shrivel. I expect him to keep his back to the doors, block my exit, but he hits a button for the next floor and stands right beside me. His looming presence makes me gulp, the scent of his cedarwood cologne wrapping around me in a lover's caress that chills me to the bone.

We stare at each other's reflections in the shiny elevator doors, his stormy blue eyes glaring through the holes in his mask and glued to my face. Melting me where I stand.

The walls close in on me as the elevator lurches, my body growing a thousand degrees hotter.

I'm literally trapped with Wes Novak.

I can't see it, but there has to be a camera in here. He won't hurt me, knowing the evidence will follow him.

Except that's why he's wearing a mask. To hide his face. Will anyone believe me if I say it was him?

My nails bite into my palms. *Shit, shit, shit.* I don't know what to do. My mind scrambles for a way out of this, away from him, but comes up empty.

The elevator grinds to a halt on the next floor. My empty lungs ache, longing for air I don't dare give them.

"This is your stop." His low command echoes in the metal box, loud and clear despite the mask.

I double-check the buttons, but this is the second floor. My dorm is on the fifth floor, the number lit up. "No, it isn't."

Wes reaches the elevator doors in a single step. The pressure in my chest eases at his departure.

Until he stops with his hand against the open doors. "I said this is your stop."

Oh shit. That wasn't a reminder—it was an order.

The last thing I want to do is go anywhere with Wes.

I grip the handrail behind me. He'll have to drag me out of here.

When the muscle in his jaw contracts, I know I've made a mistake.

He smacks the Stop button and strides for me, scooping me up in his arms so fast, I don't have a chance to fight him off.

"Put me down!" I hiss.

He carries me like I'm air. Under different circumstances, if that night hadn't happened, I would be swooning. One of his arms supports my back while the other is hooked under my knees. Like I'm his bride and he's carrying me to our wedding suite.

Except that night did happen, and I'm not the girl he's carrying to his bed. I'm his victim, and he's carrying me to my crime scene.

"I'll scream," I warn.

"God, I hope so." The words come out in a guttural groan that makes me blush. Almost like the thought of me scream-ing . . . turns him on.

When he backs into the door to the stairwell with a creak, my heart drops before he dumps me onto the ground. I collide palms first with the unforgiving concrete.

Pain lashes through my hands and knees. But I barely have time to register it before I'm hauled back by my bag onto my feet and pinned against the wall.

My hands are already trembling, but Wes looming in front of me is enough to melt me into a puddle.

"I warned you, Violet." His distorted voice rakes down my spine like fangs.

"I'm sorry," I sputter, tears spilling down my cheeks. The words I've been aching to say to him for months, but he's never given me the chance. "I'm *so sorry*, Wes—"

His hand wraps around my throat in a viper's death-grip. "Don't fucking fake-apologize," he growls.

"I'm not. I swear I am s—"

Wes squeezes tighter, shutting me up. Stopping the flow of oxygen. He could crush my windpipe with one hand. I claw at his arm, trying to pull him off me, but it's like fighting a tree.

"I could kill you right here. No one would have any idea who did it." He leans in, the edge of his mask brushing my cheek. His soft breath drifts through the holes to cup my ear, sending goosebumps down my arms. "No one would care."

Some wild, absolutely insane part of me stirs at his voice in my ear, his hand wrapped around my throat. Adrenaline shoots through my veins as my air is restricted and liquid heat pools between my legs.

I almost think he's about to kiss me, and if I could catch my breath enough to speak, I'd beg him to. Maybe that brush of our lips would remind him of what it used to be like between us. Before I ruined everything.

But then he squeezes my neck with both hands, the pleasure vanishing as he lifts me off my feet. His hands are my noose. The last thing I'm going to see before I die is Wes Novak's ice-blue eyes salivating at the light leaving mine.

"You deserve to die for what you did."

He's right. I deserve this. If he kills me right here, it'll be a death I earned.

"Maybe if I kill you, I'll get acquitted too. I'm sure the judge would understand."

Just as my vision goes black, the pain pulling me under, Wes releases his grip on me.

My feet hit hard concrete. I gasp for air, clutching at my throat with scraped, bleeding palms, the pain in my hands long forgotten. I don't know what hurts more—my head or my throat.

I'm unable to run. Unable to move. I'm completely at his mercy as I take ragged breaths, each one tearing through my scorched throat. He squeezed so hard, bruises will appear on my neck by tomorrow. No idea how I'll explain those to Aneesa.

If he lets me live long enough to see her again.

Wes is still looming over me, peering down through his mask like I'm shit on his shoes. "But I'm not like you. I don't go around killing people. You got lucky there."

When he steps back, my gaze lands on the bulge in his pants. My mouth goes dry. *Oh my god.* Choking me and nearly making me black out made him hard.

Hurting me turns him on.

I never thought Wes Novak had it in him to be sadistic. To get off on inflicting pain. Eliciting fear.

He leaves me with one final promise. "By the time I'm through with you, you're going to wish I'd killed you."

Chapter 11

After

Wes

GOD, it felt so good to have my hands wrapped around her throat. Her eyes were wide while she was bleeding and trembling. Watching her cower in front of me, feeling her delicate little throat beneath my palms, made me want to wrench open that pretty mouth and make her suck me off.

I can't do that, though. Can't give in to that last bit of stupid, lingering attraction.

Violet has always been beautiful. Long brown hair, usually tied up in a ponytail begging to be pulled. Stunning hazel eyes, button nose, and a pouty little mouth. She's so tiny. Can't be more than five-three. More than a foot shorter than me. I can't count the number of nights I've spent daydreaming about her tiny hands and perfect mouth wrapped around my cock.

Sure, in my fantasies I mix the pleasure with a bit of pain. Have her choke on my cock, drive into her from behind so hard she screams. But I've never actually thought I would do any of that. I'd be gentle, do whatever she asked to keep her around.

But I don't care about keeping her around anymore.

In the locker room, I scrub the grime of practice off in the showers. In the other corner, Luke does the same in silence. Before Chloe died, Luke would belt some country song in an exaggerated Southern twang until I'd holler at him to shut up. He hasn't been the same since my sister died either.

All because of Violet Harris.

My vision pinpricks when her heart-shaped face and round eyes pop into my mind. I squeak the shower off, wrap the towel around my waist, and stomp to my locker, shaking thoughts of Violet from my head.

Out in the locker room, my teammates watch while a puck bunny blows Trey in the middle of the room, his hand pressed against a locker beside him while he smirks down at her.

He smacks her cheek when he spots me. "Give the captain a turn. He needs a pick-me-up."

The girl turns to me, chestnut eyes framed by hair of the same shade. Wrong complexion, different nose, thinner lips, but the color in her cheeks reminds me of Violet.

She flashes me a salacious grin, saliva coating her chin. My cock throbs when I picture Violet doing the same.

No. I block the images of her out of my mind as Trey tears open the puck bunny's top, exposing her tits nearly spilling out of her bra. She gasps before giggling. Normally, we have a few girls in here at a time, their high-pitched moans and cries echoing. But I like when we get to focus on one girl too, admiring how many cocks she can handle at once.

I stride for her, ripping down her bra to expose her peaked nipples and pinch her cheeks between my thumb and forefinger, a flash of fear in her dark eyes that makes my cock twitch. "Hey, bunny," I murmur.

I'm squeezing too hard for her to respond, but I don't need her talking. I need her sucking. Making me forget all about Violet.

My cock springs out when I drop the towel around my

waist. The smile fights to pull across her face. I slap her cheek with my dick a few times before placing the tip on her lips and finally releasing my hold on her cheeks to slide in.

Her wet tongue caresses the underside of my shaft, her cheeks sucking in because she knows exactly how to get a guy off. She lets out a little yelp when I push in all the way to her throat. She gags, and Trey groans behind me, already wanting back inside her.

I thread my hand in her hair, rubbing the back of her head like I'm giving her a scalp massage. She groans until I drive my cock deep into her throat in a hard thrust, keeping her head in place with both hands while I fuck her face.

Her nails bite into my thighs as she gags and chokes, but that only makes me fuck her harder. Rage pumping in my veins as I picture Violet on her knees before me, mouth wide and jaw coming unhinged to accept her punishment.

"I need to be inside her," Trey groans.

I nearly growl when he interrupts us, pulling the puck bunny to her feet. He tugs her shirt and bra off while Brody yanks her shorts and panties down. She's naked in seconds, every inch waxed and plucked in preparation for this moment.

"Bend over the bench, bunny," I instruct her, leaning back against the locker.

She does as she's told, bending with her eyes peering up at me as Trey drools over her ass. "My name is—"

"Shh, bunny." I press a finger over her lips. "It doesn't matter."

Before she can say another stupid fucking word, I shove my cock down her throat. She blinks back the tears, but they eventually start to spill when Trey spits in his hand and slams into her pussy.

She cries out around my cock, gagging every time Trey's thrusts send my dick down her throat. Brody stands over her, jerking off as her ass bounces. A couple of the guys crouch and suck her tits into their mouths. Her eyes roll with pleasure.

Luke walks by and out of the room without a word. He's never been into sharing. If I gave a shit about the girl, I wouldn't either. Wouldn't want another guy even looking at her, let alone burying himself inside her.

Trey gets on the floor, spinning her to face him and pulling her down onto his cock. "What a good fucking slut," he growls, pounding into her like she's a blowup doll while her tits bounce wildly.

Brody kneels and sucks on his finger before nudging at her ass. "You're going to love this, baby."

She whimpers when I snap her head back to me, forcing her lips to part again even though her jaw is aching.

When Brody enters her ass, she cries out, lurching forward. I slam into her mouth over and over, dark makeup mixing with her tears and I smear the mess across her face before slapping, turning her flushed skin a brighter red.

She manages to wrap her hands around two more cocks, pumping them while she gets fucked in every hole. I squeeze her neck, restricting her airflow until she's gasping around my cock.

Her saliva drips down to my balls just as they tighten. One of the guys cums on her back, and the room fills with the slap of skin on skin. Brody grunts, slamming into her tight ass just as Trey thrusts up into her and shouts, "Oh, *fuck!*"

The puck bunny's scream around my cock sends reverberations all the way to my toes, and I release her neck as my hot cum spurts out and down her throat. She chokes, pushing at my thighs. But my hand crushes her head to me, her nose nearly brushing my pelvis as she's forced to swallow my cum or drown in it.

"Good girl, bunny."

With both hands, I mix her spit with her makeup and tears, spreading the concoction across her face.

Exactly what I would do to Violet Harris if I ever had her in this position. Getting off on her tears, her terror.

Violet

THE INSTANT ANEESA spots me waiting for her in the dining hall, she gasps and hurries to the seat across from me, dropping her plate onto the table. "What happened?" She immediately digs out the med kit from her bag, scoots her chair next to me, and dabs at the scrapes on my hands.

"I tripped and fell." The practiced lie comes out easily. I managed to cover the freshly blooming bruises on my neck with concealer.

I can't tell Aneesa what really happened. She'll demand to know who pushed me, and when I refuse to give her the name of my assailant, she'll figure out who it is. Then she'll do something stupid. Either track Wes down herself and demand that he leave me alone, which would only make my torment worse, or she'll go to the administration and report it. And once Wes finds out I reported him, he won't let me leave this campus alive.

No, Aneesa can't know about any of this. I just need to suck it up and deal with it. Any punishment that Wes wants to dole out to me, I deserve anyway.

Thankfully, she buys the lie. "They should heal in a few days. Just make sure you keep the wounds clean and watch for infection." I can't help but smile. She's so obviously pre-med. She slips the med kit back in her bag and stabs at her salad.

"Anyway, I hope you have a cute outfit to wear because we're going to a party tonight."

I shake my head. "I'm not—"

She holds up a hand. "Stop, you're going. A bunch of my friends will be there too. We'll all look out for each other. You can't spend your whole semester locked up in our dorm. You need to enjoy college."

"I'm here to study and work, not to party." I've been there, done that. I know exactly how a party ends.

Aneesa clicks through her phone, ignoring me. "I'll even let you wear my favorite little black dress."

"Aneesa—"

She shoves her phone in my face, a sexy black dress on her screen. She reminds me so much of Chloe. Stubborn, demanding, athletic, outgoing. The kind of girl who won't take no for an answer only because she wants the best for you.

If she'd gotten a chance to meet Chloe, they would've been friends.

If I hadn't fucked everything up.

So I sigh and tell her, "Fine. I'll go."

Chapter 12

Before

Violet

At the Sigma Chi party, I adjust my too-short skirt. Everything I'm wearing tonight belongs to Chloe. She went through my entire dresser and decided none of my clothes were suitable for my first frat party.

When she snaps a selfie of us, I hardly recognize myself. She curled my hair and covered my face in concealer, foundation, eyeshadow, liner, mascara, blush, and cherry lipstick. The crop top she threw at me plunges so low, my bra almost peeks through the top. When I complained that my bra was showing, she simply told me to take it off.

Though I feel like I'm wearing a costume, I've got a new sway to my hips, and even next to the radiant beauty that is Chloe, some of the guys check me out.

In the crowded living room, she digs her nails into my arm.

"Ow!" I try to shake her off, but there's no getting rid of Chloe once she sinks her claws in you.

"I'm not normally into redheads," she whispers, "but look at that guy. He is so cute."

"I thought we were here for Luke."

"*I* am, but we've gotta find you a man too."

My stomach twists at the thought of forcing myself to try to fall for a guy who isn't Wes.

But it's just a silly crush. Once I find some other guy, a nerd from the library like he suggested, I'll get over him.

I follow where Chloe is blatantly pointing at a redhead, tall and reedy with thick glasses. "Oh, I know him. That's Maxwell. He's in my Intro to Fiction Writing class.

Chloe gasps. "A fellow writer? Oh my god, you have to go over and flirt with him."

"What?" My body temperature spikes. "I'm not doing that."

She pinches me. I'm starting to learn her love language is violence. "Why the hell not? He's cute, and I bet you two have a ton in common."

"Because I have to see him in class every week, and I don't want things to be awkward between us."

"I'm not telling you to *date* the guy. Just flirt with him. Get some practice in. I bet he's the type of guy who would be flattered you even looked in his direction. Give him a compliment and he'll be begging for your hand in marriage." When I fold my arms and make it clear I'm not budging, Chloe adds, "I dare you."

Shit. I dared her to flash a guy at a crowded hockey game and she didn't even bat an eye. If she can do that, surely I can flirt with a cute classmate for five seconds.

Chloe and I grab drinks for the three of us as an icebreaker. When we reach him, she bursts out with a loud "Hi!" I shove a red plastic cup wordlessly into his hand.

His eyes widen, frightened. "Uh. Thanks."

"Violet." Chloe's voice comes out artificially high. "What were you just saying about his hair?"

I'm going to kill her for this. "Oh, yeah. It's . . . nice."

Chloe manages to hide her cringe, but Maxwell slips into an easy smile. "Thanks. You're in my fiction writing class, right?"

The tight knot in my chest starts to loosen. "Yeah, I am."

"How did you do on the last assignment?"

Chloe squeezes my shoulder. "I'm going to get another drink!" she shouts over the pulse of the music and the cheers from the kitchen.

She leaves me with Maxwell, giggling and flirting with Luke in the kitchen as they play a drinking game. Maxwell and I talk about class, writing, and books for the next half hour. He's cute, he's nice, he's easy to talk to. The ideal guy to have a crush on, to date, to take my first kiss. Logical, practical, rational.

Yet my heart is still full of irrational feelings for Wes. When I imagine myself leaning in to kiss Maxwell, all I see is Wes Novak's face.

Just as Maxwell drapes an arm across the couch behind me and his gaze falls to my mouth, Chloe stumbles from the kitchen and bumps into my legs.

"Luke left." Her bottom lip puffs out in a pout. "Now I'm b-bored."

She avoids alcohol so she can stay in the best possible shape for figure skating, but she's clearly drunk now.

"Sorry," I tell Maxwell. "I need to get her home."

Before she passes out and becomes dead weight. Secretly, I'm glad she interrupted before Maxwell could kiss me. I know I wouldn't have stopped him, but I also don't want to share that first with him.

I want that with someone else.

"No problem. See you in class."

I manage to get Chloe outside and onto the porch before she drops to her butt and leans against the railing, eyes fluttering shut.

"No, not here, Chloe. Come on. We don't have that much farther."

She waves me off, and no matter how much I tug on her arm, she's not budging.

I dig in her front pocket for her phone and convince her to open her eyes long enough to unlock it. Wes is in her emergency contacts.

If you end up in a bad situation, you call me.

Both of you.

The phone rings, and I hope he's not drunk or passed out at a party too.

On the third ring, a low baritone hums in my ear. "What's up?"

"Hey, um, this is Violet."

"Violet." His voice floods me with a warmth that makes my thighs clench.

"Chloe and I are at the Sigma Chi party, and she's kind of passed out. Could you come help me get her back to the dorm?"

"I'll be right there." He hangs up without another word.

Chloe is drunkenly snoring by the time Wes shows up five minutes later. He shakes his head before scooping her up effortlessly.

An insane part of me wishes that I was the drunk friend and Chloe was the one who called Wes for help so I'd be the one in his arms right now.

When he fixes his gaze on me, he halts. I melt under his stare as he takes in every inch of me, from my curled hair to the low-cut top down to the thighs that are almost entirely exposed by the tiny piece of fabric that barely passes for a skirt.

No one's ever looked at me like this before.

Wes clears his throat. "You ready?"

I manage a nod.

He tucks Chloe into the backseat of his car, and my heart

nearly stops when he opens the passenger side door for me. A small gesture that shouldn't make me swoon as much as it does. Maybe he's checking out my ass as I slide in.

God, I hope so.

When he's behind the wheel and we're headed for Nohren Hall, Wes asks, "How many drinks did she have?"

I bite my lip. I should've been watching her more closely. "Honestly, I'm not sure. She was playing a drinking game, so I think she had a few."

"I'm amazed she lasted a whole month before getting hammered." His gaze flicks to me, making the nerves in my stomach stir. How my heart doesn't explode every time he peers at me through those dark lashes is a mystery. "How much did you drink?"

"I only took a few sips. It tasted pretty gross to me," I admit, knowing that makes me sound like the nerdy loser he already thinks I am.

He chuckles, and the sound is enough to spread a grin wide across my face. "Shitty beer tastes like piss. That's why I don't really give a shit that Coach doesn't let us drink during hockey season."

"So you don't go to parties?"

"I go to some, but they're not as fun when you're one of the only sober people there." He lifts an ebony eyebrow in my direction. "That how you felt tonight?"

Earlier, I left our dorm expecting to hate every second, to feel like a little kid playing dress-up, but having Chloe by my side made the night fun, exciting. Even when she was in another room, she helped me do something I never would've done otherwise. Adrenaline is still coursing through my veins. "I actually didn't have a bad time. I hung out with Chloe and one of my classmates."

"Who's this classmate?" I don't know Wes well enough yet

to interpret his tone, but the question doesn't sound wholly casual.

"I don't think you know him."

His shoulders stiffen, grip tightening on the steering wheel. Almost like he's . . .

No. Not jealous.

"Did you hook up?" There's a steely edge to his voice now.

"No," I say quickly, wringing my hands. "It's not like that with him."

"Why not?" A careful question.

"He's nice, but I only see him as a friend."

Wes's blue eyes land on me again, playful and roguish. "What do you see me as?"

My heartbeat stutters. There's no way I'm imagining this now. He's definitely flirting with me. But whether it means anything more to him or it's just a fun way for him to pass the time, I can't say for sure. "A mystery," I admit.

My answer both surprises and amuses him. "Huh. No one's ever called me mysterious before." He pulls into a parking lot outside of Nohren Hall. "Guess we'll just have to get to know each other better. Now that you're living with my sister, after all. Gotta make sure you're not a psycho killer."

I giggle. "I'm definitely not. Although, I think you should've found that out before you gave me a ride."

He grins, and I nearly combust. "That sounds like something a psycho killer would say."

Wes carries Chloe up to our dorm, the scent of her vanilla perfume hitting us. The smell is comforting now. My home away from home.

He lays her on her side and covers her with the blanket, our room about sixty-five degrees because Chloe likes to curl up under four layers while she sleeps, even in the summer.

My heart squeezes at Wes's tenderness toward his little sister as he tucks her in before I force myself to turn away and grab the trash can in the corner in case she pukes in the middle of the night.

I sit on the floor to watch Chloe. During the ride to campus, Mom warned me that if you're drunk and puke while you're lying on your back, you could drown in your own vomit. I have a feeling I won't be sleeping tonight, terrified about what might happen to my new best friend if I shut my eyes. "I think she was trying to impress Luke," I tell Wes. "I don't know why she thinks she has to impress him, though. She's great. He'd be lucky to date her."

"No guy on this fucking campus is good enough for her." Wes lowers himself to the floor beside me. He says it like a fact, and I smile. He's right. "You have a boyfriend yet?"

Warmth creeps up to my cheeks. "No, I've never had a boyfriend," I admit. I hate that every conversation we have further confirms how far below his league I am. "What about you?"

"I've had one girlfriend. That was plenty." His jaw clenches, features stony now as he returns his focus to his sleeping sister.

The subject is clearly a touchy one. Likely off-limits entirely. But the adrenaline from tonight is making me braver. "What happened?"

He lifts a dark brow. "You really want to hear the whole story?" Like maybe no one else has ever been interested in hearing it before.

"I like stories." I nod to the stack of books under my desk where I keep my collection.

A smile flickers across his face, lighting a candle in my chest. "All right, well, I'm not much of a storyteller, but I'll give it my best shot." He bends a knee and rests his arm on it. "I dated this girl all through high school. Head over heels, thought we'd get married."

Stupidly, my heart sinks. I picture a model who was probably also an athlete and smart and funny and everything I'm not. He's already been in love before. So in love, he thought he'd marry her someday. He'll probably never love anyone like that again, let alone me. If his life turns out anything like the books I read, he'll get his happily ever after with her. Not me.

"We graduated and went to different colleges. I didn't even blink. We were rock-solid. Plus, we were only two hours apart. We could visit each other every weekend. Talk every night. No big deal." He shifts, growing more uncomfortable with the memories, but I'm relieved he keeps going, eager to learn as much about him as I can. "First semester, she starts acting differently. I go from waiting an hour between texts to not hearing from her until the next day. Stops returning my missed calls and then stops answering my calls altogether. Acts like I'm bothering her when I do manage to get a text back. She said I was smothering her. I figured it was the distance and we just needed to spend some time together again. How am I doing so far?"

I nod, hanging on to every word. "Good. I definitely want to hear what happens next."

He manages a smile. "So I show up at her campus to surprise her. Get a couple of her friends to help me out. Her roommate lets me borrow her card to open the door, and when I walk in and flick on the light, my girlfriend's riding some other guy in her bed."

My hand flies to my mouth too late to cover the gasp.

Wes lets out a humorless laugh. "It was almost fucking funny, watching her eyes bug out of her head when she realized it was me. She yelled my name, and that motherfucker was still inside her when he said, 'That your boyfriend?'"

"That's awful," I whisper. I can't even imagine how he must've felt. How that kind of betrayal would shape you, change you. Now I know why Chloe told me her brother doesn't date.

"I beat that motherfucker to a pulp. Made sure she wouldn't get any use of his dick, tongue, or fingers for weeks."

Knowing Wes is capable of that much violence sends a shock of fear down my spine. But there's something else mixed with the fear.

Excitement.

That same excitement I felt when Wes sent his opponent tumbling to the ice during the hockey game.

My thighs clench, imagining that aggression directed at me. His hand around my throat, anger in his eyes while he fucks me into the mattress.

I shake the images away, ashamed. What the hell is wrong with me? I should want someone who treats me like a queen. Who's gentle and kind. Not someone who's jealous and possessive and beats the shit out of a guy just so I can't fuck him again.

Wes is unhinged. But I'm more unhinged for liking that about him.

"How'd I do?" he asks. "Decent story?"

"I'm sorry that happened to you."

He shrugs. "So why have you never had a boyfriend?"

"I thought that was obvious," I say. Wes frowns, tilting his head and waiting for me to continue. "You said I'm a loser who should only date nerds from the library. I guess I just haven't found the right one yet."

"I never said you were a loser. You're gorgeous and sweet and smart. You could date any guy."

The compliments throw me off so completely, I can't formulate a response. Wes Novak thinks *I'm* gorgeous?

But that doesn't matter because he had his heart so thoroughly broken by his first love, he's determined to never love again. That much is clear.

"So why did you say I should date a nerd from the library?" I ask.

"Wasn't meant to be an insult. I figured you'd want to date a guy who's like you. Reads books. Writes. A nice guy who will treat you right."

I shrug. He's not wrong, exactly. That is the exact type of man I've always fantasized about meeting and falling in love with. The type of man I write about in my stories.

"You can't tell me no guy's ever been into you." A lopsided smirk that gets my heart fluttering. "I refuse to believe it."

"I thought one boy liked me in ninth grade," I admit. The memory makes me cringe, but it's nothing worse than what Wes went through, so I keep going. "He was really nice, said all the right things. He even sat with me during lunch a few times. I usually sat by myself and read a book, so it was nice having someone to talk to for once, especially a cute guy. I even shared some of my stories with him." I swallow and squeeze my eyes shut like I might block out the memories flashing through my mind, but they're engraved in my brain. "I wrote a new story the night before that I was really proud of, so instead of waiting to see him in class, I went to meet him at his locker before homeroom. He and his friends had their backs to me, so they didn't notice me standing right behind them. But I stopped when I overheard him reading one of my stories out loud to his friends. They were all laughing, even him. It's stupid, but I spent an hour crying in the bathroom after that and never let anyone read anything I wrote again."

My heart is pounding at simply reliving the memory. Even years later, I can hear the words from my story in Randall's mocking voice. Words I poured my heart and soul into. Words I believed in.

He was the first person I trusted with them, and he crushed them into dust. I don't know how I'll ever let anyone read anything I've written again. How I'll fulfill my dream of becoming an author if I'm terrified about how people may read my words and twist them into something ugly. How I'll be able to bare my soul like that to anyone again.

"That kid was a dick," Wes says simply. "Definitely the kind of asshole who'd fuck another guy's girlfriend."

I giggle, relieved he can make a joke about our old wounds. "Definitely."

"But if you're passionate about something, you should go for it. No matter what anybody else thinks," he says, serious now. "Plenty of people think I'll never make the NHL. That hasn't stopped me from going after it. Don't let that little shit stop you."

I hide behind my curtain of hair so Wes doesn't spot the shimmering tears. I've needed to hear those words for so long.

The thought of sharing my writing with anyone still gives me hives, but Wes is right. I shouldn't let some freshman punk like Randall dictate my life. One person's opinion doesn't determine the worth of my words. I'm a good enough writer to secure a spot in Diamond's prestigious writing program. I'm a good enough writer to at least give my dream a shot. I may not ever be a bestselling, full-time author with millions of fans and movie deals. But I at least need to try.

And even though Wes has never read a word I've written, his faith in me gives me the confidence to believe I can someday make my dream a reality.

Chapter 13

After

Wes

WHILE I'M in the kitchen pouring myself another Jager bomb, there's a knock on the door. I don't know how many more bodies we can squeeze into this cramped apartment. But if it's another cute girl, I'll let her in. At least one of them should be able to take my mind off Violet tonight.

When I swing the door open, a beautiful girl with a bright smile stands in front of me. She's exactly the kind of girl who could distract me tonight. Tall, slender, dark hair and eyes. I recognize her from the soccer team, but I've never caught her name. "Hey, come on in."

"Thanks!" She points over her shoulder, but she's too tall to see whoever's behind her. "My roommate and I are very excited to be here."

I snort. Definitely a freshman.

The second she passes me, another girl squeals and pulls her through the crowd by the arm. Then I'm left with the girl who was standing behind her. Her roommate.

My teeth grind together. Not fucking *her*.

70

She actually had the balls to come to my party, knowing how the last party she attended ended.

She's even wearing a skimpy black dress. Almost like she thought she might tempt me into forgiving her. Seduce me into bed, so maybe I'll quit terrorizing her before it gets any worse.

Too bad for her, I have plenty of puck bunnies waiting in line to ride my cock. I don't need pussy from her when I can get it anywhere.

But I'll play the game. Let her think for a few minutes that I'm falling for her tricks until I pull the rug out from under her.

I let my gaze rake over every inch of her tiny body. From the round, hazel eyes framed by thick lashes, down to the red-lined lip she's biting, to the plunging *V* of her dress, exposing the top of her tits. The thin material clings to her hourglass figure, hugging her little hips and just barely hiding her ass before stopping high on her thighs. She's small, but in this dress, her legs go on for miles.

Before, I would've scooped her into my arms, carried her to my room, and kissed up every inch of those legs until I had her squirming. Begging for me. Now, I still want to make her squirm, but in an entirely different way.

I lean against the doorframe, and Violet swallows under my gaze. "Password?"

"You didn't make Aneesa give a password," she points out, no conviction in her voice. She should know better than to mouth off to me.

I'll teach her exactly how I expect her to speak to me from now on. "Pretty girls like that don't need a password."

Violet's eyes drop to the floor. She actually believes I don't think she's pretty. Tormenting her is going to be a whole lot easier than I thought. "If you say everything I tell you to, you can come in."

Her gaze flashes up to mine. She doesn't actually want to

be here, but her roommate dragged her, and she doesn't want to walk back in the dark alone. Smart. Not all of the Devils are here yet, and if they see her wandering around at night by herself, there's no telling what they might do.

"Say you love sucking cock."

Her pretty little mouth falls open. "What?"

"Say you love sucking cock, or you're not getting into this party."

She keeps her mouth clamped shut, gaze darting to the people chatting and laughing around us.

I narrow my eyes. "I dare you."

Her face falls at those familiar three words. The three words that doomed my sister.

Violet's gaze drops to her feet again before she murmurs almost imperceptibly, "I love sucking cock."

I hold my hand up to my ear and lean in. "Couldn't hear you. Say it again."

She sighs and blinks furiously at the floor. Already trying to fight back tears. I almost snort. She has no idea how much worse this is going to get. "I love sucking cock." Her voice is watery, but she manages to say it louder.

"Good girl. Now say you're a little slut."

"I'm . . . a little slut," she repeats, more obedient this time.

Trey and Brody listen in, wolfish grins on their faces. "Now say you want to ride my cock."

She swallows. "I want to ride your cock."

Even though I'm commanding the words from her lips, my dick still hardens in my jeans. I never thought I'd hear anything so filthy from Violet Harris's mouth. But I fucking like it. "Say you want me to shove it in your ass."

She swipes at a tear that slides down her cheek. "I want you to shove it in my ass."

Trey, Brody, and a few of the guys behind me step closer, hooting now.

"Now moan when you say this next part: *make me come, Wes.*"

Her hazel eyes finally fly up to mine, full of tears. They make me grow harder. I want to fuck her face while tears stream down her cheeks. She shakes her head.

I shrug. "All you have to do is say that and you can come in."

She takes a long, shaky breath. "Make me come, Wes," she whispers.

Chills race down my spine, but I pull myself together. "That didn't sound like a moan to me."

The guys are cracking up and a few girls snicker behind their hands.

"Make me come, Wes," Violet moans softly.

I grin. The words on a moan from her mouth make me salivate. Almost as good as if she were saying it for real. "That's a good girl."

She takes a hesitant step past me when I stand aside. Probably expecting me to grab her and push her to her knees. But I let her shuffle by and into the crowd, searching for her only friend left on this campus.

I'll let Violet think that was the worst of it tonight. At least for a little while.

SHE TOLD ME HER NAME, but I didn't bother remembering it. Her mouth slides up and down my cock and I try to focus on her red hair, not let my imagination turn it brown. The girl clearly doesn't know what she's doing. She's just bobbing her head, not sucking or using her tongue. What a waste.

"Suck," I command.

Her eyes widen. She's been following me around like a puppy since last year, hungry for this moment, and it's not going at all like she hoped. "I am."

"Suck harder."

She drops her head back to my cock and pulls in her cheeks. Better, but she's still not the girl I want sucking me off.

Violet's words ring in my ears again.

I love sucking cock.

No, I can't let my mind go there. Violet killed my sister. She's dead to me.

I want to ride your cock.

I force myself to concentrate on the curvy girl in front of me. Violet's complete opposite. Red hair, big tits, fat ass, and thick thighs. The kind of girl every man would love to see bouncing on his cock. A girl who dresses in tiny shorts and crop tops, who throws herself at every guy on the hockey team, who waltzed up to me five seconds ago and offered me a blowjob. A confident, outgoing girl who goes for what she wants.

Nothing like Violet, with her unassuming brown hair always tied up, boring gray sweats covering her slim curves, face void of makeup because she thinks that makes her stand out less. As if that could ever be possible.

Make me come, Wes.

Fuck it. I can't stop myself this time.

I push the redhead off me, and her eyes widen. "What's wrong?"

"Open your mouth."

She does as I command, and I pump my slick cock in front of her. Her hair darkens to brown, wrapped in a ponytail that I twist around my hand. The green eyes she flicks up to my face turn hazel.

"Stick out your tongue," I instruct her.

In my head, Violet flattens her tongue on the underside of my shaft and pumps my cock with her tiny hand. Then she swirls that soft, wet tongue around my tip.

I want to ride your cock.

"Fuck, Vi—"

I stop myself just before I groan her name as my cum launches into the redhead's mouth. She keeps her lips parted while I empty into her, but then she spits out my cum and I shake my head. I would make Violet swallow.

I pat the puck bunny's cheek before stuffing my cock back in my jeans. "Good girl."

She gives a little scowl, but I don't care. Violet will like being called a good girl.

The redhead straightens and fixes her hair. "I'll see you back out there. Maybe you can return the favor next time."

Like there will be a next time.

As soon as she's out the door and I'm alone, shame slowly washes over me like oil. I shouldn't be getting off to my sister's killer.

When I jump to my feet, I ache to punch something. I yank the door open, letting it slam against the wall.

Luke pats my shoulder as I pass and tries to hand me another plastic cup, but I shrug him off.

My apartment isn't big, so it doesn't take long to spot her. She's in a corner of the kitchen, mouth shut and doing her best to be invisible. Her roommate chats amiably with a group of girls next to her, but Violet doesn't join in. Lost somewhere in her mind.

Good. I don't fucking feel bad for her. I hope she's suffering in there.

I grab the punch bowl from the counter, still half full, and approach the group of girls. Fix on my usual, charming smile. "You ladies need another drink?"

They smile at me and start to answer when I pretend to trip, the punch sailing through the air. Landing right on my target.

Red liquid washes over Violet's hair and down to her feet. She gasps, completely drenched.

She should look like a drowned rat. Her makeup should be running, her hair sticking to her face. The punch was supposed to make her ugly, but now her dress clings to her body and her nipples poke through the thin fabric. *Fuck.* She's not wearing a bra.

All I want to do now is throw her on top of the counter, rip that dress down, and suck those hard nipples into my mouth. She must've covered those bruises I left on her neck with makeup because the faint yellow spots peek out now. Oh god. The sight makes my balls tighten. I love seeing my mark on her skin.

Her expression is a mix of horror and embarrassment. A delightful combination that somehow gets me hard again. Apparently, cumming in the redhead's mouth was nowhere near enough to cure me of my lust for Violet Harris.

"Nice nips!" Brody shouts.

Her roommate is horrified by what just happened, but the rest of the girls giggle. Everyone on this campus knows who to be loyal to, and that's not Violet Harris.

"Way to go, Wes," one of the girls calls, but she says it with a laugh.

Violet's roommate's eyes flash to me. "Wait. You're Wes?" She angrily grabs a roll of paper towels and starts pointlessly dabbing at Violet's soaked skin and clothes. "You did that on purpose, didn't you?"

I don't let the easygoing smile slip off my face. "Of course not. It was an accident."

"Yeah, right," her roommate grumbles, tossing the soaked paper towel at the trash and missing.

I grab Violet's arm and drag her from the room, ignoring her roommate's protests. She tries to follow us, but she can't part the crowd like I can. Violet pulls against me, trying to free herself from my grip, but her attempts are laughable. She's a bird fighting a brick wall.

Once I get her in my bathroom, I slam the door behind us, flick the lock, and whirl on her. She's cowering near the shower, trying to get as far from me as she can.

"Why the fuck are you wearing that?" I growl.

She glances down at her soaked dress, scared and confused. "Um. I don't know . . . it's a party. Aneesa told me to wear it."

I roll my eyes. Right. She still does whatever anyone tells her to do. Her mom tells her to stay at Diamond University, she stays. Aneesa tells her to wear a dress, she wears it. If Chloe had told her to jump off a bridge, she would've jumped.

She doesn't know how to stand up for herself. How to fight back. She never has. That's what makes this so easy.

I grab a towel and close the distance between us. Her back hits the shower and she's got nowhere else to go. My finger hooks in her plunging neckline, her tits still wet and glistening, mere inches from my touch. She gulps.

With my other hand, I wipe the punch off her arm, her shoulder, her chest. Even with the cloth between us, I can feel her heart thumping against her ribcage.

I lean toward her neck and leisurely lick the spiked punch off her skin, the sweet flavor mixed with a hint of hard liquor and the delectable taste of Violet. She shivers but doesn't shove me away or tell me to stop.

Her nipples peak again and I wonder how wet she already is for me.

"Don't ever wear something like this around me again," I warn her, glaring into her wide hazel eyes. "Unless you want to get bent over the nearest table and fucked."

A flicker of arousal in her eyes before she remembers to fear me. She presses her back against the shower, finally pushing my hand away. "Please just let me leave."

"You shouldn't have come here in the first place." I drag her out of the bathroom, shoving a protesting Aneesa out of the way, and slam my bedroom door behind us before throwing my sweats and an old jersey at her. She'll drown in them, but at least they'll hide her delicious curves. "Change."

Violet stares at me wide-eyed, clutching the clothes to her chest. "What—"

"Change. *Now*."

She drops my clothes on the bed and starts to bend until she notices I'm still watching. Her mouth pinches. "Can you at least turn around?"

I fold my arms, leaning back against the wall to settle in for the show. "No." She sighs but decides arguing won't get her anywhere. Smart girl. She grabs the sweats, but I shake my head. "Take the panties off."

"What? Why?"

"Because you're soaked, Violet." I'll let her mull over that double entendre.

"Because you threw punch on me," she grumbles, but she does as I say, tugging her panties down her legs. My cock hardens.

"You're the one who showed up here."

"I didn't know it was at your apartment. Otherwise, I wouldn't have."

"How you can even go to a party while your best friend is dead is sick."

Her eyes flash up to mine as she hikes the sweats to her waist, fabric bunched at her ankles. She debates whether she's going to retort until she decides to go for it. "You're partying while your sister is dead."

I'm up against her in three steps. She balks, instantly realizing her mistake. "But I didn't fucking *kill* her, did I?"

Aneesa pounds on the door. "Let her out of there, Wes! Or I'll call campus security!"

Violet turns away from me, scrambling to yank her dress over her head. My erection grows rock-hard at her half-naked inches away from me. She slips on my jersey, and I hate that I love seeing her in my clothes.

Violet ducks to grab up her panties, but I step on the flimsy black fabric. "Leave them."

She doesn't bother objecting this time. She heads for the door, wrenching it open, and I don't stop her.

Aneesa glares at me like a bull about to charge, but she takes Violet's hand instead. "Come on, Violet. Let's go."

Violet doesn't say a word or even nod. All she does is shake and let Aneesa pull her out of the apartment, giggles and whispers following in her wake.

I grab up her panties, ball them in my fist, and tuck them in my pocket. With every brush of my sweats against her bare ass, she'll be forced to think of me. Of everything I'm going to do to her.

Chapter 14

After

Violet

IN MY ADVANCED Fiction Writing class, Professor Tate returns our graded writing assignments. A short story that focuses on the setting, adding specific details to make the characters' surroundings come to life. I'm not surprised by the seventy circled in red at the top of the page. Setting has never been my strong suit, but everything I've tried to write lately has been a painful extraction. Like yanking out my fingernails and scratching out the words in my own blood.

When she dismisses us, Professor Tate calls out, "Violet? Hang back for a second?" She perches on her desk and waits for my classmates to file out of the room, wearing a rare frown.

My stomach twists. I'm sure this is about the most recent assignment. "Setting isn't my strong suit," I blurt.

She holds up a hand. "This isn't about your story. At least, not only that one. All of your work so far this semester has been a far cry from the writing you turned in last year."

Words shouldn't be enough to physically make my chest ache, but they do. Writing has always been the only thing I've ever been good at. Now I don't even have that anymore.

"You're a strong writer, Violet. Stronger than the work you've been turning in lately. Where's the heart? Your soul is missing from the page."

Of course it is. My soul is cold and darkened, if it's even there anymore at all.

Professor Tate hops down from her desk and drops into her seat, shuffling through folders. "You need to bare your soul for your work to have any meaning. Keep that in mind for your next assignment."

I swallow down the lump in my throat. "I will." A promise I know I won't be able to keep.

Before she can say another word, I scurry out of the classroom and head back to my dorm.

I swear my hair still smells like punch, despite spending an hour in the shower after the party last night scrubbing every inch of my body clean. Trying to wash away the feeling of their eyes on me.

But there's one pair of eyes I can never seem to shake off.

His little trip with the punch bowl last night was no accident. A small humiliation that Wes could shrug off as unintentional, but everyone knows the truth.

I still can't believe he licked my neck clean. Made me strip off my panties and leave them behind, and then made me wear his clothes as a reminder of what he did to me with every step. His sweats and jersey are buried at the bottom of my dirty laundry.

I reach for the student ID in my bag just as my eyes land on the door to my dorm.

I stop dead in my tracks.

Words in black and blue are painted on the door. He chose those colors purposely—he's going to paint me black and blue next.

The variations in handwriting tell me he must've had his

teammates help him with this prank. *Murderer. Killer. Psycho. Crazy. Bitch. Slut. Cunt. Little cum slut. Loves taking it in the ass. Get your dick sucked here.*

I'm frozen until my eyes land on a string of numbers. Bile turns in my stomach. They wrote my phone number.

I rush into my dorm and soak a paper towel, propping the door open while I scrub. A couple walks by and laughs. No matter how hard I scrub, none of the paint comes off. I scrub harder and harder until my fingers and nails ache, but it's useless.

I need to get these words off the door before Aneesa gets back or she'll flip out. I call maintenance, even though that's the last thing I want to do. I don't want anyone else's eyes on these disgusting words written about me.

First the party. Now this. Wes is doing everything he can to humiliate me at every turn.

I blink back the tears. I don't deserve to cry because I've earned this. The insults, the torment, the assaults. I've earned each and every one.

"Get your dick sucked here, huh?" A sickening male voice calls out. My spine goes ramrod straight. "Don't mind if I do."

I squeeze my eyes shut, praying I'm imagining this before reluctantly turning to find whoever is approaching.

Four hulking men saunter toward me, solid white masks concealing their faces.

The Devils.

Their faces are almost entirely hidden behind the masks, but I'm familiar enough with their eyes, statures, and smirks to know exactly which Devils they are.

Trey, Brody, Luke, and Wes.

They stop mere feet from me, Trey making a big show about punching my number into his phone even though I know he already has it saved. I'm sure I can expect a barrage of dick pics at two in the morning.

"Maintenance is on their way," I mumble, like that's any sort of threat to them. They got what they wanted—public humiliation.

"What do you say, Novak?" Brody asks, stepping closer. His brown eyes flat, almost bored even as he looms over me with predatory intent. "You take her mouth first?"

My pulse picks up speed. They can't do anything to me here—we're in a hallway. Sure, we're on the fifth floor in the middle of the day and most students are on campus, but they can't seriously think they can force me to blow them right here, out in the open.

Wes doesn't say a word. His ice-blue eyes are murderous through the holes in his mask.

Of course, if the cameras catch them forcing me to suck them off, the only footage the university will have is of four unidentified masked men.

My gaze darts to Luke, but even his normally kind, friendly eyes are hard. I took Chloe away from him. The girl of his dreams. He resents me too.

Trey approaches, forcing me back against the door. They tower over me, blocking me from view from anyone who might exit the elevator behind them. Blocking me from signaling to anyone who may be able to help. I'm cornered.

Trapped.

"I say we fill all of the little cum slut's holes," Trey purrs, hot breath curling around my neck through the cluster of small holes in his mask.

I flinch away, but Brody smacks a hand on the other side of my head, blocking me in.

No, no, no. The panic mounts. Trey's hand slowly slips

from my cheek to my collarbone. Then down to my breast, where he cups me in his huge palm and squeezes.

I hiss through my teeth, flattening against the door, but it does nothing to help me escape his touch.

Brody grabs my other breast, squeezing and shoving my flesh up before twisting my nipple.

"Stop!" I try to push them away, but they're immovable concrete barriers in front of me.

Over their shoulders, Wes glares. But he doesn't move. Only watches.

After that first time he kissed me, he told me I was his. More warning than promise.

Now he's letting his teammates touch me. Grope me.

His way of confirming I'm not his anymore.

He doesn't care who touches me or where. He doesn't care what they force me to do. Right in front of him.

I don't matter any more to him than a nameless puck bunny now.

"Shh," Trey whispers in my ear. "Or we'll make it worse."

My eyes sting when Trey's heavy hand on my shoulder shoves me down until I land so hard on my knees, my teeth clack together.

"Let go of me," I beg.

Brody claps a revolting hand over my mouth. "Novak, shove your cock down her throat and shut her up."

Wes steps between them. He's finally going to stop this. Even he has to realize this is crossing a line.

Until I spot the long, solid bulge in his pants. He's rock-hard at the sight of me on my knees before him, Trey's hand still on my shoulder holding me down and Brody's on my mouth keeping me quiet.

To my horror, Wes pushes my hair over my shoulders before his hand drifts to his belt.

Behind us, the elevator dings. "Maintenance!" a voice calls out.

My heart is in my throat, and Wes yanks me to my feet, nearly popping my arms out of my sockets before the four of them retreat, leaving me alone in the hallway with the maintenance worker as they escape down the stairwell.

I clap a hand over my mouth and run for the girls' restroom, stomach churning.

The next time they trap me, I might not escape.

Wes

SHE'S GOT her hood pulled over her head again today. She's stupid if she thinks that's a disguise. Today, she's ditched the sweatpants for shorts, though, and I allow myself one sweep down her legs before I pull over.

Violet jumps away from my car when the tire hits the curb. Her eyes widen when she spots me and she braces to make a run for it. But my window's already down and I shout my command, "Get in!"

When she hesitates, my hands twist around the steering wheel. Someday she'll learn to fucking listen to me. "Get the fuck in this car."

"I-I need to get to class," she stutters.

"Get. In."

Finally, she does as she's told. She clasps her hands in her lap to stop them from shaking and drops her hood, the shitty disguise useless now.

"You know no matter what you wear, I can spot you from a mile away."

She wrings her hands together. Her legs are smooth and pale. She doesn't stay outside long enough to get any sun. Too afraid of how being outside around other people might end for her. My hand aches to reach out and grip her thigh. Feel how soft she is. Then I'd grab her ponytail, yank it, and push that pretty face down into my lap.

I could. I could drive us around as long as I want, make her suck me off and swallow it. She'd hate it, and I'd love every second, but I don't want to enjoy a single moment with Violet Harris.

At least if I had made her suck me off in front of the guys, it would've been about more than the blowjob. Public humiliation, degradation, control. But enjoying her in private is too intimate to rationalize.

Besides, I know she's fantasized about sucking my cock before. Maybe she still does. I refuse to act out her fantasies.

Only her nightmares.

"I know this doesn't help." Her voice is small, a shell of the girl she used to be. "But I swear it was an accident."

I clench my jaw and pull back out onto the road. "You're right. That doesn't help."

She grips the door handle when I pull off campus, but she doesn't dare jump out. She knows she won't get far. "Where are you taking us?"

"Wherever the fuck I feel like."

Her panic escalates when I sail past the center of Diamond, nails digging into the upholstery. But she tries to keep her voice even. "Congrats on getting captain."

I fucking hate that she knows that. Hate that she gets to know I made captain but my sister never will.

When I don't say anything, she adds, "Chloe would be proud."

My sister's name from her mouth sends my fist flying into

the dashboard. Violet flinches, scooting as far away from me as her seat will allow. "Don't fucking talk to me about her. In fact, don't let her name come out of your fucking mouth again."

Silence falls over us. Violet remains statue-still for a few seconds, letting me calm down. But there's no calming me down anymore. I've been pissed every day since my sister died, and my fury only grows with each day that passes without justice.

Violet slowly pulls out her phone as if I don't notice every single move she makes.

"Put your fucking phone away."

"I just need to text my boss—"

"You don't need to text anybody. Nobody gives a shit about where you are or what happens to you. Now put the phone away before I rip it out of your hand."

Violet slips her phone back in her pocket. She knows I'm right. No one gives a shit about her, not even her mom who made her come back to Diamond University knowing I'd be here. Knowing what I'd want to do to her if I saw her again.

Tears flood her eyes and my cock twitches in my jeans. I grab her hand and flatten it against my hard-on. "This is what your tears do to me."

Her nose scrunches, disgusted, and she tries to pull away, but I don't let her.

"Remove your hand and I'll make you use your mouth instead."

She freezes, suppressing her tears and not daring to move a muscle. The threat of what my cock could do to her jaw a constant reminder beneath her palm.

I stroke her hand up my shaft, biting down on my lip to suppress a groan. She doesn't get to know the kind of effect she still has on me. The only bit of power she continues to wield.

The rest of the ride passes in silence. I take random turns

and backroads so she can't track our movements. I brush off her hand, the feel of her palm on my cock over my jeans too good for comfort.

When I finally pull over, I tell her, "Get your phone out."

Wordlessly, she does as she's told. Guess she still has some sense left in that head.

"Turn the passcode off."

When she does, I hold out my hand. "Give it to me."

She obeys, and I slide her phone in my pocket.

Her entire body's shaking now. Nothing but empty fields around us. I could kill her out here. I could get away with it. Too bad I can't stomach being anything like her.

"Get out."

Her head whirls to me. "What?"

"Get. Out."

"But . . . how will I get back to campus?"

I shrug. "Not my problem."

Fuck. She needs to stop crying or I'm going to get too hard to resist her anymore.

"Why are you doing this?" she whispers.

"Why did you kill my sister?"

Violet drops her gaze to her lap. Her voice comes out barely audible. "I didn't mean to."

"That doesn't matter. You fucking did it. And you got away with it. Until now, anyway. You deserve this, you know that?"

To my surprise, she nods.

"So get out of my fucking car, Violet."

She listens this time. She's barely shut the door behind her before I slam on the gas, leaving her in a cloud of dust.

If she survives, if she makes it back to campus, she better prepare for the Devils to rain hell down on her.

Chapter 15

Before

Wes

"You KNOW if you keep bringing her around, she's going to fall in love with me."

Chloe rolls her eyes, hands planted on her hips while she watches Violet waddle toward us on her skates. She's got about five layers to cushion her fall if she hits the ice.

Not if. When.

"Why do you need me here, anyway?"

"I told you, I need you to help me teach her how to skate. I don't want to be alone if she cracks her head on the ice. Besides, she's already terrified enough. She'll feel better having us both here, ready to catch her."

I bet she would. I bet Violet Harris would love to fall into my arms. And I'd love to play hero. "If she's so terrified, why is she trying it?"

"Because I dared her to," Chloe says simply.

I lift a brow in her direction. "So?"

"So that's our *thing*, Wes," my sister huffs. "Come on. If she falls the second her skates hit the ice, we'll never convince her to try again."

"Funny how it's *we* all of a sudden," I grumble, but Chloe takes off to the edge of the rink, ignoring me.

Violet's hair is swept back in a pretty braid. Must be Chloe's doing. Somehow, she looks goddamn adorable in all those layers. Part of me wishes Chloe wasn't here so I could persuade her to take them off.

"You know you don't have to do something just because she dares you to," I tell Violet. "What if she dares you to jump off a cliff?"

"If Chloe dares me to jump off a cliff, there's water below, and she's jumping with me." They grin at each other, and I can't help but grin too.

I love my sister, but she hasn't exactly had many friends. The girls she skates with all see each other as competition, and Chloe's hectic schedule leaves little room for friends. Not to mention most people are intimidated by her single-minded drive and can't relate to her dedication.

Even I wonder if I'll ever live up to my father's and sister's accomplishments.

"Take her other arm," Chloe instructs me.

We both grab one of Violet's arms. I'm touching her through at least three layers—a winter jacket over her hoodie and a long blue shirt dangling right above her ass—so the contact shouldn't have this effect on me. Heart picking up speed, cock swelling in my pants, balls tightening.

I love how fragile she is. A primal urge to take care of her sweeps through my veins. To protect her in public so she'll worship me for it in private.

Violet stares down at the ice with wide eyes, but she nods. "I'm ready."

I can't help but admire that she's willing to do something she's so scared of, especially because it's for Chloe. Chloe adores sharing her love of the ice. They haven't known each other that long, but Violet's already proving herself to be the best friend Chloe's ever had.

If she means this much to my sister, there must be something special about this girl.

Violet

CHLOE IS DYING. Surely, her lungs must be bruised by now from all the laughing.

She swipes at the tears leaking from the corners of her eyes and wheezes. "Oh my god. How is a book with such a cute cover so filthy?"

"I didn't know!" I'm laughing right alongside her.

"*Come on, little duck. Be my good girl.*" Chloe squeals, kicking her legs in the air. "I love him *so much!* Why are fictional men so much hotter than men in real life? This is my new favorite book. If all books were like this, I'd be a voracious reader."

"You told me you haven't read a book since you were twelve."

"Exactly." She waves the romcom in the air. "You need to write a book like this. And dedicate it to me."

"I am *not* writing a book like that. My mom will read it!"

Chloe whacks my knee with the book. "And she'd love it! You have to write a smutty story. I dare you to."

Well, shit. Neither of us has backed down from a dare yet.

She jumps up when there's a knock on the door, revealing Wes on the other side. My stomach immediately twists with nervous anticipation.

Chloe heaves a heavy sigh. "What are you doing here?"

He rolls his eyes. "Bringing you the snacks you were bitching about."

Wes holds out a plastic bag, and Chloe snatches it from his hand. "I don't bitch."

She spills the contents onto her bed. Mostly protein bars and sugar-free beef jerky to help her stay fit and lean. She holds up chocolate peanut butter cups with a furrowed brow. "I didn't ask for these."

Wes's startling blue eyes land on me. "They're Violet's favorites."

How does Wes know that chocolate peanut butter cups are my favorite candy? I don't remember telling him that.

However he found out, he went out of his way to get them for me.

I grin, opening up a peanut butter cup and popping it in my mouth. "Thanks."

Chloe's eyes flick back and forth between us. She flashes me a knowing little smirk before flouncing out of the room. "I need to pee!"

Leaving me entirely alone with Wes.

"Thanks for the chocolate. I forgot I told you they're my favorite."

He sits on my bed like he belongs there. "You didn't."

I swallow down the nerves mixed with delight. "Then how did you know? Have you been following me around?" I tease, even though part of me is certain it's true.

"I'm a busy man, Violet. I don't have time to follow pretty girls around campus, no matter how much I wish I did." His lopsided smile tells me he's lying through his teeth. "But I've noticed some things about you."

"What else have you noticed?" I dare to ask, not sure I want to know the answer.

He leans back, arms folded casually to show off his enormous, corded biceps. "You're the kind of girl who doesn't have any confidence in what she says or thinks, even if she's smarter than everyone else in the room. You're prettier than you realize. You think you're lucky just to have a man glance your way, when really a man would be lucky to fall to his knees before you. You think you're the type of girl who should only want the things that are sweet and nice, even if that's not what you really want deep down. You're an iceberg girl—most people only get to see the five percent that's on the surface, what you choose to show them. But there's a lot more to you hiding underneath."

His words utterly silence me. I have no idea what to say to that. No idea how someone who hasn't known me for long at all could already understand me so well. I am fully clothed, but I might as well be nude in front of him.

"That's . . . shockingly accurate," I admit.

"I bet what's underneath is pretty interesting too." His ice-blue eyes rake down my body, taking in my flushed neck and chest, hovering over the mounds of my breasts under my sweater, trailing down to the slopes of my hips and my legging-clad thighs.

I swallow around the lump in my throat. Wes doesn't want a relationship. Not with anyone, and certainly not with me. But if it wasn't crystal clear before, it is now—he's interested in me, even if that interest extends only to my body.

Part of me wants to save my first time for the right guy. The guy who will be gentle and caring and loving. My first boyfriend. My first love.

Another part of me wants my first time to be with Wes, no matter what that entails. Even if I'll never be his girlfriend, even if he'll never love me, some wild part of me wants to know what it would be like to be naked beneath him. To feel his mouth on my skin and his hard length between my legs.

His eyes dance with amusement, almost like he can read my thoughts. "So what were you two in here giggling about?"

Thank god he changes the subject. I cannot keep thinking about having sex with Wes Novak right in front of him.

"We were reading."

To my horror, Wes picks up the book splayed open at the end of my bed.

"No—" I reach for it, but his eyes are already skimming the page.

"'*You like my hard, throbbing, monster cock buried deep in that sopping, wet pussy?*'" Wes laughs. "Holy shit. The porn I watch isn't this graphic."

I reach for the book again, but he stands, holding it well out of reach.

"*She moans. 'Ugh, yes, daddy. My pussy is weeping for you.' 'Good girl. You're going to take it deep. I want every single inch of my cock buried inside you.'*"

Even though I'm mortified by what's happening right now, a thrill zips down my spine at his low, rumbling voice reading the seductive words out loud. My thighs clench. If Wes was a narrator, I would only read audiobooks.

"Is this what you like to write?" Wes asks.

My face is actually on fire. "No, but Chloe dared me to."

"How are you going to write a smutty story if you've never been with a guy?"

"That's a great question." I finally manage to snatch the book out of his hand and clutch it to my chest.

His grin turns wolfish. "Maybe someone needs to give you a little inspiration."

"Next year, we're getting an apartment with a private bathroom," Chloe declares, striding into our dorm. She hops on her bed and glances back and forth between us. "What did you two talk about while I was gone?"

I flush and can't meet either of their gazes.

Wes grins like he scored the winning goal at the championship. "Violet was just telling me she's looking for some inspiration."

Chapter 16

After

Violet

MY FEET ARE SCREAMING by the time I hobble into Nohren Hall, dark long since descended over campus. When I reach the elevator, I ache to collapse on the floor, but I know if I stop now, I won't be able to stand again. My legs are jelly, heels of my feet numb.

When I returned to Diamond University, I had no idea the punishments Wes had in store for me. Humiliating me at a party, nearly choking me to unconsciousness, deserting me in the middle of nowhere with no way to contact anyone for help, nearly forcing me to blow him in front of his friends.

I'm not sure how much more I can take, and I have a sickening feeling this is just the tip of the iceberg.

The second I'm through the door to our dorm, Aneesa leaps to her feet. "I thought you'd been killed! Where have you been? Some guy answered your phone and told me to stop calling. I'm pretty sure he blocked me."

I collapse onto my bed, groaning at the sweet relief before I peel my shoes off. By some miracle, my socks are free of blood. I don't know how many miles I walked, and I'm still not totally sure how I made it home. "I lost my phone, and there wasn't anyone around to give me directions."

"This campus isn't that big. How did you get lost for half a day?"

"I . . ." I scramble for a decent excuse. ". . . went off campus."

Aneesa hovers at the edge of my mattress, peering over at me. Long, luscious black hair dangling down, almost brushing my face. "Why would you leave campus?"

"I just needed to get away for a while. I wanted to go for a walk, get out in nature."

The lie is flimsy, and Aneesa's eyes narrow. "Stop with the lies, Violet. Tell me the truth. What's really going on with you?"

My back protests when I sit up to face her. I take a slow, deep breath. Aneesa's not going to let me get away with lying any longer. The words spill out of me in a rush. "It was Wes. Wes and his teammates have been basically terrorizing me since I got back to campus. Wes is captain, so they'll do whatever he says. And he wants to make my life a living hell. His words."

Her eyes widen. "So Wes is the guy who has your phone?"

I nod. "He told me to get in his car and drove us off campus. Then he made me hand over my phone and get out."

Aneesa gapes. "That *asshole*." She holds out her hand to me. "Come on. We need to go report this."

"I can't report it."

Her brows furrow. "Why the hell not? He left you stranded without any way to call for help. He can't just get away with it."

I already know exactly what he would say to that. *No, Violet can't get away with it.* "No one will do anything. There's no evidence, and even if there was, he's Wes Novak. He's the star hockey captain, and I'm the killer responsible for his sister's death. No one would believe me."

Besides, what he's dealing with is way worse than what he's putting me through.

Nothing he does to me will ever hurt as much as losing Chloe. Nothing.

"He doesn't get to keep punishing you forever for an accident." Aneesa turns and grabs her bag from her bed. "If you don't report it, I will."

My heart leaps to my throat, panic making the words burst out. "Aneesa, if you report this, it'll only get a thousand times worse for me. Please. Just keep this between us. He'll get bored of it eventually."

She debates for a few seconds, chewing on her lip. Then she shakes her head and drops her purse. "I still don't get why you think you deserve all of this. But if that's what you really think is best, I'll keep my mouth shut. For now. If this keeps getting worse, though, I'm reporting it."

I want to tell her there is no *if*. This *will* keep getting worse. Wes will make sure of it. And there's nothing she or I can do to stop him.

"It won't," I lie.

THE NEXT MORNING, an RA calls me to the front desk to let me know that a "good citizen" found my phone. I'm pretty sure Wes only returned it so he could harass me via text too.

After Aneesa and I spend two hours in the first-floor study room of Nohren Hall, she drags me to the gym when it's clear I'm not going to get more than five words written.

The latest assignment from Professor Tate is to write a love story. If Chloe was still here, the assignment would be an easy one. I could write about friendship, family, romance. Drawing inspiration from Chloe, Mom, the Novaks, Wes.

But now, each concept makes me draw a blank.

Aneesa insists that getting up and moving will help my brain start working. I have zero confidence in her theory, but I also have zero motivation to argue with her. After we lift weights and she guides me through pilates poses, she suggests we do some laps in the pool to cool off. While she dives in, I hover at the pool's edge.

The last time I was in a pool, my best friend died.

Aneesa swims the entire length of the pool and back before she realizes I still haven't joined her. She grabs onto the edge, not even a little bit breathless. "Aren't you getting in?"

I swallow and nod. It's easier to suck it up and get in than try to explain my hesitation to Aneesa. I'm not the one who drowned, after all.

She takes off again, and I ease into the shallow end. The cool water laps at my hot, sweaty skin, soothing every inch of me. At the first stroke through the water, I'm reminded how much I love swimming. There's something calming about floating on the surface. A sort of peace I haven't felt in months, not even between the pages of books.

Aneesa backstrokes across the length of the pool three more times before she yells to me that she's going to shower.

"I'm doing a few more laps!" I call.

When she disappears into the locker room, the only sound is the rush of water past my ears and the slosh of each of my strokes as I glide through the water.

I'm nearly to the shallow end when I hear a splash behind me. I tread and glance back for Aneesa. Maybe she decided to do more laps. Or maybe someone else decided to workout in the pool.

There's no sign of anyone anywhere. No break or ripple in the water's surface. I kick out, aiming for the shallow end again. I'll hit the showers and let them have the pool to themselves.

But when I kick out again, my foot catches on something.

No, something catches on *me*.

An enormous hand circles my ankle and yanks me down beneath the surface.

Water rushes past my ears, up my nose, into my open mouth.

My lungs scream for air. No chance to suck in a breath before getting pulled under.

I land a kick on what feels like someone's shoulder with my other foot and manage to break the surface, coughing and gulping down a bit of air before they pull me down again, this time by the waist.

Their hands release me and instead find my head, pushing me down. I claw at their arms.

His arms.

Through the spinning water, I can just make out the swim trunks on Wes Novak as he attempts to drown me.

This is it. This is when he really kills me.

He lets me break the water's surface to gulp down a breath only to shove me under again. Over and over. My lungs are burning, chest caving in on itself.

This is how Chloe must've felt in her final moments. Floating in the water, unable to move. Unable to save herself.

They say drowning is painless, but nothing has hurt this much since they told me Chloe was dead.

I claw at Wes's arms holding me down, kick at his knees. Fighting to survive. Fighting for one more breath, one more chance to make things right.

Just as the muscles in my arms and legs start to give out, my chest collides with the hard metal edge of the pool so violently, I heave. The hands that were just drowning me finally release me and I cough up water onto the tile. My entire body aches and convulses as my lungs simultaneously hack up water and try to suck in air.

Water sloshes as Wes climbs the ladder. He saunters in front of me, stopping with his feet just inches from my fingers.

He waits for me to look up at him. Waits for me to peer at the face of the man who nearly killed me. The man I destroyed.

"Now imagine I'm your best friend," he says.

I squeeze my eyes shut. I have imagined the betrayal that Chloe must've felt in her final moments a thousand times. Knowing I was the one sending her to an early grave.

Now Wes wants me dead. There's no question about it. But he's going to drag it out as long as possible.

Water drips down from his dark hair to his pecs, a few drops trailing to the abs he doesn't need to flex. The hard muscles on his biceps and calves could wrap me up like a python and snap me in half.

His body is exactly as I remember it, but I haven't recognized his face since she died.

I miss the old Wes. The Wes with the cocky grin and the mischief in his eyes.

But he died with his sister.

Chapter 17

Before

Wes

Mom calls to tell me Chloe is coming home for the weekend, so I am too. No excuse to get out of it, even when she tells me Chloe is bringing Violet.

As soon as I pull into the driveway, she rushes toward me with hands up and a watery smile. "My boy! Oh, my sweet, handsome son!"

After the fourth cheek kiss, I pull away. "Mom, I've only been gone a couple months."

"*Only* a couple months, he says!" She grins and whispers, "Did you know Violet is single?"

I grab my bag from the backseat. I know exactly where this is going, but I stupidly ask anyway. "So?"

"So you should ask her out!" Mom smacks my shoulder. "Oh, Wes, she's *so* sweet and a little cutie! Why don't you ask her on a date? What could that hurt?"

"Mom, *please* stop trying to play matchmaker."

She puffs out her bottom lip. "I just want you to be happy. You haven't had a girlfriend since Britt."

"That's why I'm happy."

Mom shakes her head and tsks. "No, I know my son. You're afraid of being hurt again. But that's life, sweetheart. You've got to risk your heart if you ever want to find the person who deserves it. Chloe just adores Violet, and your father and I are already smitten. I bet you would be too if you gave her a chance."

What Mom doesn't know is I already hate exactly how smitten with Violet I am.

They've known Violet for all of five minutes, and they already like her better than they ever liked Britt, even before she cheated on me. She never fit with us. Clamming up at family dinners and wanting to spend all our time up in my room. Acting like she was inconvenienced when my parents suggested family activities like mini golf and beach days. As soon as Chloe found out Britt cheated, she called her a "walking red flag." Wish I'd seen the signs earlier so I didn't waste my time.

Now all I do is watch for signs.

I squeeze Mom's shoulder as I pass and head for the house. "Mom, stop trying to pimp out your son."

DESPITE MY BEST efforts to avoid Violet as much as possible this weekend, Mom insists that I go hang out in the pool with her and Chloe.

I sit at the pool's edge, taking my time inflating my raft and can't help watching Violet swim and bob in the shallow end. Her long brown hair is slicked back, soaked and plastered to her delicious, creamy skin. Every time she bobs up out of the water, her glistening tits flash, making me ache to pull down the flimsy fabric covering her nipples.

Chloe smacks my raft and pulls herself half out of the pool to hiss in my ear, "Stop eye-fucking her."

The sliding glass door opens behind us. "Chloe!" Mom calls. "Come help me with the lemonade."

My sister groans and pulls herself out of the pool. "I'll be right back." A promise to Violet and a threat to me.

As soon as we're alone, Violet keeps her gaze on anything but me. Her shyness is cute. Makes me want to take her to my bed and break her of it. Watch her blush deeper and deeper shades of red as I peel every layer off her body. Listen to the way she moans and screams as I make her feel things no man ever has.

"You know Chloe hasn't had a friend sleep over since middle school. Pretty sure Mom embarrasses her too much."

"That's funny, she told me you're the one who embarrasses her," Violet teases. A surprised laugh bursts out of me. Then she admits, "I've never had a friend sleep over."

"Never? Not even when you were a kid?"

She shakes her head. "Mom had to work a lot. She never had time. I spent most of my time at home alone, actually."

"Damn. That sucks." A twinge in my chest at the image of Violet as a kid, all alone at home with no one to talk to. "What about your dad?"

"He died when I was really young." She shields her eyes against the sun as she glances my way, face scrunching adorably. "Before you say sorry or anything, I barely remember him."

"Good thing I wasn't going to say sorry. I'm not the one who killed him."

Her turn to bark a surprised laugh. "Thank you. No one likes when I make jokes about my dead dad. As if he's not *my* dead dad to make jokes about."

"What happened to him?"

"A car accident. I was actually in the backseat. I don't remember it," she adds in a rush. "Mom was terrified she lost both of us. But I made it out without a scratch."

She was resilient, even back then.

I flash her my cockiest smile. "So you could live long enough to meet me."

She lets out a musical laugh. "That must be it."

"And Chloe. I'm glad you're friends." Chloe's never had a friend like Violet. She's been waiting for Violet her whole life.

Part of me thinks I've been waiting for her my whole life too.

"I'm glad I have a friend like her. And that she has a brother like you looking out for her."

"I'll look out for you too," I promise.

Her pretty lips twist just a little. "Like a sister?"

"No," I tell her. "Not like a sister."

Her smile widens. "Thanks. I'd like that."

"Do you want to try out the raft?"

She flashes me those adorable, bashful eyes through thick lashes. Always gets my heart going. "You just spent all that time inflating it. You should get your turn."

What I really want is to see Violet's body in a bikini floating across my pool. "I'm cool hanging out with my feet in the water. You're the guest—you should try it out. I'll help you in."

No way she doesn't see right through my flimsy excuse to touch her wet body, but she still moves toward the ladder and climbs out. My mouth goes dry as Violet emerges from the pool, every exposed inch of her nearly at my fingertips. Her tits could easily fit in my hands, and I want to yank that top down with a single finger and suck her nipples into my mouth. Then when she's squirming hard enough, hook a finger in her bottoms and slide those down slowly. Explore her thighs with my mouth first and then between them.

She moves behind me, wet feet slapping against the concrete. I hold out my hand for hers, and when she slides her palm into mine, I can't remember what I'm doing. So distracted by her that I'm lost in a trance until she finally reaches for the raft herself.

"Here." I hold the raft while helping her ease her tight little ass down onto it.

When the raft settles, every inch of her perfect body glistens in the sun. Fuck yeah. I want her living in this pool.

Maybe if I fuck her once, I can get it out of my system. Get her out of my head.

"So what do you want other than the NHL?" she asks, leaning her head back and basking in the sun.

"What?" My mind is so overwhelmed with thoughts of getting Violet naked and being the first guy to make her come that I barely understand her question.

"What else do you want after college? A house? Kids? Or are you trying to be a Leonardo DiCaprio?"

"Dating hot twenty-year-olds for the rest of my life doesn't sound too bad." Even as the words leave my mouth, I know they aren't true. I want what my parents have. The kind of marriage that's like a forever honeymoon. The loyalty, the commitment, the love.

But I need a loyal girl. A ride or die.

"Really?" Violet lifts a brow, hazel eyes locking on mine. She's getting braver now. I like it. I want her meeting my gaze when my head is between her legs, when she finally comes around my cock. "That doesn't seem like you."

"What do I seem like?" I tease. Last time, she called me a mystery. Doubt she knows much more about me now. It's easy to learn as much as you want about a girl when you follow her around campus and your sister is her roommate.

Violet chews on her lip for a second. "The kind of guy with

a big heart he doesn't like to show. You drop everything to be there when your sister needs you. You come home for the weekend just because your mom misses you. You don't date because you put your whole heart into the relationship, and when it's broken, it takes a long time to repair. You want the big house and kids, but you're too afraid to admit it to yourself. Because if you let yourself want something, if you put your heart on the line again and it breaks, you're not sure you'll ever be able to fix it."

Fuck. I'm supposed to be the one who knows her better. The one who knows things about her that she never told me. Her favorite candy (chocolate peanut butter cups), the scent of her shampoo (honeydew melon), the sub she orders (turkey with mayo, lettuce, tomatoes, and bell peppers on wheat bread). Who understands things about her she's never admitted out loud to anyone.

Somehow, she sees right through my bullshit to everything I've been hiding so well from everyone else.

I play it cool, leaning my hands back on the concrete. "So you've got me figured out, huh?"

She shrugs. "Not entirely. I still need to figure out your favorite candy."

A chuckle rumbles from my chest. "Gummies."

"There. Now I know everything." She flashes me a smile.

"Oh, little flower. There's so much more for you to learn."

The cocky little grin slips off her face before she swallows. "Maybe you should teach me then."

"Who wants lemonade?" Mom calls, and I jump into the pool to hide my stiff cock beneath the water.

Jesus Christ. The effect Violet has on me. How the hell I'm supposed to keep my hands off her while she spends the entire weekend at my house, I have no idea.

Maybe I won't.

Violet

THE NEXT MORNING, Chloe's parents announce it's beach day. They've already got a cooler packed with sandwiches, sodas, and water.

When we parallel park along the sidewalk, I offer them gas money, but Mrs. Novak gasps and swats the money away. "I will *not* be taking money from any child of mine."

My heart swells. She's known me for less than twenty-four hours and I've already been adopted.

"She's not your child, Mom," Chloe objects. "She has a mother."

Mrs. Novak waves her off. "A girl can never have too many mothers."

On the beach, Wes and Mr. Novak set up the chairs and two umbrellas while Chloe and I lay out towels.

The air between me and Wes is charged. After our conversation in the pool yesterday, I've been bracing myself every time he's around, waiting for him to get me alone so he can teach me everything I still need to learn.

Despite lathering herself in a thick layer of sunscreen, Mrs. Novak parks under an umbrella and settles in.

Mr. Novak unzips a bag and beams at me. "Chloe tells me you're a big reader, Violet. I've taken up reading since I retired from the NHL, so I took the liberty of bringing a few to keep you busy."

He pulls out a stack of paperback mystery novels. Not the romances I usually gravitate toward, but the kind gesture has me grinning and reaching from my towel for the paperback on top of the tower.

I haven't known the Novaks long, but I already feel like I belong.

"Dad, the point of bringing her to the beach was to get her to do something *other* than read," Chloe tells him.

"She can do it all," her dad insists.

"Everyone put on sunscreen," Mrs. Novak calls, waving her bottle of SPF-eighty in the air.

Behind me, a low voice murmurs in my ear, "I've got you."

Wes squeezes a dollop of sunscreen into his palm from his crouched position. As soon as his massive, calloused hands massage the lotion into my shoulders, I have to bite down on my lip to suppress the moan. Chills race down my limbs despite the heat.

I pray my face doesn't betray the effect Wes has on my body. The last thing I want is for his family to know their son and brother turns me on.

His hands drift down my back, callouses scraping deliciously over my skin. My eyes ache to fall shut.

Chloe grabs my hand, pulling me up off the towel and out of my trance. "I'm hot! Let's get in the water!"

"You kids have fun," Mrs. Novak calls, nose already in a mass-market paperback. On the towel beside her, Mr. Novak is sprawled out, sunglasses on and snoring lightly.

Chloe's feet fly across the sand while I stumble along behind her. The sand turns dark and smooth where the tide has been rolling in, and I stop at the water's edge.

"What are you doing?" Chloe asks. "I want to swim."

"I am *not* swimming in the ocean," I object. "There are sharks and jellyfish and about a thousand other things that will kill me in there. Have you seen the way orcas literally *torment* seals? They're called killer whales for a reason."

Chloe plants her hands on her hips. "First of all, wild orcas have never harmed humans. Second, we did not come all the way to the beach for you to refuse to get in the water."

"You've never been in the ocean?" Wes's rumbling voice is suddenly beside me. Too close. As half-naked as he was when I met him. But instead of a towel around his waist, he wears a pair of red swim trunks. My mouth goes dry at the sight of his sloping muscles, hard pecs, and the abs lining his stomach. A sprinkling of freckles dust his shoulders and make me long to rub sunscreen on his back too. Maybe my hands on his skin would have the same effect as his on mine.

"I've never been to the beach before," I admit.

"How have you lived in Rhode Island your whole life and never been to the beach?"

I don't ask how he knows I've lived in Rhode Island my whole life. At this point, I wouldn't be surprised if he knew my social security number.

"I dare you to get in the ocean!" Chloe calls, already backing into the gentle waves. She turns and dives into the water.

"Shit," I mutter.

Wes holds his hand out to me. "I'll help you. I'll make sure you don't drown."

Panic bubbles in my stomach, but Wes Novak is holding his hand out to me and I can't not take it.

His fingers thread through mine, sending a bolt of electricity through me.

The water is colder than I expected, making my nipples peak under my bikini top. Wes lets me take my time slowly submerging, deeper and deeper into the water.

Until I'm waist-deep, when he wraps an arm around my hips beneath the water where no one can see our connection.

He squeezes so hard, my flesh pinches between his fingers. I gasp.

His touch isn't tentative or uncertain. Not the touch of a man testing the waters.

This is the touch of a man who knows what he wants and takes it. Who knows I want it to.

Rough. Dominant. Possessive.

The touch of a man claiming what is his.

"They like you, you know."

I'm so flustered by his hand on me, I have no idea what he's talking about. "Who?"

He nods back to the shore. "My family. They hated my ex."

"Really?" I squeak. The infamous ex who broke his heart.

"Maybe my parents didn't *hate* her—Chloe did—but they didn't like her either. They faked it the best they could, but you? You already kinda belong with us."

I beam. *Belong with us.* Belong with *him*. The days I spent alone while Mom was working one of her three jobs or grabbing a few hours of sleep in between shifts, all I longed for was a family to belong to.

Now I've found one. I know when I introduce them to Mom, she'll fit right in too. An image of all of us together on Thanksgiving flashes through my head. At my birthday. At my and Wes's wedding—

Whoa. What the *hell* is wrong with me? We haven't even kissed and I'm already planning my vows. I am truly unhinged.

"Violet?" His soft but commanding voice.

I meet his eyes until his gaze drifts to my lips. Focusing on my mouth with so much concentration, it feels like the only visible part of me. The only body part that matters.

He's going to kiss me. I'm so sure of it, the butterflies in my chest burst free from their cocoons and take flight.

But when I expect him to draw nearer, to brush his lips against mine, they part instead. "Chloe doesn't want us together."

"She doesn't?" That's the first I'm hearing about this. She hasn't said a word about me and Wes since I first met him, when she confidently declared that I'm attracted to him and he doesn't date. "Why not?"

"Supposedly, she doesn't want us breaking up and getting caught in the middle." Despite his words, he keeps his hand on my bare skin.

I can't blame Chloe for her concerns. If Wes and I actually did date and break up, the situation would be, at best, incredibly awkward. At worst, she might feel like she has to choose between us.

Wes is family. She'd choose him. My chest aches at the thought of losing her.

"But I don't believe it," he adds.

I lift a brow in his direction. "You don't?"

"Nah. She just doesn't want me all over you every time we're together. She knows if I get my hands on you, I won't be able to keep them off. She'd be happy for us, but we'd annoy the hell out of her."

I laugh, even as his words set me ablaze. Uttered with so much conviction and certainty. Like a promise.

I imagine Wes Novak's hands all over me and hope it's a promise he doesn't break.

Chapter 18

After

Violet

AFTER MIDNIGHT, three texts come through from Wes.

> We need to talk.

> Meet me outside the university center.

> Now.

My heart gallops in my chest. Finally. The conversation Wes and I have been needing to have for months.

I'm not sure why he's changed his mind out of the blue, but I don't care. As long as he's willing to talk to me, to hear my apology, that's all that matters.

I slip on my shorts and vans, careful not to wake Aneesa, a sleep mask covering her eyes.

The University Center is named for its central location on campus. But at this time of night in the middle of the week, the campus is deserted and eerily silent. I wrap my arms tight around my middle, shivering more from nerves than the chill in the air. The occasional lamppost lights my way, and I stick to the sidewalk, head swiveling to make sure I'm alone and some creep isn't lurking in the shadows.

When I finally reach the University Center, I don't see anyone around. Is Wes standing me up? Or maybe this whole thing was just a ploy to get me out here in the middle of the night, alone and defenseless.

Panic bubbles up until someone moves in the shadows, where he's leaning back against the building.

Wes.

I recognize his towering stature and swagger, even within the shadows.

When he emerges, the light from the lamppost behind me illuminates the solid white mask covering his face, revealing nothing but his piercing blue eyes through two large holes and the outline of his smirk behind a cluster of pinprick holes at his mouth.

Liquid heat pools low in my belly. Overwhelming terror mixed with an impossible dash of arousal.

He lured me out here. Not to talk.

For something far worse.

"Welcome to your nightmare, little flower."

Before I can scream, a rough hand claps over my mouth from behind. "Don't make a fucking sound." Trey's threat churns the acid in my gut. "Or you'll regret it."

He holds me in place while Wes saunters toward us, every thud of his combat boots chilling me to the bone.

Behind him, the rest of the Devils emerge from the darkness.

I'm completely alone, surrounded by twenty-five men in identical masks. Each of them following their captain's orders.

Trey keeps his hand on my mouth until Wes reaches me. He trails the back of a finger down my cheek while his other hand clamps down on my shoulder, keeping me firmly in place.

Tears already burn my eyes, yet his touch ignites a fire low in my belly.

I want to puke. Scream. Run. Throw myself at him. Kiss him. All at once.

"What is this, Wes?" I whisper.

"We're going to have some fun, little flower."

Trey chuckles behind me.

My blood runs cold. That's exactly what I was afraid of.

"Ever play manhunt?" Wes asks, low rumble distorted by the mask.

"No." I squirm beneath his hand, but his grip on me is hard as steel.

"This is how we play," he purrs. "We give you a ten-second head start. Then we hunt you. And you better hope we don't catch you."

Ice slices through my spine. "What happens if you do?" I whisper.

His wolfish smile spreads. "You don't want to find out."

My stomach twists. No, I don't.

"Ten. Nine. Eight—"

"Please don't do this, Wes." The ragged cry makes the Devils surrounding us snicker.

His eyes are flat, unaffected by my plea. "Seven, six—"

"Can we just talk? *Please!*"

"Five, four—"

"*Wes—*"

"Better run, bitch." Trey's sinister warning in my ear and his slimy hand on my hip make me lurch out of their grip.

They don't chase me. Yet.

"Three. Two—"

There is no reasoning with Wes. No talking him or any of them out of this.

So I spin on my heel and sprint off the concrete and

through the parking lot as fast as I can, heart pounding and fear pumping through my veins.

"One."

Howls echo from behind me like the hockey team has shape-shifted under the full moon. A stampede of heavy footsteps follows and terror like I've never felt before rockets through me.

Even with a head start, I don't stand a chance against the best athletes on campus. I can't outrun them. I can't fight them off.

The darkness is my only advantage. If I can disappear into the shadows, I may be able to hide. Wait them out until they grow tired of searching for me.

I veer off the sidewalk and dart between brick buildings, my feet already screaming, still raw from the miles I was forced to walk back to campus. The hoots and shouts get closer, the hockey team yipping behind me like a pack of coyotes on the trail of wounded prey.

Tears threaten to obscure the little vision I have left in the darkness. I blink them away, pumping my arms and ignoring the sting already growing in my calves.

I can't let them catch me. I can't let them catch me.

They will hurt me beyond recognition.

If I survive them at all.

Near the library, I spot a brick wall the height of my waist surrounded by hedges. Heart in my throat, I scramble onto the wall, skin on my hands scraping and peeling. I jump down, crouching as low as I can to blend in with the shadows.

Two pairs of sneakers slap against the concrete, slowing when they realize they've lost my outline in the darkness. I freeze and hold my breath, not daring to move a single muscle.

"I can't wait to fuck her," Trey sneers. "Been wanting to destroy that sweet pussy since day one."

Bile rises in my throat. If there's anyone I'm scared of just as much as Wes, if not more, it's Trey.

He's gotten his hands on me before. If he manages to do it again, I'm not sure I'll escape him this time.

"You take her pussy; I'll take her mouth," Brody tells him. The two laugh together, their footsteps fading as they pass.

I wait for their footsteps to come back or others to arrive, but when they don't, I take a slow, calming breath before inching back up the brick wall and bracing my hands to push myself up and over.

I'll run back to the dorms. I'll stick to the shadows near the buildings and blend in, escape them—

Watching me from the sidewalk five feet away are two Devils.

Trey and Brody.

"Ready to play, pretty girl?" Trey drawls.

My heart nearly explodes in my chest, and I attempt to launch over the wall and escape, but both of their hands are already on me, dragging me back.

A scream rips from my throat, my last weapon to save myself. But they only laugh, not even bothering to cover my mouth.

They're well aware we're alone out here. Me, and twenty-five Devils.

"We got her!" Brody shouts to his teammates. A few whoops in response before more come running.

Trey bends down to my ear and hisses, "I'm disappointed. I expected a better fight."

I flail in their arms, but it's no use. A repeat of the day they forced me to my knees in the hallway, holding me in place and preventing my escape.

Except this time there are twenty-five of them and no chance of anyone saving me.

117

Trey's threat rings in my head. Now that he's got his hands on me, he's going to destroy me.

They throw me onto the concrete in front of six other pairs of legs. More are slinking through the darkness to surround me. Terror makes my head pound, the pain in my hands and knees already throbbing. My heart racing so fast, it could compete in the Olympics.

I scan the eyes behind the masks in front of me. None of them belong to Wes.

How can he let this happen to me? How can he orchestrate this? I get that he wants to punish me. But this is worse than I ever thought he'd be capable of.

I expect them to wait for their captain to show up, but Trey grips my hair, yanking down and forcing me onto my back.

I claw and kick at him, but several pairs of hands quickly pin me down. Their laughs and masks swirl above my head.

An errant hand drifts up my shirt, another down my shorts. I squirm, eyes stinging as I try to get away, but they don't budge.

Trey leans down before cupping my breast and squeezing. "God, I love when they fight."

He yanks my shirt up so hard and fast over my tits, I gasp. The night air kisses my newly exposed skin, and Trey groans.

Someone roars a warning from the darkness. "Fuck! *Cops!*"

A series of curses and shouts and most of the hands leave my body, sneakers squeaking as the Devils run for it.

Except for one pair of hands still holding me down. A mask still hovering above my head, staring at me with ruthless intent.

"Trey!" Brody shouts, nudging his shoulder. "Come on! Cops!"

"I don't give a fuck," Trey seethes, green eyes boring holes into my skull as his hand fumbles with the button on my shorts.

But Brody yanks his arm. "Let's go, man!"

Trey gives my tits one last painful squeeze, a promise to

return for more, before he releases me and takes off with the Devils.

I gasp in a long breath before a sob racks through my body. In the silence, I let the horror over what just happened, what *could've* happened, settle into my bones and make my limbs tremble until I force myself to stand.

I need to get the hell out of here before any of them decide to risk coming back.

But when I get to my feet, I realize I'm already too late.

One of the Devils has already returned. Or he never left in the first place.

Wes.

The smile beneath his mask is sadistic. A wolf that's found his dinner.

"Wes," I whisper, one last attempt to appeal to the human heart I hope is still beating somewhere beneath the predator's skin. "Please, don't—"

He takes a step toward me, and another cry escapes my lips. "The cops will find you."

His grin widens, head tilting just slightly. A predator amused by his prey. "There are no cops."

I try to replay the warning shout in my head. In the moment, overwhelmed by terror, I didn't recognize the voice belonged to Wes.

Of course there isn't anyone here to rescue me. Wes simply wanted me all to himself.

I bolt, spinning on my heel and racing down the sidewalk and into the parking lot.

I dare a glance over my shoulder. Wes is sauntering after me, so confident he'll catch me that he doesn't bother breaking into a run.

We're completely alone now. Predator and prey.

Pavement gives way to dark grass below my feet as I sprint

119

for the woodline. Before I break into the trees, I find Wes behind me one more time.

Sprinting after me like I've stolen his most prized possession.

Like I killed his sister.

I crash into the woods, twigs and leaves crunching beneath my shoes and low-hanging branches smacking my arms and face. One sharp enough to draw blood across my cheek. The pain doesn't register yet, buried somewhere deep below the terror.

His boots smash into the woods behind me, entirely too close. He's closed the distance between us in seconds. If I keep running, he'll track me and catch me.

I duck behind a tree and glue my back to the bark, heaving but trying to keep my breaths quiet. All I can hope for is that I can hide long enough that Wes grows bored and leaves me here. To resume the hunt another day.

My ears strain, trying to pick up the crunch of his boots across the ground. But there's nothing. Did he head in the other direction?

I'm alone. *I'm alone.* My heart hammers, on the verge of exploding. Maybe I'm going to survive another night.

Soundlessly, I peer around the massive trunk of the tree—

Wes slams me back against the bark, knocking the breath out of me.

When I part my lips to scream, one hand clamps over my mouth and the other around my throat. "Don't you fucking dare."

Fuck. *Fuck, fuck, fuck.* I'm dead. This is where he kills me.

My feet scramble to kick his legs, my nails dig at his arms. I manage to pry his hand off my mouth, but he keeps me pinned. "What do you want from me?" I plead.

Wes leans close, hot breath hitting my ear through his

mask. "Get out of my fucking head." His growl fills me from my ear to my toes.

God, I wish I could. Wish I could erase my existence from his memory. Except part of me aches at the thought of us forgetting everything we shared before Chloe died.

While she was still here, I thought . . . I thought I was falling for Wes. And I thought he was falling for me. I don't want to erase those moments. They're some of my happiest memories.

But that's all they are now. We'll never, ever get that back.

His grip around my neck tightens. "You should be dead. Not her."

"I know," I whisper. "I wish that's what happened."

Something in his eyes changes. Like he didn't expect that. How could he not? He knows how much I love Chloe. She's always been a better person than me, destined for bigger things. She was going to be an Olympian. Known around the world for how she sailed across the ice. How she made every movement look effortless. How she made *life* look effortless. More people loved her, more people were devastated by her loss than would ever be hurt by mine.

If one of us needed to end up in a grave, it should've been me.

A shout from the parking lot pulls us out of our staring contest. "Novak!" Trey has returned for his captain.

I kick out at Wes, managing to shake him off with the element of surprise.

But I don't get far. He knocks me to the ground, hard as a brick wall behind me. I cry out as the pain lashes through my body. He flips me so I'm on my back and plants a hand over my mouth, his body flattening me into the earth.

My heart slams against my ribcage, but Wes doesn't yank my clothes off. He doesn't move, listening for Trey to find us.

When the shouts grow distant, he returns that laser focus to me.

I should be terrified. I'm entirely at the mercy of someone who hates me. Who wants me dead.

But all I can think about is the way his lips felt against mine when he finally kissed me for the first time. The way my heart soared and my toes curled. And all the times I've imagined us in this position, in my bed, in his bed, on the floor. Wherever he wanted to take me.

His piercing blue eyes remain glued to my face. He's trembling with restraint until something clicks and his restraint dissolves as his hand moves to his belt. "Don't make a fucking sound."

The leather hisses as he pulls it free from his jeans. I'm pinned beneath him as he straddles me, his other hand fastened across my mouth. My hands tremble, but I'm not consumed by the same overwhelming terror I felt with the rest of the team.

Part of me—an insane, unhinged part—wants to know what Wes is going to do with that belt.

He leans forward, mask filling my vision as he slides the cool leather behind my neck and loops it around, tightening and securing it against my throat. So tight, I gasp in a breath, panic rising as my airway is restricted.

With one hand, he holds the belt out, keeping it tight. "If you scream, I'll make sure you stop breathing."

His other hand finally drifts from my mouth and down my shirt.

Even with his threat wrapped around my throat, I could scream. But I don't. Trey would be the one to find us, and he wouldn't have rescue on his mind.

He'd join.

Wes inches the hem of my shirt up, the opposite of Trey's

rough touch. Like he's trying to talk himself out of this with every new inch of my exposed skin.

When my shirt is over my bra, he tugs the wire down, making my tits pop out.

His throat bobs, and his breathing turns ragged beneath his mask.

"You like this. Don't you?" A finger suddenly slips down between my legs, into my shorts, and swipes up.

I jerk and gasp, unexpected pleasure electrifying me.

With that one stroke along my panties, he knows exactly how wet I am for him.

He reaches for his fly and tugs down.

"Hey!" An authoritative female voice shouts.

Wes freezes as a light sweeps through the woods.

Oh my god. A security guard. Finally, someone's found us.

Except the crazy half of my brain is screaming at her to leave us alone.

Before the flashlight can land on him, Wes removes the belt from my throat, scrambles off me, and runs.

Chapter 19

After

Wes

VIOLET HARRIS HAS DESTROYED ME. I can't focus on anything anymore. Not on classes, which my professors keep reminding me I can't slack off in just because I'm a senior. Not on practice, which sends Coach into a fucking meltdown every time I fumble a play or miss an easy goal. Not on the game, even when I'm in the fucking middle of it.

"Novak!" Coach shouts over the buzz from the crowd and the yells from the guys on the ice. "Eyes on the puck!"

I spot it in the Hawks' control and long to beat the player with my stick.

Violet's face keeps popping in my head. Her small body writhing and aching for me while I had her pinned down in the woods, my belt wrapped around her throat. The way her legs shook and her eyes fluttered shut when I stroked a finger up her pussy and felt how fucking soaked she was for me.

One of the Hawks shoulder-checks me and I go after him, forgetting all about the puck. I slam into him from behind, sending him face-first to the ice. He lands with a thud and a groan.

"Novak!" Luke shouts from the net. "Where's your head at?"

Back in those woods with Violet. Listening to her tell me she wished it had been her instead of Chloe.

But something snapped in me even before those words left her mouth. When I saw her held down and surrounded by my team, all of them groping and ogling her, I about lost it. Which didn't make any goddamn sense. I let Trey and Brody force her to her knees before me. I ordered them to put on their masks for a night of manhunt. Told them to chase down our prey.

Yet the second they ensnared her in their trap, I nearly ripped each of their fucking heads off.

They can't have her.

That's the thought that rang through my head.

Mine.

The puck sails past my head, over Luke's arm, and into the net. Half the crowd groans, the other cheers. Coach is spitting, face crimson as he screams at me. I'm captain. I'm supposed to keep this shit running right. I'm failing him, my team, myself.

All because of her.

Because I can't get her out of my fucking head.

I've been following her again. Without my mask, without any intent to confront her or torment her. Without her knowing I'm behind her, watching. The same way I did when she first got to campus her freshman year. Consumed by a foreign need to know everything about her. To know where she is and what she's doing at all times. A pulsing urge to reach out and touch her.

Take what's mine.

Violet

I ARRIVE at my philosophy class early, hoping the professor will provide a distraction from my thoughts of Wes with the works of Aristotle.

Two minutes before the start of class and most of the seats in the lecture hall are filled. I can't wait until next year when I'm taking classes that are actually relevant to my major and the class size drops from fifty students to twenty.

Someone takes one of the two empty seats beside me. When a large hand lands on my knee, I freeze.

In the chair next to me, Wes is leaning back casually.

My mouth goes dry at the sight of him. Dwarfing the tiny chair, button-up shirt straining over his muscles, and dark slacks that disappear into combat boots. Combined with the piercing blue eyes and the cool, stoic expression, he's the most devastating man in the room.

But he's not supposed to be here.

"What are you doing here? You're not in this class."

He shrugs. "I'm in whatever class I choose to be."

At the front of the room, the professor still hasn't noticed his non-student in the back row. Once he does, he'll instruct Wes to leave the class, and my racing heart can slow.

But then the professor starts writing on the whiteboard and begins his lecture, keeping his back to us.

Heat crawls up from my toes to the tip of my scalp.

Unless I want to make a break for it and cause a scene, I'm stuck here with Wes. With his hand on my leg.

His thumb begins to rub circles on the side of my knee, and I try to remain motionless. If I don't give him a reaction, he'll get bored and leave. All I have to do is pretend his touch isn't setting me on fire.

Wes Novak is my tormentor. A bully. He's seeking revenge

and I am his target. I shouldn't enjoy his touch. Shouldn't crave more of it. Not when his touch, his attention, has already caused me so much pain. I can't trust him. Can't let my guard down.

But every cell in my body is fighting against my mind. Warring against the memories of how his lips felt on mine, how much I wanted him last night in the woods.

His hand drifts further up my thigh, so slowly and imperceptibly I almost wonder if I'm imagining it. His fingertips dig into my flesh, but not to hurt me. To massage away the tension in every fiber. Under his expert touch, my muscles loosen, my thighs falling apart, just a little.

When his hand drifts higher, dangerously close to the hem of my skirt, I tuck my hands in my lap, pinning my skirt down.

He releases me, and I almost think I've won.

Until his hand finds the nape of my neck.

He massages careful circles there, nearly eliciting a moan from my lips. Just before his fingers twist in my hair and give a sharp tug.

I hiss through my teeth and clamp my mouth shut before anyone around us hears.

At the front of the classroom, the professor drones on, the students around us taking notes or texting under the table. They're totally oblivious to what's going on at the back of the room.

"I'm going to take what's mine, little flower." Wes grabs my hand and pulls it toward him. My spine goes ramrod straight. He's not going to do what I think he is. Not right here, in the middle of class.

He plants my hand on his leg. A silent command: *Don't hide from me. Let me touch you.* Then his fingers find their way further up my thigh and under my skirt.

I can't move. Can hardly breathe.

His fingers delicately glide up my skin. I didn't think he could be this tender, the pressure no more than the faint kiss of a butterfly's wings. Goosebumps race down my limbs.

"You shouldn't," I whisper, not taking my eyes off the words scrawled across the whiteboard, my mind unable to decipher any of them.

"But you want me to." His murmur reverberates down to my toes.

He's right. I hate that he's right. Hate that I'm so weak, I fall apart under my bully's touch.

His pinky glides down my panty line. My breath catches in my chest. I clamp my thighs together.

Wes lets out a low growl. "Don't pretend you don't want this."

We are in a stalemate. Me with my thighs clenched together, him with his fingers digging into my leg. But he's not prying me apart. He could so easily take whatever he wants from me. Yet he doesn't.

That wouldn't give him the satisfaction he wants. He wants my acquiescence. To know that, despite everything he's done to me, I gave in to him.

He grips my hand still planted firmly on his thigh and moves it to the bulge in his pants.

I whimper, his erection hard and long beneath my palm. A promise or a threat? I can't tell with him anymore.

He strokes my hand up his shaft to the tip. "Mmm," he groans.

Liquid heat pools between my legs.

Wes and I are in public, touching each other where anyone could see us, yet it feels like we're the only two in the room. Like he could pull me into his lap and slide me on his cock right here, and I would let him.

My legs fall apart.

"That's my good girl," he murmurs.

His fingertips slide further up, trailing along my panties to just below my belly button, the soft caress making my heart stutter.

I swallow a hard lump in my throat, expecting his hand to dive beneath the fabric of my panties. But he trails his fingers over the single layer separating us. Until he stops at the spot between my thighs.

Blood thrums in my ears, my chest heaving with ragged breaths. Wes stifles a groan with his palm when he feels the dampness through my panties. Every sound he makes turns me on more.

My thighs shake, wanting to clench together at the shame of my arousal. But doing so wouldn't keep Wes away this time. It would only pin him to me.

"Fuck, Violet," he whispers. With a finger, he pulls my panties to the side. A cool breath of air brushes against the wetness waiting for him. "You have no idea how long I've been wanting to do this. How many fucking times I've imagined you like this. Exposed and ready for me."

Then his finger lands on my clit.

I shudder into my palm, gaze darting around to make sure no one is aware of what we're doing.

"You like that you might get caught, don't you?" Wes murmurs. "That everyone knows you want to be my own personal plaything. You love when I make you get on your knees for me. You get off on that edge of fear."

I shake my head quickly, eyes stinging even as the pleasure sings through my body.

His expert finger swirls around my clit and I bite down hard on my lip to prevent the cry from escaping.

He grinds against my hand, and I inadvertently wrap my fingers around him as he increases the pressure on my clit.

"*Wes*," I whisper.

My pulse hammers wildly in my neck. I'm going to explode any second, bits of me flying all around the room. Then everyone will know exactly what Wes Novak was doing to me in the middle of class.

A clap at the front of the room makes me jump.

"All right, everyone. That's all for today. You can head out early. Have a good weekend."

Abruptly, Wes pulls his hand from under my clothes and stands like someone tossed a bucket of ice water over us. Every cell in my body is screaming to reach that crest of pleasure. My heart thuds hard, skin on my chest and neck flushed, swollen clit begging for release.

Dread washes over me when Wes heads for the door without looking back.

He has no intention of giving me what I want. He took his time, knowing he'd bring me right to the edge before snatching the pleasure away from me without a second's warning.

A new form of torture.

Chapter 20

After

Violet

I CALL MOM. She answers on the third ring with a tired, "Hey, hon."

My heart squeezes. I'm hon again. Even for just a second, she's forgotten to be disappointed in me.

"Hey, Mom. I have a favor to ask." She sighs into the phone and I press on before she can object. "Can you take me to Chloe's grave today? It's her birthday."

Chloe and I had already made our plans for her birthday by the end of April. We'd go to the movies first thing in the morning and sneak from theater to theater, watching as many movies as we could until we got kicked out. Her favorites were romcoms and horror, a dichotomy I could never wrap my mind around. Then we'd head to the ice rink and we'd "skate," which would translate to her skating and me watching safely from solid ground. My plan was to have my book written by then so I could print it and sign it and give her the first copy of my first-ever book. Dedicated to her.

She and I thought my first book would be inspired by my life. Fun, romantic, maybe even smutty.

Now if I were to write a book based on my life, I'm pretty sure it would be shelved as horror. I've been jumping awake the past three nights, just as Wes squeezes the life from my throat in my nightmares. As all twenty-five Devils track me down and pin me to the ground while they each take their turn.

What would've happened to me if that security guard hadn't found us? Would Wes have fucked me? Shoved his cock down my throat? His hand was on his fly.

The crazy part is . . . I wouldn't have tried to stop him.

Mom lets out another sigh, this time with a note of sympathy. "I can't today, hon. I'm working a double. Maybe this weekend."

Panic rises in my chest. This weekend isn't Chloe's birthday. I need to be there for her today. "Please, Mom. It won't take long—"

"Violet, you shouldn't be going to the cemetery today, anyway. The Novaks will be there."

I flinch. I know she's right, even if I don't want to admit it. Before the accident, Chloe's parents loved having me around—it's hard to imagine them celebrating her birthday without me. "I need to give her this gift."

The little stuffed duck that I won at the carnival. Chloe coveted Ducky as soon as I held him in my hands. It's not much, but I want to give it to her for her birthday. Especially since I never did manage to write that book.

If that night had gone differently, if Chloe was still alive, would I have written my first book? Would Wes be my boyfriend instead of my bully?

"You can leave it there this weekend. You don't need to be stepping on her family's toes today."

If I can't get a ride to Chloe's grave, I'll just have to walk. Diamond really needs a bus system, but luckily the cemetery is only a few miles away, just outside of the town square.

I don't care what I have to do. I'm visiting my best friend's grave on her birthday.

Sunlight beams onto the rows of gravestones, some of them fading under the sun's harsh rays.

The cemetery is blessedly empty. Even though Chloe was my best friend, I don't want anyone to see me visiting her grave. They'll only hurl horrible insults my way. All I want is to be left in peace to mourn my best friend. I may be the one responsible for her death, but I didn't want her gone either. That's what no one seems to get. I'm just as devastated by her loss as everyone else. If I could take back what I did, if I could take back that whole night, I would. I would switch places with Chloe in a heartbeat.

I kneel in front of her headstone. *Chloe Novak. 2003 to 2023. Beloved daughter, sister, and friend.*

The words blur, and I tuck the stuffed duck at the base of the stone. I can almost feel Chloe's ghost grinning next to me, whispering *thanks.*

"Happy birthday." And those two words are all I get out before the sobs wrack through my body. "I am so sorry," I whisper. "I'm so sorry, Chloe."

"Still willing to switch places?" a deep male voice asks behind me.

I jump out of my skin and whip around, the sob caught in my chest.

Wes looms above me, a bouquet of flowers clutched in his hand, dangling down at his side.

Shit. I didn't think he'd be here until later with his parents.

"What?" I ask, my brain scrambling, trying and failing to make sense of his words.

"You said you wished you were the one who died that night." His voice and eyes are flat, emotionless.

"I do." I mean it with every thread of my being.

Part of me—a stupid, moronic part—hopes he'll sweep me up in a hug, rub the back of my hair while we cry together over the girl we both miss so much that her loss is a weight pinned against our chests, crushing and suffocating.

He doesn't, of course, and the sob builds in my throat, but I manage to swallow it down.

When silence falls over us and Wes doesn't make a move to strangle me, I try one more time. "I know you don't want to hear it, Wes, but I'm s—"

"Shut the fuck up, Violet." He lifts a hand, the words coming out without his usual venom, but the order makes my lips clamp shut. Like he's too exhausted for his revenge plot today. "Get the fuck out of here or I'll bury you here myself."

I hold up my hands, backing away from Chloe's grave. "Okay. I'm leaving. I'm s—" But I stop myself, knowing that for some reason, *sorry* is the last word Wes Novak wants to hear from my mouth.

I half run toward the parking lot, getting away from Wes as fast as possible before he changes his mind about letting me leave unscathed. Before he shoves my face in the dirt and makes me eat it.

When I reach the parking lot, my breaths heave from my chest. Wes sits in front of Chloe's grave, the side of his body facing her stone and his arms resting on his knees, like he's chatting with her casually. Until he swipes across his cheek with a thumb.

I turn away, giving him the privacy he deserves. Toward me, his exterior is cold, hard. But somewhere deep down, that softer part of him, the part that made him the Wes I knew before, is still in there.

I've always known he has a big heart. Bigger than he ever likes to show. I once thought I had a place in it.

But I never will.

Wes

THE FUCKING STUFFED DUCK. The prize she won at the carnival. The little duck Chloe instantly squeezed and cooed over the second it was in Violet's hands.

The duck that reminds me of our first kiss. When I pressed my lips to hers and wondered how I'd gone an entire lifetime without kissing her. When I knew there was no way I'd be able to stop myself from kissing her again.

Watching Violet sob in front of my sister's grave stopped me dead in my tracks. Like I almost forgot she had a heart in there. That before Violet killed her, they were best friends.

But the last person on this Earth who deserves my sympathy is Violet Harris.

If it weren't for her, I wouldn't be celebrating my sister's birthday at her graveside. I wouldn't have bought her fucking flowers because when she was alive, she didn't even like them. Said they were boring, unoriginal. The type of gift every girl got. The kind of gift that didn't require any thought.

If she were still alive, she'd be mocking me right now. *You're so unoriginal, Wes.*

Without her, I am.

A deranged part of me wanted to drop to the ground beside Violet and pull her in for a hug. Mourn over my sister together like we would have if Violet hadn't been the one responsible for putting her in the ground in the first place.

The sickest part of all of this is the one person I want to comfort me is the reason I need comfort.

Mom and Dad arrive carrying trays full of saplings and hand shovels so we can plant them around Chloe's grave.

"Wes, your father and I were just talking on the way over. Remember that summer when Chloe was about twelve and she got really into gardening? Then that wasp stung her on the foot?"

I chuckle. "Yeah, and she got mad at me for killing it."

Mom laughs. "Not a single thing grew, but she was out there every day."

I swallow down the lump in my throat.

"Is that Violet we just saw?" Dad asks, like she's an old friend and not our worst enemy.

"Yep."

Mom sinks to the ground beside me. "Did you get to have a nice chat?" she asks in her soothing honey voice.

"No, Mom, it's Violet." I grab a shovel and stab into the ground. "We don't have nice chats."

"You used to," Dad says, as if I need the fucking reminder.

"I've always thought you and Violet would make an adorable couple." Mom plants a sapling in the shallow grave I dug, patting the soil around it.

"I know." There was a time I wanted Violet. Wanted her in every sense of the word. But that's never happening now.

Mom grabs my hand, hers covered in dirt because she forgot gloves. Or she didn't want to bring any, hoping the cool earth between her fingers would make her feel closer to my dead sister on what would've been her twentieth birthday. "I just want you to be happy."

"We both do." Dad pats his shovel against the soil where

136

he's planted a sapling on the other side of Chloe's grave. She'd love to be here doing this with us.

"Not sure how to be," I admit, staring at the words on her headstone until they start to blur.

"You start by forgiving Violet," Mom tells me. I open my mouth to object, but she cuts me off. "Violet is a good girl, Wes, and she was such a great friend to Chloe. She genuinely feels bad about what happened."

"She should." I still don't get how they can forgive her so easily. How they can just shrug off Chloe's death like someone else didn't cause it. Like her *best friend* didn't betray her in the worst way possible.

Mom faces me, brows furrowed but gaze tender. "You can allow yourself to feel happy, Wes. That doesn't mean you've stopped grieving your sister or love her any less." I can't swallow down that fucking lump in my throat now. "You and Violet are both grieving someone you loved so much. You can help each other through this, but instead, you're making her loss worse for you both. Chloe would be so upset if she knew you were closing your heart off to her best friend just because you're ashamed of feeling happy."

Chapter 21

After

Violet

"Where's your short story, Violet?"

I freeze, Professor Tate hovering by my desk. *Shit.* I completely forgot about the assignment. Everything going on with Wes and the Devils has completely distracted me.

Sorry, Professor. I meant to do the assignment, but then I got hunted down by a group of masked men in the middle of the night and forgot about it.

"Um. Sorry. I forgot to do it. I can get it to you tomorrow."

Professor Tate's lips thin. "I'll extend your deadline this once. If you don't get your story to me by tomorrow, you'll receive a zero for this assignment." I nod, but Professor Tate isn't satisfied. "There is very little graded work in this class, Violet. Failing to turn in any of your assignments could easily lead you to fail this course."

Sweat pools under my arms when I imagine Mom's disappointment if I fail any of my classes and need to scrounge up thousands to pay to retake them. "I understand. I'll definitely get it to you by tomorrow."

I have no idea how I'm going to manage that when I haven't

written a single short story that quickly all semester. But I'll just have to sit down and do it, even if every word feels like yanking a tooth from my gums.

As soon as class is over, I head for the library and duck behind the circulation desk. My stomach twists when I spot Wes and a few of the Devils shove two tables together and crowd around them. Wes actually has a textbook open while most of his teammates elbow each other and bark out laughs.

"Boys never change." Edith tsks, peering at them over the rim of her glasses, the latest Nora Roberts installment open in her lap. "Wait until they're men, Violet. Then they'll be worth your time."

"I thought you were just telling me the other day how much you love their attention," I tease.

"I'm sixty-nine. Of course I do. But just because I wouldn't mind having one in my bed doesn't mean I want to marry one."

I chuckle and shake my head. Edith snaps her book shut before waving it in the air. "I'm going to read in the back. Do you think you can handle this place?"

Other than the Devils, the library is vacant. I nod, even though their presence makes my hands tremble. These boys are the real-life nightmare I can't escape. "Go enjoy your book."

She points at my closed laptop on the desk. "You get writing, little miss."

I try to hide my cringe by forcing a smile. "I will."

As soon as Edith is gone, I pull out my latest book. A dark romance that was advertised as including knife play and "hand necklaces." I'm not a hundred percent sure what that means, but I have an idea, and even worse, I think I'm going to like it. This is the first book I've read in months that has actually made me want to read. I'm still a fractured version of the girl I used to be, but I can't help smiling at finding this piece of myself again.

A chorus of laughter breaks out at the hockey team's table.

A wave of dread washes over me. They can only be laughing at one thing.

Me.

But when I dare a glance over my book, it's not me they're watching—it's the team's newest recruit, a freshman. Mason. How he made the team in the first place is a mystery. He's short and slim. The kind of guy who will get rag-dolled on the ice.

Trey slams Mason's laptop shut, making some joke about porn. They all burst out laughing, and Mason pretends to join in.

Wes clenches his jaw. "Shut the fuck up or leave. I'm actually trying to work."

At least it's not just me he snaps at.

A mousy girl appears in front of me. "Hi. I can't find the book I'm looking for. Can you help me?"

"No problem." She tells me the title, a thick tome for her philosophy class, and I look up the call number.

She frowns. "I checked there."

"Let me see if I can find it for you. Wait right here."

I leave my post and head back for the stacks. The eyes of every hockey player at the table follow me, their stares turning my blood to ice.

I scurry back to the shelves, cheeks burning, and scramble for the book so I can get back behind the safety of the circulation desk. I chose my outfit carefully today. Sweater, cardigan, long skirt, and hair pulled up in a tight bun. All of it meant to make me invisible. Apparently, it didn't work.

They can't do anything to me here. We're in public during the day. They're just trying to scare me.

Before I can reach the desk and the girl waiting for her book, Trey's spine-chilling voice calls out to me. "Violet! We need some help over here."

I freeze, halfway between them and the student. Her wide

gaze darts to the Devils and back to me before she rushes forward, snatching the book from my hand and murmuring, "Thanks," before scrambling from the room.

When I remain frozen, Trey's feline smile spreads. "Come on over, beautiful. We won't bite. Too hard."

They're all watching with blood-thirsty amusement. All of them except Wes.

His blue gaze sears into me, but he's somehow not delighted by whatever torment they're about to inflict on me this time.

I don't have a choice. If I don't comply, whatever punishment they dole out next will be worse.

I step toward them slowly, hoping Edith will emerge from the back room and call for me. A student will rush through the door needing my assistance.

But the room stays silent.

As I near, Trey pats his lap. Nausea roils in my gut. I balk, but I'm too close now. He grabs my wrist and yanks me down onto him, my ass directly over the bulge in his pants. Nothing but his jeans and my flimsy skirt between us.

I squeeze my eyes shut, but that doesn't stop me from hearing the low moan escape Trey's lips. "Mmm. I wish we hadn't been interrupted the other night. I would've had you *screaming*."

I swallow down the bile and dare a glance in Wes's direction.

A muscle feathers in his clenched jaw, his gaze melting me and Trey with the raging heat of lava. This isn't even my fault, and he's going to punish me for it.

To Trey's right, Brody leers before his hand lands on my knee, drifting up and up to explore beneath my skirt.

My legs clench together and they chuckle. Tears prick my eyes. They don't care where we are or who might see. They didn't bother with the masks this time. They know they'll get away with doing whatever they want to me.

Trey pulls the scrunchy from my bun, hair falling past my shoulders in waves. "Should've worn this in a ponytail so we could pull it." My stomach twists just as he pushes me onto Mason's lap, bony and painful. "Give him a lap dance. He's still a virgin."

"I'm not," he seethes. Mason's hands, massive despite his leaner frame, go right to my breasts, squeezing hard over my sweater and making me wince.

I flatten back against his chest, trying to escape the pain, but he only squeezes harder.

Trey slides out of his chair with a slimy grin, crouching under the table where he's hidden. "Don't let her make a sound." He pushes my skirt up my thighs and pries them open, making me gasp at the sudden, violent intrusion. Brody clamps a hand over my mouth.

A wild glance in Wes's direction tells me he's not happy, but he's not moving to rescue me either.

Of course not. He was the one who pinned me to the ground in the woods. He was the one reaching for his fly to fuck me into the dirt.

Trey's hot breath hits my panties. I try to scramble away, but Mason and Brody hold me down, Trey keeping my legs in place like guillotines. "I bet she tastes so fucking good," he murmurs.

A chair screeches, making all of us jump.

Wes is at my side, grabbing my arm and hauling me up and off Mason. His face is stormy, and for a second, I think he's going to rescue me.

But then he sits and hauls me onto his lap.

He's rock-hard between my ass cheeks. So hard, if he pushed inside me, it might be the worst pain I've ever felt.

His arms wrap around me, and this isn't about him rescuing me or giving a shit about me.

This is possession.

"Get out," he growls at his teammates.

Trey emerges from beneath the table, still grinning. "We were just starting to have some fun."

"Get. Out."

Now the smile slips from Trey's face and his eyes narrow. "What? She's all yours now?"

"That's how it works. I claimed her. She's mine."

His words send a thrill through me, even if they shouldn't. *She's mine.* I might not be safe in Wes Novak's arms, but they're the only arms I want to be in.

Trey rolls his eyes, grabbing his bag. The other guys follow suit. "Whatever, man. I've got a line of puck bunnies waiting to suck my dick."

Wes and I remain motionless as the rest of the team leaves the library. When it's just us, I brace myself for his lips to brush against my skin. His hands to drift up my thighs or to squeeze my breasts. To do everything to me that his teammates were doing, everything that got him hard and made him want to try for himself.

Instead, the cocoon of warmth from his arms disappears and he shoves me from his lap. "Get the fuck off me."

I'm on unsteady feet, free from his clutches, and I should be rushing to get away. Take advantage of this moment of freedom, of safety. But I'm frozen in place. I can't read him. One minute, he can't stop himself from wanting me, and the next, touching me repulses him.

A gaggle of giggling freshmen enters the library, gathering around a table in the opposite corner, and I head for the circulation desk, hands shaking and mind spinning.

I should be glad he didn't grope me like his teammates. Glad he didn't take advantage of me.

He hates me. He loves tormenting me. He's my bully.

But part of me is still hanging on to the Wes Novak I used to know. Part of me even wants the Wes he is now.

I don't care if he's rough. I don't care if it hurts.

Against my better judgment, against every instinct in my body warring with my mind, I want him.

Wes

THE REDHEAD IS BACK, but this time, she brought a friend.

I could've studied in my apartment with my noise-canceling headphones, which is usually my preferred place to study, especially after Trey's gotten a few beers in him and passed out. But being here means keeping Violet in my sights, so that makes putting up with the puck bunnies bearable.

She even dresses like a librarian. Long, flowing skirt, frumpy sweater under a cardigan. She doesn't want to be noticed, and I wish I didn't. Wish I could go even more than a second without thinking about her.

Fucking Trey had to pull her onto his lap. Put his filthy fucking hands all over her. I tried to contain myself, tried to fight against the urge to rip her from their grips, bend her over the table, and fuck her right there in front of them, show them all exactly who she belongs to.

He pulled that scrunchy from her hair and kept it. Like a fucking trophy.

Once I knew he planned to taste her, I couldn't hold back anymore.

At the circulation desk, she smiles at a student. My stomach twists. Been a long time since I've seen a smile on her face. Since she smiled at me.

"I'm so excited for your game, Wes." The redhead squeezes my bicep. I forgot she was next to me.

"We should go out to celebrate after," her raven-haired friend suggests.

"I plan on it," I tell them.

The redhead trails her finger up and down my arm, and I want to shake her off. "We're really good at celebrating."

The girl wouldn't know subtlety if it bit her in the ass.

"Have a good day," Violet calls to the student.

Even after everything, she still has it in her to be kind, sweet. After everything she's done. Everything we've put her through.

Her bright hazel eyes find mine across the room. I lean into the redhead's touch. "Yeah, baby. Let's celebrate all night."

Violet can't hear anything we're saying, but it doesn't take a genius to see this girl's basically offering to climb onto my lap and ride me right here.

That familiar pink creeps up Violet's cheeks and she glances away. I grin. My cock stiffens at her jealousy.

The redhead notices, but she thinks my hard-on is for her. She simpers and skims her hand across my thigh. "Remember how your cock could barely fit in my mouth?"

All I remember about that night is imagining Violet's face while the redhead sucked me off.

She gets close to my erection now, grazing a sharp nail up my inner thigh, dangerously close. Driving me nuts and not in a good way.

Violet would wait for my instructions. And then she would do everything exactly as I tell her.

The librarian emerges from the back room, and Violet

shoos her. From the way the woman hobbles, it's rough being on her feet. Every time she tries moving up out of her chair or pushing a cart, Violet takes over. She's like that. Bends over backwards for people who deserve it. And the people who don't.

This time, the librarian's not backing down, though. "Go get your lunch!" she barks. Not the typical librarian keeping everything to a whisper.

Violet scurries out of the room with a smile, and for some stupid reason, I'm mesmerized by every step she takes—the sway of her hips, the swish of her long skirt—and wish she'd packed a lunch.

The librarian locks her beady eyes on mine over her glasses and gestures me over with a crook of her finger. "Gotta go, ladies." I'm all too relieved to shake the redhead's palm off my thigh. "I've got a hot date."

I saunter up to the desk and lean against it, flirty smile fixed in place. Old ladies love me. "Hey, beautiful. What can I do for you?"

I've noticed how she fans herself anytime one of the student-athletes or professors waltzes into the room. Even saw her at the gym once pretending to lift weights while she gaped at the biceps of the football player doing curls next to her. Bet those romance novels she's always reading are absolutely filthy, if the half-naked men on the cover say anything about the contents.

But she throws me when she rolls her eyes at my charm. Then she points a finger in my face. "Don't you hurt her."

I stiffen. Did Violet tell her about what I've done? She should've known better than to open her mouth. Or maybe she means the redhead I was basically ignoring while she groped me. "Hurt who?"

"Don't play dumb with me, boy. Violet's a sweet girl. Sensitive. And she's already heartbroken. She doesn't need you breaking her heart too."

Jesus Christ. She's not worried about me literally hurting Violet—she's worried Violet's in love with me. She's worried about something as inconsequential as heartbreak.

I force a smile, even as the charm is slipping away. "No need to worry about that. It's not like that between us."

The librarian rolls her eyes again. "Oh, please. I see the way you stare at her. The last time a man stared at me like that, he married me."

Chapter 22

Before

Violet

I don't realize I'm on a double date until the four of us are already at the carnival, stars barely visible above the yellow and purple lights and the fully illuminated Ferris wheel.

Ahead of me, Chloe laughs flirtatiously at something Luke says, her head tipping back. At my side, Wes stays quiet, the air between us charged. I bet he didn't have any idea about Chloe's surprise double date either.

I loop my arm through hers and pull her away from the guys toward the cotton candy stand. "What happened to 'don't date my brother'? Now you're playing Cupid?"

Chloe rolls her eyes dramatically, pulling out a few crumpled bills for cotton candy as if that's actually why I brought her over here. "Who did you want me to set you up with instead? Trey?"

My stomach twists. Definitely not Trey.

She reads my expression. "That's what I thought. You know Wes, and you're comfortable with him. I figured you wouldn't be *totally* miserable hanging out with him."

I don't know how she can think I'm comfortable with Wes.

I'm on edge every time I'm around him, palms slick and stomach twisted into knots.

But I guess she's right on some level. I'm comfortable enough to talk to Wes. I don't worry over every word that leaves my mouth the way I do with nearly everyone else. I even flirt with Wes, and I've never successfully done that with anyone before.

Maybe I've become more comfortable with him than I realized.

"But why do we even need to be here? Wouldn't you rather be alone with Luke?"

"No, I want my best friend with me, silly." She flashes me her winning smile. "But I didn't want you to be a third wheel."

"What can I get you?" the pimply teenager asks from the cotton candy stand.

"A pink and a blue, please," Chloe tells him.

"I hope you're not planning on paying for that yourself," Luke says, stepping up beside Chloe.

I smile. I still don't know him well enough, but if I had to pick someone who *might* be good enough for Chloe, it would be Luke.

A hand flattens against the small of my back. *Wes.*

Warmth radiates from him. He's so handsome with his clean-cut, onyx hair, bright blue eyes, and hockey jacket emblazoned with his number three.

Chloe has no idea the trouble she's causing. If she wants to keep me and Wes from falling for each other, she's doing a pretty terrible job of keeping us apart.

His hand on me is at once comforting and arousing. I love when he touches me like he owns me. I long to be his. To belong to him.

To my surprise, Luke pays for Chloe's cotton candy and Wes pays for mine.

"You don't have to do that," I object. This isn't a real date. We were both tricked into being here.

"Yes, he does," Chloe corrects, ripping off a chunk of her cotton candy and feeding it to Luke, who opens his mouth with a grin. They're already so cute together.

"Yeah, I do," Wes agrees. "Especially because I'm about to eat half of it."

"Good," I whisper. "I actually don't like cotton candy."

Chloe lets out a horrified gasp, even though I hoped she wouldn't hear me. "Who doesn't like cotton candy?"

"Crazy people," Luke says, the two of them leading the way.

Once they're safely out of hearing range, I ask Wes, "Can you just eat it for me?"

He flashes a wicked grin. "I'll eat whatever you want me to eat."

My cheeks burn, and I shove the cotton candy into his hand. Now I can't stop thinking about Wes pulling me away to a dark, private corner and kneeling before me, his tongue between my legs.

We hop on every spinning and swinging ride we can until Chloe complains that if she rides one more, she's going to puke pink, even though she's the one who insists on hitting every ride.

When we reach the row of carnival games, Chloe spots a stuffed duck and challenges Wes to compete with her for it.

"Aren't you supposed to win a goldfish?" Luke asks.

"All out of goldfish," the bearded carnival worker informs us in a monotone.

Chloe and Wes shout and groan as they toss ping-pong balls, failing to dunk them through the tiny rings. These are the moments when it's painfully obvious that they're brother and sister. Other than their vibrant blue eyes, they couldn't look more dissimilar. But that competitive streak runs in the family.

"I really like her," Luke admits to me, his hands buried in his pockets. "Wes won't like it because no one's good enough for his little sister, but I know he'd rather her date me than any of the other assholes on the team."

"She likes you too." I know she wouldn't mind me saying so. She's made her attraction to Luke obvious. Knowing her, she's already told him exactly how she feels. Hell, she was probably the one to ask him out. And she didn't even need me to dare her to do it.

Chloe is the kind of girl I've always wanted to be but never had the guts to try.

Until now, maybe. Being her friend has made me believe I can do anything. I can finally write that book. I can flirt with a guy as out of my league as Wes. As long as I have Chloe by my side, I can be brave.

"I know you've probably already gotten this from Wes, but if you hurt her, I *will* kill you."

Luke gives me an easy smile, as if he knew this conversation was coming. "I'd be more worried about her hurting me. I've been trying not to scare her off by coming on too strong, but Chloe's pretty much the girl of my dreams."

My heart squeezes, so unbelievably happy for my best friend.

"Violet!" Chloe calls. "I need you to tap in for me."

Wes flashes me his heart-stopping grin. My stomach flips.

I take Chloe's spot beside him. "I've got a deal for you, little flower," Wes murmurs in my ear. "Winner gets to come tonight."

"What—"

But Wes is already tossing ping-pong balls at the rings, Chloe screaming at me from behind to win.

Did he really say what I think he did? I'm not sure if he meant it or if he just wanted to fluster me so I would lose.

Either way, I've never been more motivated to win a game in my life.

I grab a ping-pong ball and toss it. It bounces off the ring with a *clink*. Before it hits the ground, I'm tossing another.

It sinks through the hoop.

Behind me, Chloe screams and cheers, jumping up and down.

"It's three to win the duck," Wes reminds her.

She stops jumping and whines. The carnival worker reaches for the stuffed duck and hands it to Chloe. "You can take the duck as long as the four of you get far away from me."

Chloe beams, not giving a single shit about the insult.

"We gotta get you playing beer pong," Luke tells me before wrapping an arm around Chloe's waist. "Are you happy you got your duck?"

"It's Violet's duck. She won it. But yes." She beams. "Ducks are my favorite animal."

"Ducks aren't anybody's favorite animal," Wes says.

"Well, they're mine." She sticks her tongue out at him. "They make gliding across the water look effortless, but beneath the surface, they're paddling frantically. That's how I feel on the ice. I spent years falling and bleeding to get where I am, but when I'm back on the ice, every bruise and scar is worth it. I don't want to be anywhere else. They're at home in the water, and I'm at home on the ice."

She does make it look effortless. Every time I watch Chloe skate, I'm mesmerized. She dances across the slippery surface like it's second nature.

"That's how I feel about writing," I tell her.

She smiles at me. Maybe that's one of the reasons why

we're such great friends. We understand each other's drive, our relentless pursuit of our passions.

"You should let me read one of your stories sometime." Wes smiles at me.

"Just kiss already," Chloe calls to us, rolling her eyes. I freeze, even though I know she's joking. Until she flashes a devilish smile. "I dare you."

Shock and dread seize me.

What the hell is she doing? Why is she pushing me and Wes together when she keeps claiming she doesn't want us dating? Of course I want to kiss him—I want to do a lot more than that with him—but I don't want it to happen in front of an audience.

I dare a glance at Wes, the smile vanished from his face.

But I haven't backed down from a dare yet.

He wanted to kiss me that day at the beach. He said the winner gets to come tonight. He wants me. I know he does.

I take a step toward him, and his eyes widen before he retreats. The word that comes out of his mouth stops me in my tracks. "No."

Mortification washes over me at the rejection. The *public* rejection, right in front of Chloe and Luke.

How could I have read Wes so wrong? I completely misinterpreted his signals. My cheeks flame, and Chloe's eyes widen for a second—just long enough to give away the horror at my humiliation—before she grabs Luke's hand and announces, "Let's go! I need funnel cake."

I follow Chloe and Luke around the carnival in silence, forcing a smile whenever Chloe attempts to include me in the conversation. Staying as far from Wes as I can get.

I've known from the beginning that he would never go for a girl like me. I was stupid to think him flirting with me was anything more than a fun way for him to pass the time. He's never actually been interested in me; he's just been humoring his sister and being friendly. Nothing more.

The carnival is closing in fifteen minutes, and I'm counting down the seconds until I can escape.

"Let's go on the Ferris wheel before they shut it down!" Chloe calls.

"Heights freak me out. You guys go." I wave them on, grateful for a chance to be alone.

"No way." Chloe shakes her head. "You're coming with us."

"If I get that high in the air, my heart will explode—"

"I dare you!" she shouts, laughing and running for the Ferris wheel. Full of a light that can never be snuffed out.

Her joy makes me smile, even with the sour turn this night has taken.

The four of us wait in line, and when Chloe and Luke climb into the pod, she shuts the door behind them.

Leaving me alone with Wes.

The operator sticks us in the next empty pod, and the silence is suffocating.

My heart pounds as we rise slowly. God, I hope we don't get stuck at the top. This night could not have gone any worse.

Wes wraps a protective arm around my shoulders, and I'm instantly enveloped in his scent, his warmth. "You're okay," he murmurs.

"You're the last person I want to comfort me right now. I would suggest scooting as far away from me as you can because I might puke." I squeeze my eyes shut, hoping the nausea in my belly will go away if I can't see how high up we are. If I forget about Wes's horrified face when I moved in to kiss him. *No.*

His fingers brush my cheek, forcing my face toward his. "Look at me."

Even though the last thing I want to do is see him, the rejection and pity etched into his features more nauseating than the ground far below our feet, I do as he says.

He pulls me closer, the side of my body flush against his. He's so warm, smelling deliciously of cedarwood, and I want to get lost in the smell and feel of him. His blue eyes bore into mine, and he cradles my jaw, rubbing his thumb back and forth across my cheek.

"Just keep your eyes on me and you won't feel scared."

My chest caves in, wanting nothing more than to let him comfort me. To let him be my safe harbor. But he doesn't want me the way I want him.

"I'd rather feel scared," I whisper.

He swallows, and there's a flicker of something new in his eyes. Regret.

"I wanted to kiss you." His grip on my jaw tightens yet somehow remains tender. My heart stops. "But I didn't want to do it on a dare. I want it to be real."

I wasn't wrong. I wasn't misreading the signs. I haven't been imagining this. Wes really does want me. As much as I want him.

I'm barely able to force the words out, my heart caught in my throat. "Me too."

He examines every inch of my face before his thumb brushes across my bottom lip. I can't help myself—I let out a small, involuntary gasp.

"I don't do sweet and gentle," he warns. "If you're looking for a prince, he's not me. I want my belt around your throat. I want to fuck you so hard, your nails leave scars on my back. If I kiss you, you're mine."

Liquid heat pools between my legs. I'm half-aroused, half-terrified by his words. But I know what I want.

"I want to be yours," I breathe.

That's all he needs to hear. He grips my hair and pulls me

to him, our lips meeting halfway in a collision that makes fireworks burst in my brain. My stomach somersaults as his soft lips move over mine, my panties growing damp when his tongue slips past my lips. I can't breathe. Can't think about anything but the feel of his mouth on mine.

When he emits a sound that's halfway between a groan and a growl, I melt.

"*Fuck.*" The word is hoarse leaving his throat, a curse and a prayer. "I hope you know what you've just unleashed, little flower. You're not going anywhere now."

There's no going back. I'm his.

I belong to Wes Novak.

Chapter 23

After

Violet

In the library, the words are pouring out of me.

Professor Tate said we had to write about love in our story. She didn't say we couldn't include sex.

Part of me knows I'll never want to show this to her or to anyone, but I'm not letting the doubts or worry take over. If a love story like the ones I've been devouring in books lately gets me writing again, I'll take it.

The words fly from my fingers so fast, I grin. I've missed this feeling so much.

When Chloe told me about why she loved figure skating, how it felt to be on the ice—like she was soaring, like she was untouchable—I told her that's how I feel when I'm writing.

I've been missing this feeling for months. I hope wherever Chloe is now, she feels nothing else.

She'd love reading the smut I'm writing. She'd be reading out loud over my shoulder, giggling right along with me.

Except when the love interest says, *Get on your knees for me*, I realize he sounds an awful lot like Wes.

The door to the library creaks open. Since it's nearing two

and the place is empty, I'm at a back table. At this hour, I assume it's a cleaner or another sleep-deprived student until the lock clicks shut.

Followed by familiar footsteps.

The slow thud of each of his combat boots is echoed by my heartbeat in my ears. I watch motionless as he approaches.

His boots stop beside my chair. Tonight, he's in dark jeans, a Diamond University hoodie, and a mask. Didn't want anyone to identify the guy crossing campus at nearly two in the morning.

My palms grow slick, throat closing up. I don't know what to expect from him anymore. I want to ask if more Devils will be joining us, but I'm afraid of the answer.

He plants a meaty hand on the table. The one he used to choke me. To rub between my legs. Behind his mask, his eyes are unreadable. "I need a book."

Right. I'm sure that's exactly why he's here. I nod and clear my throat. "Um. Okay."

"Up," he commands.

I rise.

He nods to the stacks behind us, gesturing for me to lead the way.

I head down the first row of books until I near the end. He strides past me, flicking the light switch and casting the shelves in shadow.

"Wes, what—"

His body pins me to the shelves and my heart leaps to my throat. "Shut the fuck up," he growls.

He shoves his mask up, finally revealing the flawless, gorgeous face beneath, before smashing his lips against mine.

Adrenaline shoots through me like lightning. His lips are so much softer than I remember, exploring mine with shocking tenderness before his tongue sweeps into my mouth.

My knees grow weak at the feel of him. This is happening. This is really happening.

I'm kissing Wes Novak.

I never thought this would happen again. Hell, I never thought it would happen the first time.

Except this time, it's not sweet or romantic or tender. It's rough and possessive and claiming. Like we're not sharing something—he is merely taking. Taking what he wants from me, what he's been restraining himself against.

I shouldn't love it as much as I do.

He bites down on my bottom lip, making me gasp, before sucking it into his mouth, sweeping away the slight twinge of pain. I can't keep myself upright anymore. Wes's hand drops from the shelf behind my head and latches onto my hip, pinning me in place.

He lets my hands land on his chest, the heart beneath my palm hammering just as hard as my own.

A new fear flutters in my gut. A repeat of what he did to me in my philosophy class. Bringing me so close to the edge before pulling away and taking every bit of pleasure with him.

He yanks my shirt up and my bra down, the cool, air-conditioned air kissing across my exposed skin and making my nipples peak. "These belong to me now," he growls before sucking my nipple into his mouth.

I gasp, and his mask falls to the floor as I clutch at his hair. He rips my hands from his head and slams them down against the shelves. I whimper, and he curls my fingers around the wood. "Don't fucking move."

He keeps sucking on my nipple, pulling it deeper into his mouth. Pleasure sings through my veins and wetness pools between my legs.

In all the times I imagined Wes's mouth on my skin, it never felt this good.

I squirm beneath him, aching to claw at his hair, his biceps, but I dig my nails into the wood instead.

Wes drops my nipple with a small pop before moving on to the other. I bite down the cry and try my best to stay still. Letting him do what he wants to me.

His hand plunges down my skirt so suddenly, I jump. "You're going to take everything I give you," he orders.

"Yes," I breathe.

His hand eases down into my panties until his finger scrapes along my clit. I suck in a breath. When he circles that sensitive spot, I moan.

Wes slaps a hand over my mouth. "Shut up. I don't want to hear your fucking moans. This is for me, not you."

My muscles and joints stiffen. I knew it. This isn't desire or affection. This is something much more twisted.

Yet my knees are still jelly and I ache for him to do whatever he wants to me.

When he kneels before me, chills run down my body.

"Don't make a fucking sound," he warns.

"I won't," I whisper.

His mouth latches onto my thigh, hard. Nearly making it impossible to follow his order. I bite down on my lip to suppress the whimper that builds in my throat. My nails dig into the wood so deep, I know I'll leave my mark. Just as Wes is leaving his mark on me.

He moves to my other thigh, sucking and nipping at my skin. I'm already weak for him, completely at his mercy, and he hasn't even reached the throbbing spot between my legs. Bruises bloom on my skin, marking his trail.

"Wes," I gasp.

"I told you to keep your mouth shut," he snaps. "Now I have to punish you."

I swallow, kicking myself. He's going to deny me that pleasure again. Or inflict a new pain now that he has me in a vulnerable position.

Wes pulls my panties to the side and groans. That sound from him is nearly enough to make me combust.

"Violet," he murmurs, and that fury is gone from his voice now. A tenderness to my name that I haven't heard from him in months.

He blows gently on the apex of my thighs and I shudder. I want to beg him to touch me, to give me that pleasure I'm aching for, but I'm terrified to see what punishment he would have in store for me.

He plants a kiss on my clit, and I can't help the whimper that escapes this time.

"You're going to hate how good this feels." His words make me stop breathing. "I'm going to be the first man to make you come, and when you think back on your first time, you'll have to think of me. The man who scares you, and you like it."

My mind spins, trying to digest every word from his mouth. *Your first time.* He plans on having sex with me? I shouldn't. My first time shouldn't be with a man who hates my guts. Who wants me dead. Who's spent the last weeks of my life tormenting me.

Yet the thought of Wes inside me, fucking me in the stacks, only makes me want him more.

Something is wrong with me. But I don't know if it's Chloe's death that changed me or if I've always had this darkness inside.

The man who scares you, and you like it.

He's right. The fear coursing through my veins, knowing that Wes could do anything he wants to me, knowing that he could hurt me, sends a shot of adrenaline down my spine. Makes my heart race and the pleasure that much more delicious.

He thinks I'll look back on this moment and not just hate him, but hate myself. Hate myself for wanting somebody who treats me so terribly. Hate myself for giving in to him.

The thing is, I can't hate myself any more than I already do.

"Show me how much I'll hate it," I breathe.

"I told you not to speak." The words come out on a low growl that makes my thighs shake.

"So punish me."

His jaw clenches, and he yanks my panties down to my ankles. His fingers dig into my ass where I know he'll leave his imprint, and he yanks me toward him. "Be fucking careful."

But then his tongue glides up my slit, and I get exactly the punishment I was hoping for. I don't bother holding back the gasp of pleasure, knowing that Wes can do whatever he wants to me and I'll want it too.

Pleasure mounts in my limbs when his tongue stops on my clit and swirls there. *Holy shit.* Wes Novak has his tongue between my legs, and it's a thousand times better than my wildest fantasies.

His hands slide up from my ass to my breasts, squeezing them roughly in his calloused hands. The scrape of his palms over my nipples sends my eyes rolling.

"Oh my god," I gasp.

He doesn't stop to bark another order at me. His tongue continues circling my clit until he latches onto it, sucking it into his mouth.

Pleasure like I've never felt before spears through my center. Almost in a way that's too overwhelming, too much. But Wes doesn't care, even as I involuntarily pull away from him, my ass hitting the shelf behind me. He simply follows me, not letting me get away from him.

His tongue dips back down, gliding up me again before plunging inside me. He thrusts his tongue in and out, eliciting pathetic whimpers from my lips. The sound of his tongue working through my wetness is obscene. So loud, it seems to echo in the silent room.

"Mmm," he murmurs. "You taste so fucking good."

"You feel so fucking good."

I swear I can feel him smile between my thighs. "You won't be thinking that in a minute."

Panic rushes through me, but I'm quickly distracted by Wes's mouth returning to my clit. He sucks while one of his hands drops between my thighs, a finger slowly sliding in.

"Agh!" I cry out, the stretch intense and foreign.

Is this what he meant? Is this the punishment? Except when he curls his finger, the stretch quickly turns to a new sort of pleasure. Deeper and multiplying the satisfaction his mouth drives through my clit.

"That's it, little flower," he mutters. "Come on my finger." It's more threat than promise. Then he adds, "If you dare."

I freeze, but he keeps going at me, and even though I fight against it, try not to give him what he wants, the pleasure mounts from my toes to my head. Climbing and climbing until it reaches that inevitable crest. The tipping point I know I won't come back from, where I can't stop the orgasm, even if I wanted to.

As if he can sense it coming, Wes pumps his finger inside me faster while his mouth sucks on my clit harder. I fall over the edge, crying out the whole way down.

Down to the pits of hell, where Wes has dragged me with him.

No. Where I dragged him.

Wes continues thrusting his finger inside me and working my clit through the throes of my orgasm. Until I'm whimpering and shaking, unable to take any more.

His mouth and finger gentle, coming back down with me. The reality of what just happened washes over me.

I just had my first orgasm with a man. With *Wes Novak.*

Oh my *god.*

He slides his finger out, making me gasp, and picks up his mask before he straightens. He settles it back on his face and looms over me. Despite what he's just done to me, his stance is menacing.

"Open your mouth." I do as he instructs, and he slides his finger into my mouth. The finger he just had inside me. "Now suck."

I don't want to, but I follow his order, the taste of my own arousal on my tongue.

He snatches his finger from my mouth before bracing both hands on my shoulders. "On your knees."

Wes doesn't give me a chance to comply. His hands force me to the floor, the thin carpet scraping against my bare skin.

One hand stays on my shoulder, keeping me in place, while the other opens his belt buckle.

I swallow as he slowly pulls the belt free from the loops before snapping it in the air like a whip. I flinch, but I'm immobilized beneath his heavy hand. He wraps the belt around my neck, tightening until it's a cool, unyielding leather collar around my throat.

He steps back, the slack bit of his belt growing taut between us. I drag air down my windpipe while I still can.

"Come here," he commands. I start to stand, but he shakes his head. "No. Crawl to me."

"What?" I can't have heard him right.

He snaps the belt, jerking my neck forward and my hands smack the thin carpet beneath me. "*Crawl* to me. Now."

Reluctantly, I obey his command, the act demeaning and

164

humiliating until I dare a glance up at him. Through the mask, lust brims in his eyes.

I stop crawling when I reach his feet and remain kneeling before him.

He reaches for his zipper. "I told you to keep your mouth shut. Now you're going to find out exactly what happens when you don't listen to me."

"Wes, please," I plead, heart thundering.

"Open up, baby."

I keep my mouth clamped shut. This isn't love or pleasure —it's punishment.

He gives the belt a hard yank. I gasp, mouth opening involuntarily as his belt squeezes my neck.

Wes rubs his rough thumb across my bottom lip. "Good girl. Keep it open or I won't let you breathe."

His hand moves back to his jeans, and his thick cock springs free, long and hard for me.

My mouth goes dry. He's even more glorious than I anticipated. There's no way I can fit his entire length in my mouth. His tip is wide, a bead of pre-cum already waiting for me. The long, thick vein on the underside of his shaft protruding.

Every inch of him is intimidating.

His free hand cradles my face. Almost tender. Almost a lover's caress. "I'm going to fuck your face now, little flower."

He rubs his tip across my lips, still open at his command. My arousal leaks between my legs. Part of me wants to return the pleasure he gave me, another wants him fucking my pussy so I can come again.

"Beg me," he growls.

"What?"

"Beg me for my cum. Beg me to let you swallow." He's growing impatient, pumping his cock in front of my face in long, luxuriating strokes and pulling on his belt.

"Please," I whisper, dropping my gaze.

"Eyes on me," he snarls, yanking the belt so I'm forced to meet his gaze. "Please what?"

"Please . . . let me swallow your cum."

"Anything for you, little flower." The murmur would almost be sweet, romantic, if he didn't have me on my knees with a belt around my throat.

He slips the tip of his already-throbbing cock past my lips and groans, the hot, smooth skin dragging along my tongue. My jaw already feels the stretch around the girth of him.

"Oh *fuck*, baby. That's it."

He eases in slowly, and I grab onto his thighs, knowing any attempt to push him will be fruitless. His taste is salty on my tongue, and when my eyes travel up to his face, the panic vanishes.

His piercing blue eyes are glued on me, and I've never felt more desired in my life. Suddenly, I don't care if he's rough with me. If he takes what he wants. I want to give him the same pleasure he gave me. Want to show him that he's not the only one with power.

I suck in my cheeks and he hisses at the suction around his cock. I take him as deep as I can until I start to feel the gag building and glide my tongue back up his shaft. A rough hand lands in my hair. "Fuck, Violet. That's a good girl."

My chest flutters from the praise.

When I reach the tip, I experimentally swirl my tongue around it, tasting the salt of his pre-cum. His hand fists in my hair. "Down your throat, baby."

I suck his length again, but when I start to come back up, he drives his hips forward, hitting the back of my throat.

His pelvis hits my teeth, and I sputter around his cock as he chokes me with it and the belt. With my hair in his grip, he controls my head, forcing my mouth rhythmically up and down his cock. "You love that, don't you? You love choking on my dick."

The hard tip hits the back of my throat over and over. My eyes sting as his fingers pull my hair and his cock wrenches my jaw.

My stomach starts to ache with every gag, but he doesn't care, and with the long, low groans emitting from his throat, distorted by his mask, I don't care either. "God, I love that you can barely take it. You want the belt tighter, baby?"

He doesn't give me a chance to answer. The belt around my neck tightens, restricting my airflow. I'm forced to open my mouth wider to try to suck down air, which only makes him fuck my mouth harder and faster. The only sounds filling the room are his skin smacking against my face and my gurgles around his cock, foreign to my ears.

My fingernails dig into his thighs, but he doesn't notice as his thrusts into my mouth get faster and faster. "You're going to swallow every last drop of my cum," he warns.

Before I can protest, he drives his cock into me to the hilt, forcing ropes of his salty cum down my throat. Tears spill out of my eyes now as I gag and claw at his thighs, but he doesn't move until his cock gives one final twitch in my mouth.

When he finally pulls his still-hard length past my lips and releases the belt from my neck, I collapse on all fours onto the floor, gasping and coughing. Knowing I'll taste him in my throat and on my tongue for days. Feel the phantom grasp of his belt on my skin.

He zips his pants with a note of finality. "Don't tell anyone about this."

I straighten, sitting back against the shelf behind me, legs too weak and shaky to stand. "Who would I tell?"

I can't tell Aneesa. She would call me crazy for hooking up

with the Devil who's been bullying me since I got back to campus. I have no one else.

"Keep it that way. I don't want anyone to know I stuck my dick in Violet Harris's mouth."

Wes turns without another word, leaving me alone in the dark library.

Shame rockets through me. I've heard the way the other hockey players talk about girls on campus. They'll jump at any chance to brag about getting their dick sucked.

But I am the shameful secret. The girl no one can know he wants.

IN MY HISTORY CLASS, the professor asks me a question, but I'm too distracted by thoughts of Wes and the rest of the Devils to get the answer right. The professor shakes his head, disappointed. I've never liked history, never been good at memorizing all the various dates and years of different wars and tragedies, but I've also never had a C in a class before.

Now I have a C in this class and Advanced Fiction Writing. The one course I thought I was guaranteed to ace. What writer gets a C in a creative writing class?

If I can even call myself a writer anymore.

After class, I stuff my books and laptop in my bag as fast as I can. As soon as I'm out the door, I find Trey leaning back against the adjacent wall, casually flipping open a pocket knife.

I halt when his emerald gaze finds mine, a terrifying smile crawling across his face.

My heart jumps to my throat, blood pounding in my ears.

I need to get the hell away from Trey before he carries out whatever plans he has for me and that knife.

I hurry down the hall and duck into a restroom that's almost never occupied, tucked away in an obscure corner of the University Center's top floor.

The room is empty. I splash water on my face and breathe slowly through my nose, pulling myself together.

I'm okay. I'll be okay. The Devils will get bored of tormenting me eventually. All I have to do is survive until Wes graduates next semester.

Behind me, the door squeaks open. When I glance in the mirror above the sink, it isn't a girl entering the restroom.

Trey shuts the door behind him, locking us in. "Hey, pretty girl."

My stomach drops.

That knife is back out of his pocket, blade flipped open.

I clutch my bag in front of me, the only shield I have against Trey and his knife.

"Get out of here." My words come out shaky in the silent room.

"I have other plans." In three quick strides, he's in front of me and ripping my bag from my hands, tossing it onto the floor. I cringe when the textbooks and phone inside smack against the tile.

I itch to run, but he's blocking my only exit. Towering above me, almost as tall as Wes, green eyes glinting. "You're not going anywhere."

I watch in horror as he drags the blade across his bottom lip, nicking himself and licking away the bead of blood as he backs me against the wall.

His breath is hot on my neck, hands pinned above my head, caging me in.

He presses the knife, just below the crook of my ear, grazing it gently down my neck. I hold my breath, terrified that he'll slice me open with the slightest movement.

In one fluid motion, he grips my ponytail with his other hand, yanking it high in the air and ripping at my scalp. I yelp, the pain making my eyes sting.

The next second, short strands of my hair tickle the back of my neck, my head suddenly lighter as his hand drops beside my shoulder.

I reach up to my ponytail—

And find nothing but air.

It's gone. He cut off my ponytail.

The curtain of hair I used to hide behind, to turn myself invisible. My security blanket torn away in half a breath.

"Fuck, you look sexy this way." A lopsided smirk that makes my stomach turn.

"Why are you doing this?" I whisper.

Trey shrugs. "Captain's orders."

Wes. Wes instructed him to cut off my hair and threaten me with a knife.

A stupid part of me thought things were changing between me and Wes. Of course I was wrong. He'll never forgive me. He shouldn't.

"Ever had a papercut?" Trey asks.

I don't want to say a word to him. Don't want to utter anything that will set him off, encourage him. But if I stay silent, he'll coax the words from my mouth with the sharp edge of that blade. "Yes."

His hands drift down to my own, grabbing my wrist and flipping my palm open. I swallow down the scream of terror when he presses the tip of the knife against my palm.

"A little papercut hurts worse than you would expect, huh? Even a small wound can do a lot of damage." He digs the tip of the knife harder against my skin, and I wince. That only turns his smile feral. "But we don't want anyone knowing where I cut you, do we?"

I flatten against the wall, attempting to create space between us. If I try to escape him, if I try to make a run for it, he'll only make this a thousand times worse.

He yanks my shirt up, exposing my stomach. I cry out when the blade bites into my tender flesh. "But here," he purrs, "no one will see the marks I leave on you."

"Please don't do this, Trey."

"You brought all of this punishment on yourself, baby girl. You gotta get what's coming to you."

His hand moves with a flash across my stomach. The slice is so quick and clean, the pain doesn't register for a second.

When it does, I clamp down on my lip to suppress my cry from the white-hot sting, tasting copper when I catch my tongue.

Trey stares in delight as blood trickles down to my belly button. He licks my blood off his knife and I want to vomit. "My girl will fucking love the pain."

He's so fucking twisted. Sadistic. Even Wes hasn't done anything this bad to me, and his are the only justifiable punishments.

Trey places the knife against my abdomen again, and this time, I scramble to get away. Desperate to escape him before he can inflict more agony.

He pins me to the wall with a forearm across my chest, making it near impossible to breathe. "You're taking your punishment, pretty girl."

Another slice across my flesh has me crying out, followed quickly by another. The delight builds in his eyes with every cry of agony that escapes my lips. My blood trickling, a few drops hitting the floor, but none of the cuts deep enough to make me bleed out. Just enough to make me scream and cry and writhe beneath him, exactly as he wants.

His rock-hard erection presses against my hip through his jeans, the evidence of just how much hurting me turns him on.

"I bet you'd lose your mind if I fucked you with this," he pants, breathless.

My gut turns watery, terror prickling up my neck. "No, *please*," I beg, knowing that my pleas are exactly what he wants, that he gets off on my fear, but I can't help it.

His low chuckle hums along my skin. "Not the blade, beautiful. I'll make sure it's a knife with a nice, long handle."

Sheer panic grips my throat like ghostly hands at the thought of Trey fucking me with the handle of a knife. Then undoubtedly taking his turn.

Outside, a few feminine giggles approach. Trey doesn't panic at the possibility of getting caught assaulting me. Instead, he narrows his eyes, annoyed that our time together has been cut short.

He licks my blood off the blade, eyes rolling up like he's a fucking vampire nourished by my essence. He shoves the knife back in his pocket before pulling out his phone, holding my shirt up.

He snaps a few photos of his handiwork before he's satisfied, dropping my shirt and smirking. He turns and leaves just before the gaggle of girls can find him in here. "Until next time, sweetheart."

Wes

As soon as those photos Trey snapped of Violet appear on my phone, I race to find her.

I'm going to knock his fucking teeth in when I see him.

172

I shove my way into the women's restroom, a girl with jagged chestnut hair bent over a sink.

Trey did exactly as I instructed. He cut off that ponytail so I'd stop imagining wrapping my hand around it and pulling. But my plan backfired.

Violet is more beautiful now than I thought possible. My heart nearly fucking stops while I admire Trey's handiwork.

Until she turns and I spot the rest of it.

The delicate skin on her belly marked with red, jagged slices. She's been dabbing at the wounds with a damp paper towel. They're shallow, but enough to fucking hurt.

My hands curl into fists that I want to launch at the wall. Better yet, right into Trey's fucking nose.

Black makeup is smeared beneath her eyes, swollen from crying. I could fucking kill him.

"Fuck," I hiss, feet still frozen as I take her in. "What did he do to you?"

She sniffles. "Everything you told him to."

I don't like the sound of that. I close the distance between us, examining her bare skin for any other damage he inflicted. "Did he hurt you anywhere else?"

If he touched her, if he fucked her, I swear I'll bury him ten feet under—

"No," she manages, attempting to step away from me, but I grip her hip, holding her in place. "But he wanted to."

I bet he did. Motherfucker. "What did you do?"

Her delicate brows furrow. "What do you mean?"

"I mean, did you scream? Claw out his eyes? Knee him in the balls?" God, I hope she got in a few good shots.

She's thrown off by my question, eyes wide. "I . . . didn't do anything."

"You just let him carve you up?" My grip on her hip tightens, thinking about her standing there, gritting her teeth while he cut into her like a pumpkin, thinking she deserved it.

"Isn't that what you wanted?" Her whisper nearly breaks me. "You're the one who sent him after me."

"No." I close my eyes and breathe slowly through my nose, forcing myself to stay calm. "Yeah, I told him to cut off your hair so I'd stop fucking fantasizing about pulling it. But not the rest. He didn't even give a shit about Chloe. That wasn't him seeking to avenge me or her—that was him being a sadistic fuck. Stop taking whatever assholes like Trey want to dole out to you. Fight back."

She swallows, forcing her hazel eyes up to meet mine. "Even you? I thought you liked me at your mercy." A bitter edge to her voice.

"Only because you like it too." I shake my head. She has no idea. No fucking clue. "You'd fucking *love* it, Violet."

I grab the paper towel from her and drop to my knees, dabbing at the cuts. She lets out a little gasp that makes my cock twitch. I rub at her gently until I'm certain she's clean, the rivulets of blood wiped away.

I should be salivating, seeing her punished like this. She's done so much fucking worse. Caused a thousand times more pain.

But I'm not getting a single ounce of pleasure from this.

I toss the soiled paper towel in the trash and stand. With my thumb, I pull her bottom lip out from under her teeth. Lean closer, let my breath caress her skin. Before dropping my hand from the wall behind her and clasping it over her throat.

Her eyes widen, but she doesn't move. I don't squeeze the way I did last time. "I'm not like him. Your pleasure gets me off —not your pain. You liked this before, didn't you? You get wet every time you think about me choking you again."

She blinks furiously, wondering how I could possibly know

her darkest fantasies. Like I haven't noticed the new books she started reading. Dark covers with seductive titles. Only took five seconds on Google to figure out exactly the new kinks Violet has discovered she's into.

"Tell me what the new book's about." I already know the answer.

Her throat bobs beneath my palm. "Um. It's, uh, about a girl who gets kidnapped. And . . . falls in love with her captor."

I smirk. "And what does he do to her?"

"He ties her up," she whispers. "He gags her. And chokes her."

I squeeze the hand around her neck, just a little. Her nostrils flare as she sucks in a shuddering breath. "That's what you like, huh?"

She debates her answer. Whether she should lie and tell me no or admit the truth. Finally, she breathes, "Yes." Then she amends, "With you."

My eyes fall shut, heart hammering now.

"Wes." Her voice gentle, uncertain. Hazel eyes wide when I finally open mine. "Can we please . . . talk about what happened? That night."

She sure as hell knows how to kill a moment. How to kill a lot of things. "What the fuck is there to talk about? You killed my sister. Nothing more to say."

She nods quickly, dropping her gaze and twisting her hands together. "You're right. I did. I didn't mean to hurt her, but I did." Her voice breaks, and fuck if I don't want to sweep her up in my arms right now, let her cry herself hoarse. Cry with her like I've been longing to since the night my sister died.

The only girl I've wanted to run to. The only girl I've wanted to hold while she holds me. The only person on this entire fucking planet I wanted to trust with my heart, my soul.

The last person I could.

"The guilt has been killing me. I know—it should be. I deserve that. But there's a lot I've wanted to say to you since that night, and I need to finally say it. I just need you to know that . . ." She sniffles, blinking fast to try to hold back the tears. Bury down the feelings we've both been keeping six feet under, knowing we didn't deserve to let them out. To find any second of relief with Chloe gone. "If I could do anything to take it back, I would. Without a second thought. I wish I'd been the one to die that night instead of Chloe. I wish you still had your sister, and I'm sorry there's nothing I can do to bring her back. I know that I deserve everything you've done to me, and worse. We're in agreement about that. I just thought you should know."

I wait for her to ask me to put an end to the torment. To feed me some bullshit line like *this isn't what Chloe would want*. But she doesn't.

She means it. The guilt is eating her alive. This whole time, I've been wanting to punish her for what she did. But her own mind has been punishing her more severely than I ever could.

My heart stutters. I want to rip it out of my chest, tear it to shreds, and stomp on it.

I shouldn't give a fuck about this girl. She ruined my life. She ended my sister's.

But no matter how much I fight against it—against those memories of her sweet lips on mine, her soft words in my ear—I can't win.

She's the last girl I should want, but she's the only girl I do.

Her tears break through my carefully crafted wall, shattering me entirely. I cradle her hips, my own eyes misting.

"I just miss her *so much*." Violet attempts to cover her face with her hands. To hide the scrunch of her features as a heart-breaking sob wrenches from her chest. "And the only person I want to talk to about missing her hates me. And you should.

You should hate me. *I* hate me. But it's been so, *so* lonely grieving her alone. Without you."

My heart splinters in two. One half for Chloe, my sister who was taken from this life entirely too soon. Who had so much life left to live. Who was my beacon of light, always shining.

The other half for Violet, the monster who took my sister away. The girl I started falling for before I even learned her name. The bright star still flickering, guiding me toward her, even in my darkest hour.

How can I love my sister and the girl who killed her at the same time?

But I know that's what this is. I can't deny it anymore. Can't keep trying to bury my true feelings under a thousand layers of wrath and resentment and hatred.

What I've hated most of all isn't what Violet did. What I've hated is that I've kept loving her through all of it, no matter how hard I've tried to stop.

Gently, I pull her hands down. Tears fall from her cheeks to the floor until I lift her chin up, forcing her shimmering gaze to meet mine. "I'm sorry I made you go through this alone."

She shakes her head quickly. "Please don't apologize. You don't have anything to apologize for. I deserved it—"

"No, you didn't, Violet." I breathe slowly through my nose, pushing down the swell of emotion in my chest.

My parents' words from the beginning of the semester ring through my head. *You know she's just as upset about Chloe's death as we are. You need to figure out a way to forgive her, son. Your lack of forgiveness won't hurt Violet, Wes. It'll only hurt you.*

"It was an accident. What you did was stupid. Really, *really* fucking stupid. But I know you loved her. You'd never hurt her on purpose."

Violet shakes her head, a new stream of tears renewed. "No, I wouldn't. I'd hurt myself before I'd hurt her."

I swipe at a tear on her cheek. "I know. But I don't want you hurting anymore."

Violet can't hold back now. She throws her arms around me, burying her face against my chest and letting the sobs wrack her body. Tears finally break through the barricade, blurring my own vision as I hold her to me as tight as I can. To make up for every single day since my sister died that I haven't held her the way I should've.

She loved my sister so much. I can't believe I ever thought I had to punish Violet for not loving her enough. Other than me and my family, there's no one alive who's ever loved Chloe more.

I've hurt Violet plenty in my plot for revenge. But none of it has dulled that deep, persistent ache. None of it has made me feel any fucking better. None of it has brought Chloe justice.

None of it has brought Chloe back.

No matter what I do to Violet now, my sister is gone. There's no undoing what's been done.

What Violet and I need now is to get through this, to move forward even when every step feels impossible. The only way we can do that is together.

Chapter 24

After

Wes

IN THE LOCKER ROOM, I snarl, "Where's Trey?"

Luke's spine straightens at my tone, but Brody doesn't notice I'm out for blood. He points to the other side of the locker room, and I stomp in Trey's direction. Luke's on my heels, ready to break up whatever fight's about to go down.

Once I get my hands on that asshole, he'll never lay another finger on Violet.

He's still shirtless when I find him bullshitting with some of the other guys, that cocky, insufferable grin across his face. Like a fucking coyote that just raided the chicken coop.

I grab him by the shoulders and throw him up against the lockers. The crash of flesh on metal gets the other guys jumping to their feet, some running toward us, but none of them dare to intervene.

"The *fuck*, man?" Trey spits.

"Yeah, the *fuck*, Trey?" I get in his face. Only got a couple inches on the guy, but I'll still ragdoll him if he makes a move. "Where do you get off cutting a girl to ribbons?"

His snarl turns wicked. "Same place you do. Balls deep."

I pin his throat to the locker with my forearm, veins bulging beneath my skin. Every fucking cell in my body longs to sink my fist into his nose, beat him until he can't walk, but Coach would have me off the team in a second. I can't throw away everything I've worked for to teach him a lesson.

"You keep your fucking hands off her. You hear me?"

"I was just," he chokes out, "following Captain's orders."

Luke grips my shoulder. "Come on, Novak. Ease up."

I dig my arm deeper into Trey's neck, fear finally flashing in his eyes and making him scramble, tearing at me to get off him.

"Your captain didn't order you to cut her up." I snarl my next words directly in his ear so he hears them loud and clear. "You ever lay another fucking finger on her, I'll rip every limb off your body."

Trey smacks my arm like he's tapping out of a wrestling hold. I finally release him, and he gulps down air before bracing his hands on his knees.

"*Everyone* keeps their hands off her," I shout to my team. "Forget about Violet Harris."

What happened between Trey and Violet in that bathroom was a fucking mess. Trey might've been the one to cut her up, but I guarantee he wasn't the only one in on it. Knowing Trey, half the team was egging him on. He lives for the attention— that's why he's still so butt hurt I got captain.

"Why forget about her?" Trey pants, straightening. "You hate the bitch. You're the one who told us to run her off campus."

"And now I'm telling you to forget about her," I snap.

"You getting soft? Or falling in love with some pussy?"

Something tells me if I confess the truth—that I'm forgiving Violet, that I've been in love with her since just about the first time I spoke to her—Trey will only become a greater danger to her.

"I'm handling her myself. You don't know where to draw a fucking line, Trey. You don't think shit through. You know what would happen to the team if you'd gotten caught?"

He rolls his eyes like the arrogant piece of shit he is. "I wouldn't have gotten caught."

"Another girl could've walked in anytime, dipshit. You didn't follow my orders. So you're out. You're all out. I'll handle this on my own."

It was stupid getting them involved in the first place. This has always been between me and Violet.

Trey shakes his head, jaw ticking. "Whatever you say, Captain."

Violet

ANEESA BUYS my lie that I had a meltdown and spontaneously chopped off my own hair, but she tsks at what a shitty job I did before grabbing a pair of scissors to fix it.

"Of course you know how to cut hair too," I tell her. It should be illegal to be this perfect.

A few girls come and go from our floor's shared bathroom, most of them chatting amiably with Aneesa and doing their best to ignore me.

"You're welcome." When she's finished, Aneesa rests her hands on my shoulders. "Honestly, I think I like this better. You look good with short hair."

I touch the ends, finally daring a peek at my reflection. To my surprise, Aneesa is right. My hair brushes against my shoulders in a perfectly symmetrical bob, framing my face and turning my jaw and cheekbones delicate.

"Chloe would love this. She told me if I kept refusing to do anything with my hair, I should just chop it off." I freeze. This may be the first time I've brought up Chloe casually to Aneesa. To anyone since she died.

Aneesa flashes an easy smile. "She sounds like she knew what she was talking about."

Relief floods through me as I return her smile. I can't remember the last time I felt anything other than devastation and sorrow at the memory of my best friend. "She did."

Part of me wants to tell Aneesa about Wes too. Confide in her about our conversation in the restroom. How Wes looked at me when he spotted the jagged haircut Trey gave me. How he couldn't drag his gaze from me even if he wanted to.

How he held me while I cried. Murmured that he doesn't want me hurting anymore.

I want to confide in her about all of it. The evidence on my stomach of Trey's attack. What else he threatened to do to me with that knife.

But Aneesa will definitely run to report the incident if she finds out. Even if I only report what Trey did, Wes will inevitably get wrapped up in it. He'll suffer too. And despite everything he's put me through, that's the last thing I want to do to him.

I just want all the suffering and pain to end.

The text from Wes comes when Aneesa and I are heading back from the dining hall to our dorm room.

Come to the beta theta pi party.

Another party. There's no way I want to go to that. I don't think Wes has any evil plans for me, but I'm sure the rest of the Devils will be there. *Trey* will be there. Who knows if he'll stop at cutting up my stomach this time.

My hands are unsteady while I text back.

> Why?

I want to see you.

Wear something sexy.

> Who else will be there?

Don't worry about them.

I told them to leave you alone.

You're mine now.

My heart pounds, but I try to keep my voice casual. "Hey, Aneesa? Do you want to go to a party with me tonight?"

She frowns. "Please tell me you're not talking about the Beta Theta Pi party."

"What if I am?"

She sighs. "You know Wes is going to be there. If you go, he's definitely going to do something to you."

"I think that's behind us now, actually. We talked and . . . we're moving forward."

Aneesa's features contort. "You don't actually believe that, do you? He's been tormenting you for months, Violet. This is just another trick."

No. Not after that conversation in the bathroom. Not after he cleaned the blood off my stomach and held me while I cried, murmuring reassurances into my hair. Wes is different now. Things have changed between us.

I'm almost sure of it.

"That's why you should go with me," I tell her.

"I can't go. I'm heading home for the weekend," Aneesa says, and the small bubble of hope in my chest pops. "And you better not be going either. In fact, you should go home this weekend too. Talk to your mom—try to mend things with her. I know it's bothering you."

I shrug. "I'm fine with it."

While not totally true, I have managed to compartmentalize enough to bury Mom's disappointment deep enough that I sometimes forget about it altogether. Forget that this time last year, she was calling or texting every day to make sure I was still alive and to tell me all about our neighbor's latest antics or —when she and Mrs. Novak met—about the funny memes and gifs they'd sent each other that day or the hilarious stories they shared while wine-drunk.

Aneesa squeezes my shoulder, forcing me to meet her wide, deep brown gaze. "Just promise me you won't go to that party tonight."

My heart skips with the lie forming on my tongue. "Fine. I have a lot of studying to do anyway."

"I'm glad." She nods her approval. "Nothing good can come from you being around Wes Novak."

I'm stiff in Aneesa's black dress. She let me wear it to the last party, so I'm sure she won't mind if I borrow it again. Especially if I wash it and she never finds out.

A slow-moving line blocks my way into the frat house. A few of the Devils are passing out red plastic cups.

As soon as I spot their jerseys, I want to run in the opposite direction, but my desire to see Wes wins out. I'm aching to watch his eyes light up when he notices me in this dress.

Once I get further up the line, Trey's predatory gaze lands on me.

I balk. He flashes his notorious devilish grin before holding out a red plastic cup to me. Like he didn't have me pinned up against a bathroom wall yesterday, slicing into me. Those wounds still fresh and tender beneath my dress.

His palm snakes around my shoulder, fingers digging in just deep enough to inflict pain. "Back for more, pretty girl?"

Wes's words ring in my ears. *Fight back.* For a wild second, I imagine throwing my drink in Trey's face.

But then I picture the rage that would contort his features, and I clutch my drink in both hands. I square my shoulders. "I'm not here for you."

I shake off his touch and keep my head high as I stride away, even as nausea roils in my gut and I brace myself for him to attack me from behind. Maybe hold that knife against my throat this time. I don't dare glance over my shoulder, but his assault never comes as I disappear into the crowd of warm, gyrating bodies.

Maybe the Devils really are listening to Wes's order to leave me alone. Relief flows through me, relaxing the tight muscles in my shoulders.

In the massive dining room, I manage to get some space to catch my breath. The place smells like old coffee and burnt toast. I sip at my beer, nerves pestering me.

"You came."

I spin, drink sloshing dangerously close to the brim as Wes approaches through the dimly lit room. "You told me to."

He's already closed the distance between us, brushing a

strand of hair behind my ear. "I love when you do as you're told."

I want to ask if I'm forgiven. If he's been touching me and kissing me and making me come because he still wants me just as much as I want him.

Despite everything we've done to each other. Despite all the damage and hurt we've caused. Neither of us has been able to shake those feelings away. To withstand that magnetic pull toward each other.

But I'm still too scared to ask, because I'm terrified to know the answer.

"Why did you invite me here?"

A mischievous grin spreads across his gorgeous face. "To make you wear that dress for me."

His eyes eat me up before he presses my body against him and squeezes my ass. His hot breath envelops my ear. "You want to come on my cock tonight?"

I take another long gulp from my cup. The liquid courage helps me nod, form the breathy words of my assent. "Yeah. I do."

"Beg me," he growls low in my ear, his husky scent wrapping around me in a delicious embrace.

I let out a shaky breath. "Please, Wes."

"Please what?"

"Please . . . fuck me."

He gives my ass a rewarding slap. "That's right, little flower. You're learning."

A thrill of anticipation skitters along my spine as Wes leads me upstairs by the hand. He's touching me in public. Not caring who sees or what anyone thinks.

My heart sings, and maybe my eyes would mist again if I could feel anything other than delight and anticipation at being led upstairs by Wes Novak.

Trey's hungry stare follows us up the steps from where he's still passing out drinks. I can't possibly hear him over the shouts and music and laughter, but I swear he mouths, *I'm next.*

Now the feeling skittering down my spine is fear.

Wes finds an empty bedroom and flattens his hand against the base of my spine, pushing me inside before locking the door behind us.

I can hardly breathe, torn between wanting this with every fiber of my being and knowing I don't deserve it. Don't deserve happiness or forgiveness.

"I'm sorry, Wes," I whisper as he grabs my hip. "I'll say it every day if I have to."

"I know," he murmurs.

He grabs the red plastic cup I'm still holding and places it on a dresser behind him before running his hand through my hair and bringing my mouth to his. The kiss is tender but insistent. His lips moving over mine until his tongue parts them, sliding against mine and making my entire body thrum.

When I pull away to catch my breath, I finally ask the question that's been gnawing at me. "Does this mean you've forgiven me?"

His eyes fall briefly shut and he exhales audibly through his nose. "I'm trying."

I'm not forgiven yet. Not fully. But he's trying, and that's all I can ask for. More than I deserve.

He guides me to the bed. My knees buckle and I fall back onto the mattress.

Wes climbs on top of me and hauls my dress up to my chest, exposing my breasts and panties. My head starts to spin. I didn't feel this way last time, but maybe it's just the beer kicking in.

"You're so perfect. Fucking made for me."

My heart nearly breaks. I feel like I've finally gotten the old

Wes back. A glimpse of who he was before Chloe's death broke him. Before I broke him.

Now it's my job to help him put the pieces back together.

He squeezes my tits. "I fucking love these," he growls.

Cool air brushes against my peaked nipples before he sucks one into his mouth, making me gasp and clutch at his hair. The warmth from his mouth and the wet stroke of his tongue makes the space between my legs weep.

"*Wes*," I gasp, pulling him closer. He sucks my nipple deeper into his mouth, so hard I nearly wince.

The room spins for a second, and a small dose of panic shoots through me. I didn't drink much, but maybe I drank enough to be sick.

"How bad do you want me, little flower?" He drops my nipple and moves to the other, and I hiss when he latches on. His cock drives up against my clit and I cry out, the pleasure sudden and intense. I feel his low chuckle all the way to my toes. "That bad, huh?"

He drops to his back beside me and tugs me toward him. "Sit on my face."

"What? I thought you wanted to—"

"Sit on my fucking face, Violet. Now."

Another order I don't dare refuse. Wouldn't dream of. Warmth pools between my legs as I straddle his chest.

His huge hands grab my ass and push me forward until I'm nearly falling onto his face. My pussy collides with his mouth, and he licks up the cotton panties between us.

He kisses and nibbles, the sensations sharp against my sensitive and aching clit. My mind starts to slip and I grip onto the headboard, trying to anchor myself to this bed, to this moment, to Wes.

Except the whole world is spinning now, flickering in and out.

"Violet?" His voice, full of concern, but like he's speaking through water.

I'm staring up at the ceiling now, the mattress soft but cold beneath me without his warmth. His face, distorted above me, as his lips form my name again.

The last thing I see before my eyes fall shut.

Chapter 25

After

Wes

"What the fuck did you give her?"

Violet is passed out in my arms. When she fell unconscious upstairs, she didn't stir no matter how many times I called her name or tapped her cheek.

I check her pulse again. Slow but steady.

Trey slouches back on the couch with a cup in hand, grinning like a fucking sadistic prick. "No clue what you're talking about."

"I know you put something in her fucking drink, Trey."

"Did you get your dick wet before or after she passed out?"

If she wasn't in my arms right now, both my hands would be wrapped around his throat. "One last time. What. Did. You. Give. Her."

He shrugs. "Just a little GHB."

Jesus. He fucking roofied her. I knew it. "How many other drinks did you spike?"

He rolls his eyes. "Only hers, Christ."

God, I want nothing more than to lay him out. "I fucking told you to stay away from her."

"Then you shouldn't have told her to come here," he says. "I know she didn't show up all on her own."

The invite I sent to Violet was a spontaneous one. A text I typed out as the redhead was feeling up my triceps and purring in my ear no matter how many times I shook her off. I needed Violet. Needed her in my hands, on my face, on my cock.

But Trey can't know that. He finds out why I really invited her here, and she'll have an even bigger target on her back.

"Of course she didn't. I told her to come here, but the point is to keep her conscious so she knows what's happening."

"So fuck her when she wakes up then." He chugs from his cup like drugging a girl is no big deal.

"Monday, I'm letting Coach know about this."

That smile drops off Trey's face and he rises like he stands a chance at intimidating me. "Yeah? What are you going to tell him? I spiked a girl's drink? Where's your proof?"

"In my fucking hands."

His eyes fall to Violet's limp body, tracing over the lines of her face with a demonic hunger. "Anybody could've slipped her something." He claps a hand on my shoulder as he passes. "See you at practice."

I wish he was wrong, but he isn't. I can't prove he's the one who spiked her drink. Even if I tell Coach he admitted it, that won't mean shit if Trey calls me a liar and I have no evidence proving otherwise.

"Oh, and Wes?" His wide grin is back. "Let me know how tight her pussy is. I can't wait to stretch her out."

He's dead.

191

Violet

SOMEONE IS SLEEPING in my roommate's bed, but it's not Aneesa.

Wes is passed out on top of her blanket, eyes shut and chest rising gently. This is the first time I've seen him look peaceful since before Chloe died. He's in the same clothes he was wearing last night at the party.

My head swims, temple throbbing. What the hell happened last night? All I remember is going upstairs with Wes at the Beta Theta Pi party and his mouth on me. Then nothing.

If Wes is still here, whatever happened can't be good.

I throw the blanket off me, preparing for the worst. But I'm fully clothed, Aneesa's dress completely intact. My panties in place. My hand rushes to my chest, the relief spilling over me. *Thank god.*

I can't remember having more than one drink last night, but maybe I had so many, I simply forgot how many I really had.

Or maybe Trey put something in that cup he handed me.

Wes invited me to the Beta Theta Pi party to hook up, not to roofie me. This must've been entirely Trey's doing.

Right?

Aneesa's words stick in my head. *This is just another trick. Nothing good can come from you being around Wes Novak.*

But no, he wouldn't do something as sick and twisted as instructing his teammate to drug me.

Still, I need to know exactly what happened to me last night.

I jump out of bed and shake his shoulder. His eyes fly open, confused for a second before a weak smile crosses his lips. "Morning, gorgeous."

The compliment makes my stomach flip. "What happened last night, Wes?"

He sits up, rubbing the back of his neck. "Trey spiked your drink."

I blink back tears even as my hands curl into fists. Trey is the worst person I've ever met. Everything he's done to me is so much worse than anything Wes has done. He needs to be stopped.

I already know the answer, but I ask it anyway because I have to hear it from his mouth. "You didn't know, right?"

Wes swings off the bed, opening up my fists and sliding his fingers through mine. I want to melt into him. "Of course not. I'd never do that to anyone, let alone someone I—"

He cuts himself off, but my heart aches to hear the rest. "Someone you what?"

"Someone I . . . care about," he manages.

Not the exact words I hoped to hear, but they're still more than I deserve. He cares about me. Even after everything.

"You passed out while we were in bed. I carried you back here. Nothing happened," he adds, even though I already know he wouldn't take advantage of me while I'm drugged and unconscious.

"So you never left me alone after I passed out? No one . . . did anything to me?"

His eyes grow more tender. "No, I never would've left you alone. Not for a second. If anyone had tried something, I would've buried them alive."

My heart soars at the words, and I manage to whisper, "Thank you."

He drags his thumb over my cheek. My breath catches. "Chloe would've haunted my ass if I'd let anything happen to you."

A surprised, relieved laugh bursts out of my mouth, even as something painful in my chest swells. He mentioned Chloe in front of me. Without rage or blame.

I miss her so much. I wish she was here to cry to. To make Trey pay for what he did to me.

"Having her as a roommate freshman year was the best thing that could've happened to me." I smile because if I don't, I'll break down sobbing again, and I've cried enough in Wes Novak's arms. He shouldn't be forced to comfort his sister's killer.

"It was the best thing that happened to her too."

The shock of his words nearly knocks me off my feet. If she'd never met me, she'd still be alive. "I don't know how you can say that," I whisper. "I'm the reason she's dead."

"You are," he agrees. Maybe we'll both spend the rest of our lives trying to forgive me for that. "But she loved you like a sister."

My eyes flood with tears. Chloe was the closest thing I've ever had to a sister. But I don't have the right to mourn her. "I loved her too. I still do."

"I need you, Violet." His throat is hoarse, pain etched into his features. "If we're going to get through this, we need each other."

I nod, wanting that more than anything. All I've wanted since she died is to find comfort in Wes's arms.

He cradles my cheek, managing a smile. "She would be talking so much shit right now if she found us alone in here together."

"Something about how we're gross and she's going to go barf now."

He laughs, and my god, I've missed that sound. "Even though she secretly wanted us together the whole time."

I shake my head, grinning. "Yeah, I don't know how I was so blind to her scheming."

He swipes a strand of hair behind my ear, sending a shiver all the way down. "Or how you were so blind to my advances."

"What advances?"

Wes rolls his eyes, amused. "I was flirting with you from day one."

"Yeah, but you didn't actually mean anything by it."

His brows furrow. "How does that work?"

"You were just a flirt. You flirted with everybody."

"Not everybody."

"I saw you flirting with Edith."

"Okay, but that's because I have a thing for cougars."

I laugh, smacking his arm.

"Seriously, though, you were different from the beginning. I couldn't get you out of my head. Followed you around campus—"

I hold up a hand. "Wait. You followed me around campus?"

A lopsided smile. "How do you think I found out your favorite candy?"

"I knew it! I knew you were stalking me," I tease.

He steps closer until there's no space between us, and I'm forced to crane my neck to peer up at him. "Yeah, I was. I was fucking obsessed."

A shiver races down my spine.

He bends down and picks me up by the backs of my thighs in one swift movement. In my ear, he murmurs, "I still need to find out how your pussy feels around my cock."

Oh my *god.*

Wes tosses me onto the bed, and I expect him to climb on top of me like he did last night, but instead, he grabs me by the hips and pulls me onto his lap. His erection intimidatingly hard between my legs.

His eyes are glued to my face. I've never felt sexier, more powerful, than when I'm burning under Wes Novak's piercing blue gaze.

"Take off your clothes, baby."

I peel the dress off and toss it at his head. He flings it off with a grin.

"That's my good girl," he murmurs, hungry gaze roaming over every inch.

My eyes flutter shut. If there's anything I've learned from the books I've been reading lately, it's that I have a praise kink.

Or maybe I just have a Wes Novak kink.

He loses his patience then, wrapping an arm around the small of my back before he sits up and sucks a nipple into his mouth. I gasp and latch onto his hair. He pulls my nipple between his teeth while I tug on the unruly strands between my fingers.

His hand drifts to my other breast, squeezing and kneading. I've never wanted him more, my panties damp against the hard cock straining in his jeans.

His eyes bore into mine. "You have no fucking clue how long I've been wanting to do this."

"You have no idea how long I've been wanting you to," I gasp.

Wes dips his mouth back down to my other nipple and I whimper. I'm already soaked for him. I grind against his erection and he growls, sending shockwaves through my nipple and down to my toes. "That's such a good fucking girl."

He guides my hips with one hand up and down his hard length, the friction sending pleasure through my clit.

"What do you want?" he asks, breathless. "My mouth, my fingers, or my cock?"

"I didn't realize I could only have one."

He chuckles. "You can have whatever part of me you want."

"In that case, I choose option D, all of the above."

Without another word, he's flat on his back, pulling me up his body by my hips. When my thighs are around his head, he guides me down.

"Relax," he urges.

I don't know how I'm supposed to. I'm half embarrassed, half terrified I'll suffocate him.

But every worry is forgotten when he pulls my panties to the side and glides his tongue up my slit.

The cool, wet sensation splits me in two and I gasp, arching forward and bracing my hands on the wall.

He groans at my taste. "Fuck, Violet. You're so sweet."

I moan, liquid heat pooling low in my belly, knowing the flood he must be tasting between my legs.

His tongue laps at my clit, and I nearly lurch away from the sudden, overwhelming pleasure. But he drags me back down, forcing me to sit on his face.

A low growl from his throat, and I know exactly what he's thinking before he even says it. "You're not getting off my face until I tell you to."

My heart is already pounding. "I won't," I breathe.

His tongue strokes me, again and again, the combined friction from my panties grinding against my clit making me squirm.

When his tongue penetrates me with an obscene sound, he shoves my panties further to the side and presses down on my clit with his thumb. I shudder, my thighs trembling around him.

He keeps thrusting his tongue inside me while his thumb presses down, harder and harder, circling my clit and making the pleasure mount mind-blowingly fast.

"Wes," I pant.

Sensing my impending orgasm, he replaces his thumb with his mouth, sucking my clit. I cry out, the pleasure making my mind spin. His finger finds my slick entrance and slides inside, pumping into me while his mouth works me.

"I can't wait to feel you come on my tongue."

At his words, I can't take anymore. The pleasure mounting to an inevitable crest—

My thighs clench around his head as pleasure barrels through me and stars burst across my vision.

I cry out and collapse, no longer able to brace myself on the wall, and moan as Wes continues sucking on my clit and thrusting his finger inside me through the waves of pleasure.

He doesn't stop even as the overwhelming sensitivity in my throbbing clit threatens to cleave my brain in two. Even as I try to pull away, his arms keep my thighs pinned in place around his head, preventing me from escaping the pleasure.

When I finally start to come down from the orgasm, heartbeat echoing in my ears, Wes guides me back down his body. The slick evidence of my orgasm glistens on his neck.

A hand flies to my mouth. "Oh my god. I'm so sorry."

He laughs. "Sorry? A girl's never been so wet for me, she drips down my neck before. That's the hottest fucking thing that's ever happened to me." He sits up and reaches for the hem of his shirt. "Should probably take my clothes off before you soak them next, though."

My face warms, but I grin knowing he likes it.

He pushes me off him to slide his jeans and boxers down, then pulls me back on top of him. He wipes at the juices on his neck before stroking his cock, lubricating it before nudging at my entrance.

"You don't want me to return the favor?"

"You're about to."

I grin, but it quickly falls away when his tip slides inside me. A slight burn from the stretch.

Wes tilts my chin up, forcing me to meet his eyes. "You want this." Like he doesn't have to ask—he already knows how much my pussy aches for him to be inside me.

I nod quickly.

"Say it," he commands.

"I want this."

"Want what?"

"I want you."

He grins. "What do you want me to do to you?"

I mirror the grin back to him. "I want you to fuck me, Wes."

That's all he needs to hear. He pulls me down onto his cock slowly, letting me stretch and acclimate to him. He rubs my clit as he works his cock in, the sting and burn from the stretch making me grind my teeth. Until a new kind of pleasure fills me. We're both breathing heavily now.

"Do you like my cock inside you?" he pants.

My hands are on his abdomen, luxuriating in the incredible six-pack beneath my palms. "Yes. I love it."

His thumb on my clit rubs harder. "I want to watch you ride me."

I oblige him. Resting my hands on his chest, I slowly drag my hips up and down, feeling the stretch of his cock filling me with every movement.

"That's it, baby," he praises. "Take every inch."

Pride fills me up, making me move faster, the squelch of our joining filling my ears. He tips his head back and groans. I want to hear that sound from him every day. Want to be the reason for it.

When I glance down at where our bodies connect, I realize there are still a few inches that I haven't gotten inside me. How is that possible? I already feel completely filled up. "I don't think I can take every inch," I gasp.

He chuckles. "Not yet. But you will."

Pleasure shoots through me. At his words, at his cock hitting that sweet spot inside me, at his frantic thumb on my clit.

"Do you want to get fucked now, baby?"

The word comes out of me in a gasp. "*Yes.*"

Wes flips me on my back and thrusts inside me, making me cry out. The angle is deep, his hard thrusts almost punishing if it didn't feel so good. The mattress squeaks beneath us, Wes's heavy body lying on top of me and fucking me into the bed. So hard our bodies might actually leave an imprint in the mattress.

He groans in my ear, and his sounds turn my body to liquid. "Fuck yes, baby. You're so fucking tight. You're going to make me cum so hard."

He braces his hands on either side of my head, pushing himself up while he keeps slamming into me. My tits bounce wildly.

"You feel so good," I gasp.

"My belt is too far. This will have to do." He wraps a hand around my throat, squeezing the sides of my neck.

At the restriction of blood flow to my head, the pleasure mounts. The same way it did when he wrapped his belt around my neck in the library before he made me swallow down his thick cock and cum.

"Wes!" I croak.

"I know, baby. You're doing amazing. You're taking my cock like such a fucking good girl."

The friction from his pelvis hitting my clit with every thrust combined with the overwhelming feel of him filling me sends me tumbling over the edge. "Wes, I'm going to—"

The cry rips from my throat, struggling to escape past his

tight grip on my neck as the orgasm barrels through me. He covers my mouth with his, swallowing down my cries, pumping into me like he's punishing my pussy for making him wait all this time.

"Fuck, baby, I'm going to cum on you. I'm going to paint you with every drop." His thrusts turn so hard, pain mixes with the pleasure. I scream, tits bouncing and body coming apart with every slam of his cock inside me. "That's music to my fucking ears."

I'm not sure how much more I can take, pussy growing sore just before he hisses, "*Fuck!*"

He jerks out of me, making me yelp, and ropes of his hot cum shoot out, spilling onto my tits and stomach as my pussy continues throbbing.

In the aftermath, we're both breathless, panting and frozen while we try to catch our breath.

Wes is the first one to recover, regaining his composure enough to grab a tissue to clean me off. Then another and another. I can't believe I managed to swallow all of that.

"Holy fucking hell, Violet." He leans down to kiss me, the brush of his lips against mine surprisingly tender after he just tried pounding me into my mattress.

He slips on his boxers and bumps back into my desk, moving the mouse connected to my laptop and stirring it awake. I race to close it, not caring that I'm still fully naked, but he's faster.

He holds me back with one hand while keeping the laptop propped open with the other. A wolfish smile spreads. "What's this? *Get on your knees for me.* Is this your new story?"

"No, it's . . ." I scramble for an excuse. "A classmate's."

His grin widens. "No, this is definitely your fanfiction of me. I want to read it when it's done."

"There's no way in hell I'm letting you read it." But I can't fight the smile flickering across my face. He still wants to read something I've written.

"Be sure to dedicate it to me too," he says, pretending he didn't hear me. He grabs me by the back of my thighs, wrapping them around him, and returns me to the bed. "Only right to dedicate your story to your muse."

Chapter 26

Before

Violet

"I just made out with Luke!" Chloe squeals in my ear.

We were supposed to meet at our dorm twenty minutes ago and head to Wes's apartment together. Chloe somehow convinced him to drive us to the nearest local bookstore so she can buy the entire ten-book series of what she affectionately refers to as "fae porn," the first book of which she devoured last week. How she even makes time for reading in her hectic schedule puts her at god-tier reader level.

"I guess that's a good excuse for ghosting me," I say into the phone.

"It's a *great* excuse for ghosting you. Besides, it's not ghosting if I'm still following through on our plans. I'm just meeting you at his apartment. Nothing's standing between me and those books—not even Luke and his amazingly soft lips."

I grin. "How was it?"

"So. Sexy. He swept me up in his arms and tipped my head back like he was the hot vampire and I was the one mortal human in the entire world he couldn't resist."

"Wow." I'm smiling so wide, it hurts. I'm so happy for her. She and Luke are the perfect couple.

"I know! I was like, 'Excuse me, sir, how long have you been seventeen?'"

"Did he get the reference?"

She laughs. "Of course not. I can't wait to corrupt him. Anyway, I'm gonna go change and I'll meet you there." She hangs up without another word.

I knock on the door to Wes's apartment. I'm pretty sure there's music coming from the other side, but after two minutes when no one opens the door, I knock again, louder this time.

A shout comes from the other side that I'm pretty sure is "Come in," so I try the handle and step into his apartment.

To the left, a bathroom door is open and music plays while a shower pours.

I freeze, visions of Wes naked and wet and covered in suds flooding my mind until he shouts, "Chloe?"

"Um, no!" I croak and clear my throat. Even after kissing him on the Ferris wheel, he still makes me nervous. "It's me! Violet!"

"I'll be out in a sec!"

I take a seat on the couch to wait. After a few minutes scrolling on my phone, a door on the other side of the room opens.

Trey stops in the doorway when he spots me, and my stomach gives a nervous flip.

I've had a bad feeling about Trey since that first day I met him in the dining hall. Every time I make eye contact with him, he leers at me. I'm not sure if he makes every girl's skin crawl or if I'm his sole, unfortunate target.

He swaggers toward me from his bedroom, a rotten smile twisting his lips as he plops onto the couch beside me. Too close. His knee bumps against mine and I reflexively scoot away.

His grin only stretches. A predator who loves the chase.

"Hey, pretty girl," he coos, draping an arm across the couch behind my shoulders. I long for a magic wand to turn myself invisible. "Come all this way to see me?"

"Wes, actually." I gulp. "We're all going to the bookstore."

A spark of amusement in those green eyes. "The three of us?"

"Me, Wes, and Chloe."

His eyelids flutter shut for a second before springing open again, a new blazing fire of interest burning there. He skims my cheek, and I'm frozen in place. A terrified rabbit bracing herself for the predator's next move.

"You know what I'd do for a threesome with the two of you?" he purrs. My stomach churns. I don't want to know. "Your sweet pussy grinding on my mouth while she rides my cock with her tight little cunt. You two squeezing each other's tits and making out on top of me."

Trey lets out a low groan that turns my stomach. God, he fantasizes about Chloe and me like that when we're both nothing but repulsed by him.

I glance over my shoulder, hoping Wes will finish in the shower soon and come to my rescue. Trey grips my chin, squeezing and jerking me back to face him.

"Pounding you both with my hard cock." His hand drifts into my hair now, twisting locks of it in his palm and tugging so hard my eyes sting. "All three holes."

I try to scoot away from him, but his hand twisted in my hair holds me in place. His lips brush against my neck, and I cringe as his tongue slides out, gliding up from the base of my neck to my jaw.

"Stop." But the word gets stuck in my throat, so quiet I'm not sure he can hear it over the pounding of my heart.

He nips along my jawline until his long, sharp face is directly in front of me again. He smashes his mouth against mine, pulling my hair back and moving his lips over mine like he's feasting on me.

I shove at his chest, but he pretends he doesn't notice me fighting him off.

From the hallway behind us, a low voice calls, "Chloe here yet?"

Trey jerks away from me, my lips tingling like they've just been smacked with a hammer. He pulls his arm from behind me and scoots a solid six inches away, leaning casually back against the arm of the couch.

Wes stops in the middle of the room, wet, inky hair dripping onto his blue shirt. The sight of him makes me want to jump from the couch and run to him. Let him envelop me in his arms and keep me safe.

"Everything all right out here?" Wes asks, a note of strain in his voice.

"Just dandy." Trey pats my knee with a smile before standing, leaving me immobile and dazed, my heart still thumping.

Wes

I SWEAR Trey pulls his arm from around Violet when I stride in the room. The same rage boils in my gut from the night I walked in on my ex cheating on me.

I warned Violet the second I kissed her, she would be mine. I made it clear how this would work. What claiming her meant.

But she wouldn't fuck around with other guys behind my back. She's not like Britt. She's sweet, careful, bashful. Britt's the kind of girl who has the confidence to go after guys. The arrogance to think she can get any guy she wants and not suffer the consequences of fucking around behind their backs. Violet isn't like that.

Trey nearly waltzes past me until he mutters, "She's got soft lips, man. And I don't mean the ones on her face."

Something in me snaps. Trey's bedroom door clicks shut behind him, and I grab Violet's hand, tugging her to my own room, cluttered and reeking of old gym shoes, but I don't care. "Did something happen between you and Trey? Be honest."

Her eyes widen, and I expect her to lie through her teeth. Offer up some excuse like Britt did. *I was drunk, Wes. I was high. I wasn't thinking straight.* Magically becoming totally sober the second someone called her out on her bullshit.

My hands ball into fists and I want to slam them against the wall, but I know that'll send Violet running for the door, and I need to get the truth out of her first.

She nods. "He . . . kissed me."

I shut my eyes, forcing a slow breath through my nose that doesn't do shit for calming me down. "Did you want him to?"

Violet shakes her head quickly. "No. I told him to stop."

Now I definitely want to fucking end him. But a sick part of me is relieved that she didn't want him. Didn't let him kiss her willingly.

She's into me, not Trey. She wouldn't betray me like that. She's not Britt. They're two different girls. I couldn't trust Britt as far as I could throw her.

But I can trust Violet.

Chapter 27

After

Violet

"GREAT WORK, VIOLET." Professor Tate sets my short story on my desk, an A circled at the top. "I would've appreciated more of a warning about the explicit nature of your story." My face warms. "But it was very well-written and moving. You're bearing your soul in your writing again." She taps the page. "Keep it up."

I'm on cloud nine when I leave class. Maxwell catches up to me. "So I heard Professor Tate call your story explicit."

I grimace, even though my professor and classmates knowing I've written graphic sex scenes doesn't bother me as much as I thought it would. "Honestly, I thought I dialed it back."

Maxwell laughs. "Sounds like a must-read. We'll have to swap work sometime. I know you were the best writer in our class last year. I'm sure my stories could benefit from your critique."

"Oh." If that party freshman year had never happened, I'd assume he's just looking to swap work with a fellow writer and nothing more. But I haven't forgotten the way he almost kissed me or the way his face lit up when I complimented him. He hasn't flirted with me since, though, so hopefully we've both moved on. "Yeah. Sure."

"Awesome." He opens the door for me and offers a smile before heading in the opposite direction. "See ya."

Aneesa is waiting for me on a bench so we can walk to the dining hall together for lunch. Her eyes light up. She leaps to her feet and rushes over to me, grabbing onto my arm. "Um, who is that?"

"That's just Maxwell. He's a classmate."

"Is he why you've been smiling so much lately? He's cute. Good for you."

A smile sweeps across my face at the thought of Wes. I can't let her think anything's going on with Maxwell, but I know she'll disapprove if I tell her the truth. "Actually, no. There's someone else."

Her mouth falls open. "What? Who?"

"I don't want to say yet. But we've been having . . . a lot of fun together."

Aneesa's smile falls, and she pulls me off the sidewalk and onto the grass to give us a little more privacy. "Please tell me you're not talking about Wes Novak."

Shit. Of course she'd figure it out. I manage to give her a reassuring smile. "Aneesa, this is a good thing. He told his team-mates to stop harassing me. And the sex is amazing."

Her eyes narrow. "You've been having *sex* with him? Violet, what the hell are you thinking? You have to know this is just another one of his pranks."

I shake my head, even as the doubt starts to creep in. "No, he wouldn't do that."

"Really? He's done plenty of other terrible things to you. Why would he draw the line at this?" She steps closer to me, eyes imploring me to see reason. "Trust me, he's just trying to get you to drop your guard so he can hurt you that much worse. Don't trust him. You need to stay away from him."

As much as I don't want to believe Aneesa, a small ember of doubt questions whether she could be right. All of this could just be another one of Wes's pranks. Another way to torment me, to hurt me. Getting my heart involved so the pain he inflicts will be that much worse.

But no. We talked. He held me while I cried. He heard my apology, and he said we need each other to get through this. We're moving forward. Together.

"I appreciate your concern, Aneesa. I really do." I squeeze her hand. She's trying to be a good friend. "But Wes and I talked through it. He was mourning Chloe. He wanted me to pay for what happened to her. I understand why he did it, but that's over now. He really cares about me. You can't fake that."

She's not buying it, expression dark as she shakes her head. "Violet, you're a writer. You should know that Wes is not the hero of this story. He's the villain."

Wes

COACH MAKES us take a break in the middle of practice to check out Luke's injured leg.

"I'm fine, Coach," Luke insists.

"You're no good to us with a broken ankle, Twenty-Two!" I shout. Luke flips me the bird.

Beside me, Trey peels off his helmet, both of us leaning up against the glass, still on the ice. "You fuck her the other night?"

He doesn't have to say Violet's name. We both know exactly who he's talking about. "Don't worry about it."

I wish we were still living in the dorms so I could put in a request for a different roommate, but we both signed a lease. I'm stuck with him unless I can convince him to leave or figure out a way to break my lease early and find another vacant apartment around campus. The semester's almost over. Maybe I can wait it out before I knock his teeth in.

Trey smirks and claps me on the shoulder. "Atta boy. How tight is she?"

I clench my jaw. "Man, what did I fucking tell you? Leave her the fuck alone. She's mine."

Trey's eyes narrow. "Holy shit. Don't tell me you're actually into the girl who killed your sister."

"Of course not," I snap. Even though that's exactly my situation.

It was an accident. It was an accident.

"Wow." He leans back, shaking his head. "I thought you wanted to kill this bitch and now you're falling in love with her? Dude, she's playing mind games with you. Don't fall for that shit."

I roll my eyes. "She's not playing mind games with me."

"Really? You know she's smart. You chase her around campus, making her life miserable, and you don't think she'd do whatever she could to get you to stop? Cry some crocodile tears, throw a little pussy your way?"

Trey's a fucking idiot. Ninety-nine percent of the time, he has no clue what he's talking about.

But then there's that other one percent when he actually makes some sense.

I went from wanting to kill Violet, wanting her kicked off campus, to wanting her in my bed.

She's smart, I've always known that. Definitely smart enough to manipulate me, mess with my head enough to convince me to stop tormenting her.

Maybe she's been playing me for a fool this whole time. Telling me exactly what I want to hear, convincing me she actually feels bad about what she did to Chloe, for what she did to me.

No. I shake the thoughts from my head.

I know her. I know Violet Harris better than she thinks I do. Way fucking better than Trey does, that's for damn sure. He's wrong. About all of it.

Violet's remorse is genuine. She cried for Chloe. She loves and misses my sister as much as I do.

I'm not falling for any sort of mind games. What's happening between us is real.

Violet was meant for me from day one. We've been through hell, and now we're figuring out our way back together. I'm not letting anything or anyone stop us.

Chapter 28

After

Violet

My phone buzzes with an email notification from the Student Affairs Office.

Hello Miss Harris,
> *Please stop by my office today at your earliest convenience.*
Best,
Dean Forrester

Shit. This can't be good.

I head to Student Affairs in the University Center, running through all the possible reasons I could be in trouble.

My knee-jerk reaction is that Wes is behind this.

But no, Aneesa's just getting in my head. Things are finally good between me and Wes. He wouldn't lie to get me in trouble with the administration. Maybe he would've done something like that to get me kicked off campus earlier this semester, but not anymore.

The second I step into Student Affairs, Dean Forrester pokes his head out of his office. He has wire-framed glasses and jet-black hair, so dark it makes me think he dyes it to cover up the grays. He flashes me a smile that tries to be welcoming, but there's something unpleasant underneath.

My stomach drops.

"Miss Harris, thank you for coming in. Please." He gestures me into his office, and even though all I want to do is run in the opposite direction, I head inside and take a seat.

A few weeks ago, I would've been relieved to get kicked off campus. Now the last thing I want to do is leave. I like living with Aneesa, I like attending my classes, I like writing my stories, and most of all, I like being with Wes.

"Mint?" Dean Forrester holds out a bowl of green mints.

I shove one into my mouth to calm my nerves. "Thank you."

He clasps his hands together on the desk. "Thank you for coming in. I'd like to discuss a pretty serious allegation another student has made."

Shit. This is worse than I thought. The mint sours in my mouth, and I search for a trashcan to spit it out. "What allegation?"

"It's been reported that Wes Novak has been harassing you on campus."

A hush falls over us, so quiet I swear I can hear my heart stop. I'm not the one in trouble.

Wes is.

"What?"

"I'd like you to be honest with me." Dean Forrester leans closer. "Are these allegations true?"

Aneesa. She must've been the one to report Wes. She said if things got worse, she would say something. Once she found out Wes and I are having sex, she must've decided that was the final straw.

But she's wrong about him. This isn't one of his pranks—

this is a new chapter for me and Wes. We're finally getting to a better place, holding hands as we make our way through the darkness together, side by side.

And Aneesa's trying to stop that.

My nails bite into my palms. I get that she's trying to be a good friend, that she's just trying to look out for me, but a good friend also wouldn't go behind my back and do something like this when I explicitly asked her not to. She didn't listen to me, and if anything happens to Wes, he'll never forgive me.

I already lost him once. I'm not losing him again.

"You're not in any trouble, Violet," he assures me. "I just want to make sure you feel safe on our campus. If true, these allegations could be grounds for his expulsion."

Aneesa thought she would be giving me an opportunity to finally make Wes and the rest of the Devils face the consequences for harassing me for weeks. For hurting me, for humiliating me, for terrifying me.

"No. It's not true." I swallow hard. *Fight back.* "But there is someone else who's been harassing me."

Dean Forrester's brows furrow as he grabs a pen. "Can you give me the name?"

"Trey Lamont."

He nods, scribbling down Trey's name, and relief relaxes my limbs. If Trey gets kicked off campus, I'll finally be able to breathe easier. Wes can handle him, but he can't be around me every second. And Trey knows Wes's schedule—he knows when I'll be vulnerable.

"Okay. Thank you for clearing that up. We'll look into Mr. Lamont. I appreciate you coming in." He stands and opens the door for me. "Have a great day, Miss Harris."

As soon as I'm out of the building and stepping into the chilly air under the morning sun, I call Aneesa.

"Hey!" Her bright, airy voice. "I have the funniest story—"

"Did you report Wes to Dean Forrester?"

"No?" Her voice drops an octave, and she almost convinces me with the confusion in her tone. "I haven't reported him to anybody. You told me not to."

I want to believe she wouldn't blatantly lie to me, but no one else cares about me enough to report him. She's my only friend on this campus. And if Edith suspected Wes was mistreating me, she would handle him herself.

"So why did Dean Forrester call me into his office to tell me someone made allegations that Wes has been harassing me?" I bite out the words.

Even if they investigate Trey, they still might not do anything if they can't find proof. Worse, if they do expel him, he'll have a new vendetta against me.

Aneesa has no clue about the ramifications of what she's done.

"I have no idea, Violet." Her words are clipped now. "Maybe someone saw something. It's not like he tries to hide it."

That's true, but no one would care enough to say anything. Especially now that his pranks have stopped. "Don't lie, okay? It's fine if you did, but just be honest about it."

It's not fine, exactly, but at least if she would be honest with me, we could talk it through. We're not going to get anywhere if she keeps lying.

"I'm telling you, Violet, I didn't say anything." She's completely lost patience now. "Maybe it was that guy from your writing class. What was his name? Matthew?"

Maxwell. He's still been friendly, so it's possible he'd want to report Wes, but I don't think he's ever witnessed anything. Plus, he's a commuter, and they're notoriously oblivious to the drama that goes down on campus. "I doubt that. Wouldn't he at least talk to me about it before going to the dean?"

"I don't know. Ask him. I have to go." She hangs up without another word.

Wes

I'M LEAVING CLASS, making my way through the maze of sidewalks around campus, when I get a call from Dean Forrester.

"Hello?"

"Mr. Novak. Is this a bad time?"

Well, this doesn't sound fucking good. "Nope, just leaving class now."

"Excellent. I wanted to inform you that someone has come forward with allegations that you've been harassing another student on campus."

Fucking Violet.

She went to the dean about me? We've already backed off. If she was going to go to the administration about what we've done to her, she should've done it weeks ago. My fists clench.

I thought we were finally getting somewhere. Finally learning to trust each other. Forgive each other.

"I asked Miss Harris to come in this morning, and she denied these allegations," Dean Forrester says.

I stop dead in my tracks, a girl running into my arm and muttering under her breath as she passes me. So Violet wasn't the one who said anything. Dean Forrester gave her the chance to rat me out, and she covered for me.

I grin. That's my girl. "Who made the allegations then?"

"I'm afraid that information is confidential."

Had to have been that nosy roommate of hers.

"I hope you're aware, Mr. Novak, that if Violet had confirmed these allegations were true and we had evidence to substantiate those claims, you may not have had a future at Diamond University."

Violet saved my ass. If I'd been kicked off campus, the hockey team and my chances at the NHL would've been fucked.

I've spent weeks tormenting her. I enlisted my team to help. We made her life a living hell here. Turned everyone against her. She had every reason to throw me under the bus.

But she didn't. She knew how much staying at Diamond means to me.

I wish she was here right now so I could pick her up and kiss her.

"Understood," I tell Dean Forrester.

"I suggest you stay on your very best behavior from now on, Mr. Novak. It would not reflect well on Diamond University if its hockey captain were expelled for harassment. Nor would many other universities be keen on accepting you as a student or employers on hiring you, nor the NHL on recruiting you."

The last threat is what really gets me. Violet saved my chances at the NHL. What I've been working toward my whole life.

"What you do on a college campus may seem isolated from the rest of the world, but I assure you that what you do here matters and could impact your future. Is that understood?"

"Yes."

I understand exactly what he's saying.

I need to thank Violet. Properly.

I sink into the pool, waiting for Violet to notice I'm here with her.

When she reaches the shallow end, she spots me and grins, standing up to walk over to me, her wet tits bouncing beneath her flimsy bikini top.

My mouth waters at the sight of her. I finally know what she looks like beneath those thin layers of fabric and now I can't stop fantasizing about every inch.

"Got a call from Dean Forrester today."

Her pretty hazel eyes flash. "Wes, it wasn't me. I think it was Aneesa. I told her not to, but—"

"You covered for me." The water rushes between us as I grab her hips and pull her toward me. "Why?"

Her hands land on my shoulders, a zip of anticipation racing down my spine. "Because I deserved the punishment you doled out. And I didn't want you to get expelled."

"Then it sounds like I owe you one."

She grins until she bites her lip. "But . . . I did give him Trey's name. I know he'll probably retaliate when he finds out, but you said to fight back."

My turn to grin. I run my hand through her hair, tipping my forehead against hers. "That's my girl. I'm proud of you." She swells at the praise and hooks her legs around my waist. "We'll handle whatever shit Trey thinks he can throw our way. No one touches you, Violet. Not with me around."

She throws her arms around me and murmurs her gratitude in my ear. When she pulls back, she trails her fingers across my jaw. "I think she'd be happy for us."

"She would," I agree, carrying Violet to the corner of the shallow end. "I know I am."

Chills dance down Violet's arms when I yank her top down. Her mouth falls open, and she drops beneath the water's surface. "Wes, what are you doing? Someone could catch us—"

"Relax." I point to the sign behind her. "No lifeguard on duty." I slip my hand down her bikini bottom. "You're the one who wanted to go swimming. I would've happily fucked you wherever you wanted."

Her eyes flutter closed, a small shudder escaping before she pushes her hand down my swim trunks. Her fingers glide over the ridges of my hard cock before she wraps her hand around my shaft and strokes.

I drop my head back and groan. "Yes, baby. That's it."

The chlorine overpowers her sweet flowery scent, the water sloshing around us with each of our movements. I press my thumb against her clit. Finally doing to her what I longed to that first time I saw her in a bikini at my house.

Her breath hitches. God, I love how easy it is to turn her on. Violet plays like she's this meek, quiet book nerd. But she's got another side. A girl who wants me to choke her with my belt and make her come on my cock where anyone could walk in on us.

I'm happy to fulfill her fantasies. "Tell me what you want me to do to you."

"I want you to make me come," she breathes.

"Tell me how, baby."

Color rises to her cheeks, reminding me of that party in my apartment when I commanded the filthy words from her mouth. This time, she says them all on her own. "I want you to rub my clit while I ride your cock."

I grin, my cock twitching in her hand.

She rises and I catch her nipple in my mouth, sucking on it hard to get her ready for me. She gasps and her hand guides my cock to her entrance.

Slowly, she eases down. "Go on, baby. Try to take every inch." She might never be able to, but I'd love to see her try.

Violet bites her lip while continuing to fit my hard cock

inside her. The walls of her pussy clench around my shaft, driving me wild. All I want to do is slam my hips up into her and make her take every inch of me, but I let her go slowly, luxuriating in the feel of me filling her up.

I rub at her clit to make it easier for her, and she hisses through her teeth. "Wes," she moans.

Fuck, I love hearing my name on her lips. I want to make her moan my name every single day. "You love my cock inside you, huh, baby?"

"Yes. I love it."

I grin like a fucking idiot. "That's my girl."

She uses my shoulders to brace herself as she rocks up and down my cock. All the way up to the tip and halfway down to the base. I smirk. So cute how she can't take the whole thing. Not yet. She will.

Her eyes roll as I circle her clit faster and her hips pick up speed. I pull her hair with one hand and wrap the other around her neck, squeezing the sides to restrict the flow of blood as her pulse jumps beneath my thumb. Her moans echo around us, making my cock throb inside her.

"You on birth control?" I pant, knowing I won't last much longer. Not with Violet looking and sounding like that.

"Yes." Another involuntary moan. "Come inside me."

"Fuck." I groan and drive my hips up into her.

I release her throat, replacing my hand with my mouth, the taste of chlorine and her delicious skin on my tongue. I stroke up her neck to her ear, biting and sucking her lobe until she's whimpering.

She's putty in my hands.

Her grip on my shoulders tightens, and her pussy starts to clench around my cock, her walls nearly suffocating.

She cries out. "Wes!"

Her pussy walls contract around my cock as she comes, and

I hold her in place while I slam up into her again and again, until my cock spurts deep inside her, throbbing with her pussy.

My vision goes dark for a second as the pleasure rockets through me, and I tip my head back to groan out a long, echoing, "*Fuuuck.*"

Violet collapses against me, the water the only reason we're not both covered in sweat.

"That was incredible," she says in my ear, and I fucking love how breathless I've made her. "You're incredible."

I freeze. No girl's ever said that to me before.

I've spent the last few months tormenting her, punishing her for ending my sister's life in an accident. And she still thinks I'm incredible.

My heart pounds as I tug her closer to me, and not just because I exploded inside her five seconds ago. I pull her wet hair behind her shoulders so I can whisper the words right in her ear. The words that terrify me just to think, let alone say. But after everything I've put her through, she deserves to hear them. "I'm falling in love with you, Violet."

Chapter 29

After

Violet

IN THE LIBRARY, I check my phone. No notifications. Despite sharing a dorm, Aneesa and I haven't spoken since I accused her of going to Dean Forrester and she denied it.

I asked Maxwell, and he said he has no idea who Wes Novak is. Apparently being an English major who commutes and doesn't attend any sporting events means not knowing about the star hockey captain who basically owns the campus. He also showed me a picture of his girlfriend, who he apparently met after I left that party with Chloe last year.

So that leaves only one person who could've possibly told Dean Forrester about me and Wes, and she's lying to my face about it.

I've been taking as many shifts at the library as I can get to avoid her and staying up late writing until my eyes are blurry from staring at my laptop screen. I haven't written in a frenzy like this in years, even before Chloe died.

Maybe Wes was right. Maybe he is my muse.

After my shift at the library, I head outside into the brisk night air. I love the campus at this time of night. Quiet and peaceful, minus the thumping music from a few dorm rooms. No one else out here but me and sometimes the astronomy club.

I've been on a high since that afternoon in the pool with Wes. When he fucked me so good I saw stars, and after, murmured in my ear that he's falling in love with me.

I'm falling in love with him too. I've been falling.

Hard.

I round the corner of the library when a heavy hand clamps over my arm and smacks me against the wall.

A blade bites into my throat.

In front of me, even the mask can't conceal Trey's terrifying smile.

I open my mouth, but he snarls, "Scream, and I slice your throat."

The knife bobs when I clamp my lips shut and try to swallow the scream back down. "What are you doing?"

"Strip."

"What?"

He presses the blade right under my chin, that too-familiar sharp edge pricking my skin. His familiar mask inches from my face. "Take your clothes off, or I'll kill you."

A tear slips down my cheek as I unbutton my jeans and push them down the best I can with the knife still pressed against my throat, cool air wrapping around my bare legs.

"I'll tell Wes about this." My words come out surprisingly strong, steady.

Trey smirks. "If you tell him—if you tell anyone—I'll kill him."

I stiffen. I want to call Trey out on his bluff, but this is Trey Lamont. He doesn't bluff, and I wouldn't put anything past him.

"You think it wouldn't be easy for me to slice this across his throat while he's sleeping? I live with the guy. It would be *nothing.*"

I can't believe he's this twisted. This psychotic.

He grabs my hands, examining them like artwork. "If you tell anybody, his death will be on your hands. You sure you want more blood on these?"

He already knows the answer. Knows how the guilt over what I did to Chloe has paralyzed me, made me incapable of fighting back. I can't risk anything happening to Wes because of me.

Trey pulls the knife a mere centimeter away from my throat. "Now the shirt."

More tears as I reluctantly pull my shirt over my head. The chilly night air makes my skin pucker, my nipples peak beneath my bra. I cross my arms over my chest, trying to keep warm and shield myself the best I can as I stand in front of Trey in nothing but my underwear.

His grin sickens me. "Good." He pulls out his phone and points it at me.

My stomach gives a violent twist. "What are you—" His camera flashes as he takes a photo, and my lip trembles. "Why are you doing this?"

His smile only grows as his cock gets harder in his pants, turned on by my fear and tears. "Turn to the side and stick your ass out."

"Trey," I plead, the drumbeat of my heart making my head pound.

He brandishes the knife again, closing the distance between us until I'm forced to back against the ice-cold brick wall. I swallow at the memory of what he did to me with that knife last time. How he licked my blood off the blade after carving me up with it. "I'm not fucking playing with you, Violet. Do what I say."

My legs and hands tremble. I turn to the side and jut my ass out, biting my lip to stop it from wobbling. He's not cutting me up like he did in the bathroom, but this is a new level of sick. Photos he's going to jerk off to later.

He guides me through more positions, the camera flashing with the snap of every photo.

"Smile for the camera," he purrs.

That may be his worst command yet. Forcing me to look like I'm enjoying this.

I manage a smile, even as a sob builds in my chest.

Trey pushes me to my knees, the harsh pavement digging into my skin. My heart stops, terrified he's going to reach for his fly next.

"Wes told you guys to leave me alone," I remind him.

He chuckles, snapping a photo of me on my knees in front of him. "So?"

"So you're not doing this for him. You're retaliating because I ratted you out."

Trey grips me by the throat, dragging me to my feet. I gasp at the pain as he throws me back against the wall, the hard bricks scraping the delicate skin across my back and legs.

His breath curls around my neck, my ear. "And that was *very* stupid of you. Guess you don't know who my father is. Hard to kick out the hockey player whose father funds the team. Even harder for them to pin anything on me when they couldn't find any evidence. I'm not going anywhere."

I twist and squirm to get away from him, away from the hand crushing my throat, but then I feel that familiar kiss of the blade against my thigh.

I freeze.

"That's a good little girl." His murmur makes me want to puke. "I think it's time I fulfill that promise I made to you last time."

Fuck. *No, no, no—*

Trey tips the handle of the knife, rubbing it over my panties against my clit. I hiss through my teeth and slam my eyes shut, trying to block out the feeling and his leering gaze.

"*Fuck,*" he groans. "That's so hot. If you start crying, I'll have to fuck you with it."

The handle travels lower, pushing aside my panties.

My knees turn to jelly. "Don't," I whisper. "Please—"

Headlights sweep over us, a car passing by, but it's enough to make Trey withdraw. The handle of the knife disappears from between my legs and cool air washes over me, replacing the hot touch of Trey's hand on me and his body looming over mine.

I gasp like a fish out of water, clutching my throat, still throbbing with the pain of being choked.

He's halfway across the parking lot by the time I'm scrambling to slide my jeans back on my shaky legs, but his sinister promise still reaches me. "Until next time, pretty girl."

DURING MY NEXT night at the library, I text Wes.

> Can you walk me home after my shift?

> Be right there.

As soon as my shift is over, I stuff my laptop and books in my bag, turn off all the lights, and hurry out of the building.

Wes is waiting directly in front of the doors in jeans, combat boots, and his team jacket. When he turns and sees me, he smiles.

A smile that stops my heart.

He holds out his hand and threads his fingers through mine. "You look beautiful, little flower."

I manage a weak smile in return. Since Trey took those photos of me in my underwear and nearly fucked me with the handle of his knife, I've been longing to tell Wes about what happened. But if Trey hurts him because of me, because I told Wes when Trey warned me not to, I'll never be able to forgive myself.

I can't lose Wes too. Not again. I won't.

He leads the way through the empty parking lot. When we reach his car, he pins me against it with his hips, threading his hands in my hair and pulling my body flush against his. He presses his lips to mine, slipping his tongue in my mouth and making my breath catch.

"What you said last time," I breathe, the impending admission making my heart palpitate. "In the pool. I'm falling in love with you too."

He shakes his head. "Not sure how you can say that when I was such a dick to you."

"Because if the roles were reversed, I would've done the same thing."

"No. You wouldn't have." He brushes a kiss as delicate as a butterfly's wing against my lips before pulling open the back door of his car.

"You don't want me sitting up front with you?"

"I would if I was sitting up front. Get in, baby."

At the delicious command, my thighs clench, and I do as I'm told.

Wes slams the door behind him. He's on me in seconds, pressing his lips to mine. "I hope you know you're fulfilling every fantasy I've ever had about you."

My heart skips a beat. "How long have you been fantasizing about me?" I tease.

"Every day since I met you."

I grin like an idiot.

He pushes me down roughly so I'm flat on the backseat, pinning me down with all six-foot-four of him. His tongue sweeps into my mouth, claiming me.

I'm not just falling in love with Wes. I've already fallen.

"I'm going to fuck your mouth, little flower," he tells me, caressing my cheek with a gentle hand. "Then I'm going to make you come on my cock."

"Please," I breathe.

"Beg harder for me, baby." The words leave his mouth on his own plea.

"Please, Wes. Please fuck my mouth."

He grins wickedly. "You're such a good fucking girl."

He removes his belt and wraps it around my neck, testing it with a tug. I smile. Then he unzips his jeans, unleashing his cock.

Saliva floods my mouth, and I part my lips for him.

He braces himself over me, eyes never leaving my face as he slides his cock past my lips and pulls the belt at the same time.

Wes groans at the first stroke of his sensitive skin across my tongue. I'm pinned beneath him, unable to escape even if I wanted to as he fucks my mouth.

He thrusts in and out slowly, gradually making me swallow him deeper and deeper with every stroke, pulling out all the way to the tip before sliding back in. His loud groans above me, his taste on my tongue, his belt restricting my breathing, all make warmth pool between my legs.

"You just keep getting better and better." He smirks. "I'm proud of you, baby."

The praise makes my heart sing and liquid heat spread all the way to my toes. I wrap my hands around his thighs and pull him toward me. That's all the encouragement he needs.

He shoves his cock deeper, hitting the back of my throat. Tears spring to my eyes as he slams into me one, two, three more times before abruptly pulling out of my mouth. I gulp down air.

Wes leans down and kisses me. "Good fucking girl."

"Now are you going to let me come on your cock?"

"No," he growls. "I'm going to make you."

My pussy clenches.

Wes slides his hands up my skirt, yanking down my panties and tossing them. He crushes my body under his, pushing my hair off my neck and kissing from my jaw to my collarbone. I shudder.

When he sucks my earlobe into his mouth, goosebumps race down my arms. I gasp.

"This is better than my fantasies," Wes murmurs.

"Yeah?" I breathe.

"Yeah. Every fucking little sound that leaves your mouth, every moan and gasp and whimper, makes me want to shove my cock in that tight little pussy and fuck you until you're screaming."

I grin. "That's what I'm hoping for."

"Don't worry, baby. I'll fulfill all your hopes and dreams," he promises.

He yanks my shirt up, covering my face, before tugging the cups of my bra down with one hand and latching onto my nipple.

"Agh!" I cry out. "Maybe we should go back to your apartment. What if someone hears us?"

"The windows are tinted, baby. No one will see you." Then he flashes a wicked grin. "But they're going to hear you."

"No, Wes, no one can—"

He sucks my nipple into his mouth again, and I stop protesting, unable to do anything other than moan his name.

When he's satisfied, he moves to the other, sucking me into his mouth as deep as he can, my whole breast moving with the suction.

His belt squeezes my throat. My eyes roll, and my pussy grinds against him involuntarily. Soaked and desperate for him.

"So impatient." A low chuckle.

"Yes," I confirm.

"You're going to take my tongue first, baby." Warmth stirs low in my belly at the promise. "I want to taste that sweet pussy and feel how soaked you are for me."

"I am," I gasp. "I'm soaked."

"Wasn't a question." He's well aware of exactly the effect he has on me.

Wes kneels on the floor and throws my legs over his shoulders before yanking my pussy to his mouth.

I gasp at the abrupt movement before his tongue glides up my slit. The pleasure makes me writhe and electricity thrums through my veins. "*Fuck.* How are you so good at this?"

"Because you were made for me," he says simply.

My chest constricts and happy tears spring to my eyes until his tongue glides up me again. "That feels so fucking good. Don't stop."

"I'm the one who gives orders," he growls.

But he doesn't stop. His tongue licks me harder, making me squirm while he alternates between restricting my airway with his belt and letting me breathe. His hands press down on my thighs, pinning me so I can't escape him.

Wes pushes his head against me harder, groaning when he slips his tongue between my folds. A hand drifts up to my bare breast, pinching my nipple before squeezing. My tit fits perfectly in his hand.

Movement in my peripheral vision catches my eye. In the darkness, a shadow moves through the parking lot.

"Someone's coming," I gasp.

"She's about to." He squeezes my breast again with the promise.

"No, someone's in the parking lot. We're going to get caught."

He straightens, laying me flat again. "Then I better make you come on my cock."

"We need to leave—"

"Sorry, baby." He nudges his cock at my entrance before slowly sliding inside me, stretching me and making me cry out. "I don't break my promises."

His thumb lands on my clit just as he slams his dick inside me to the hilt. I scream, clapping a hand over my mouth.

The car rocks with every thrust of his cock inside me. We're definitely going to get caught now. "The car is rocking," I warn.

"I don't give a fuck," Wes growls.

He spreads my knees wider, driving into me deeper while his thumb keeps working my clit and his belt nearly stops the air making its way down my throat.

My hand barely muffles my screams, my tits bouncing wildly with every one of his thrusts.

Wes groans. "Take it, baby. Take it like a good girl."

I can't speak with his belt around my neck, can't even nod. My head is growing lighter, the pleasure ricocheting through me like never before.

Wes pins me down with his whole body, slamming into me and driving pleasure through every cell. "Come for me, Violet. Clench that tight little pussy on my cock. I want that pussy squeezing every drop of cum out of my cock and your beautiful screams filling my ears."

My heart pounds wildly, my head growing dangerously light as his belt coils around my neck harder.

A loud groan. "Oh *fuck*, Violet."

At the sound of my name on his lips, my pussy clenches and I scream, pulling at his hair and not bothering to cover my mouth. The orgasm barrels through me as Wes pounds into me, the sound of skin on skin and the squish of his cock inside my soaking wet pussy filling the car along with my screams and his groans.

"*Fuck*," he hisses before collapsing on top of me, his cock throbbing inside me as he finds his own release.

Our chests heave against each other as we both struggle to catch our breath. My limbs and toes tingle, the waves of pleasure crashing over me again and again, pulling me under.

Wes. Fucking. Novak.

Thank god no one came knocking. "I guess that person in the parking lot didn't notice us," I pant.

Wes peers through the window over my head. "He's giving me a thumbs-up."

I gasp. He laughs, and I slap his arm. "Not funny," I say, even as I'm smiling.

"I'm always funny." He pushes off me, finally loosening the belt from around my neck and letting me sit up and tug my clothes back into place. "When I'm not being sexy."

"You're always sexy."

He kisses my neck and murmurs, "So are you. Sexiest fucking thing I've ever seen. Every part of you"—He grabs between my legs—"belongs to me now. Got it?"

"Yes," I whisper.

I belong to Wes Novak.

I am his. And he's mine.

Chapter 30

After

Wes

I F I T H O U G H T I couldn't get Violet Harris out of my head before, now she's fucking engraved on my brain. Miraculously, my grades aren't slipping and the team's doing better than ever, even if I can't stop thinking about her. The nights I can't have her, I jerk off three times just so I can fall asleep. And the nights I can? I cum in her so hard, I want to erect a statue of her and make every goddamn person on this campus kneel before my goddess.

I'm running late to my Entrepreneurial Finance class because I need to see her. My cock is already throbbing in my pants at the thought of getting her into some supply closet or in my car and making her swallow my cum in the middle of the day.

She doesn't just make me hard or get me off. She understands this side of me that no one else does. The part of me that wants to sob and burn the world down simultaneously every time I think of my sister.

I'm Chloe's brother—I've known her for her entire life. But in a single year, Violet managed to get just as close to her as I was. I thought I was the only person who got Chloe, the only person who could understand her passion for figure skating and her drive to work at it every single day. Until Violet came along.

She understood Chloe. Now she gets me too. We understand each other in a way no one else can.

Her short story was due today for her writing class, and I want to be the first one she shows her A to. Plus, if she forgot to dedicate it to me, I'm making her waltz her little ass to a printer to make a new copy for me.

A girl with short brown hair is beaming as she leaves the Fine Arts building. My heart flutters.

My girl.

I leap to my feet, ready to sweep her up and kiss her, until I spot the reason she's smiling.

Some redhead guy with a douchey haircut and a sweater vest.

She smiles and nods, unable to take her eyes off him as he talks. Her book is clutched to her chest, pushing her tits up like she wants him to take a look.

My fists clench.

She's got to be fucking kidding me. Last week, she was saying she's falling in love with me. Now she's about to go hop on some other guy's dick?

Maybe I didn't make it clear enough to her that I don't fucking share.

"Violet!"

She waves when she spots me, but says something else to the prick before hurrying toward me with a big grin on her face. Like I didn't just witness her with some other dude.

He keeps on strolling to the parking lot like he's not bothered the girl he wants to fuck just ran to me. Either he's playing it cool or he has no fucking clue what he's missing.

"Professor Tate gave me an A!" she squeals, giving an

adorable hop that would probably make my heart melt if I wasn't questioning who inspired her to write that story in the first place.

Him or me.

"Congrats."

"Thanks! You want to go celebrate? I'm dying for some ice cream."

"Who'd you dedicate it to?"

Her grin widens and she pulls out a printed copy of the story, flipping to the second page. "Professor Tate said students don't normally dedicate short stories to anyone, but I told her this one was an exception."

To Wes, my muse.

I nod after the ginger. "Is he your muse too?"

Her smile falters and she follows my gaze to his retreating back. "Who? Maxwell?"

I grit my teeth. Even his name is pretentious. "You two seemed to really be enjoying each other's company until I showed up."

Violet's brows furrow, puzzled, until realization dawns. "Oh my god—Wes, no. He's just a friend. Honestly, he's not really even a friend. We talk sometimes in class. That's it."

I take a step toward her. "Five seconds ago, you were hopping on my dick, and now you're flashing that asshole your fuck-me eyes."

She arches a brow. "I have fuck-me eyes? That's good to know. I'll have to use them on you more often."

Despite the anger still churning in my veins, my dick twitches. She's not cowering in fear like she would've a few weeks ago. "This isn't a fucking joke. I don't share. Remember?"

She closes the distance between us, placing a hand on my arm and purrs, "I don't want you to. I'm all yours. I'm not like your ex. You can trust me. I know I've already caused you enough pain, believe me. I would never do anything to hurt you again."

Fuck. I need to be inside her *now*. Slam my cock balls-deep in her sweet pussy until we both forget that anyone else exists.

I take her hand and guide her to the athletic center. She doesn't bother asking where I'm leading her—she already knows.

When I pull the door to the locker room open, I lock it behind us and pin her to the lockers with a metallic crash.

She gasps, and I grab her thigh, lifting her leg. But she shoves me off, sinking to her knees before me. My balls clench as she slowly pulls my fly down.

My cock springs free, and she gulps.

"Suck me, baby."

She wraps her hand around my cock, stroking it the way she knows I love. I brace a hand against the locker over her head and groan as she takes me into her mouth.

Violet swirls her tongue around my sensitive tip, making me growl. "Deeper," I command.

She swallows down my hard cock, attempting to take every inch. I hiss when she pulls back up slowly, dragging her tongue along the underside of my shaft and the thick vein pulsing there.

"That's enough. Stand up."

When she does, I spin her around. She flattens her palms against the lockers and I turn her face, nudging her mouth open. I slip two fingers inside. "Suck."

She does as I say, and when my fingers are lubricated, I dip them between her legs. Swirling them over her swollen clit before penetrating her sweet pussy.

Violet gasps. I keep thrusting my fingers inside her, slow

and hard, the heel of my hand grinding into her clit. She shudders with pleasure.

"That feels so good," she moans into the lockers.

"Beg." My breath caresses her ear. "If you dare."

Her thighs are trembling now. "Please, Wes."

"Beg harder."

She shivers at the command. "Please fuck me, Wes. Make me come. *Please.*"

"Good girl," I whisper, before sucking on her earlobe and eliciting a moan from her mouth at the surprising pleasure.

My cock finds her entrance before I slide slow and deep inside her pussy. She stretches so good around me, walls tight and soaked, and I groan when she cries out.

"Fuck!" I shout. "You're so fucking tight. Squeeze your pussy on me, baby. Drag the cum out of my cock."

She's already trembling, the hard length of my cock fully filling her, but she still clenches around me. I groan, sharp and strained. So good it hurts.

I let her rock her ass back into me and hiss through my teeth. Her pussy stretches around me and takes more and more of my cock as her pussy grows wetter for me.

My fingers dig into her hip. "Don't. Fucking. Stop."

"I won't," she gasps. "Not until you cum inside me."

"*Jesus*, Violet. You're gonna make me cum so hard."

"Good. I want to make you cum harder than you ever have in your life."

I growl and grip her hips with both hands, thrusting inside her so hard, she screams.

I wrap my arm around her and rub at her clit frantically, an attempt to make her come for me so I can fit inside her easier.

My heart pounds hard, chest constricting and making my breath lodge in my throat. My eyes roll as she keeps backing up into me and I press down on her clit harder, ramming into her and catching her earlobe between my teeth.

Her pussy clamps around my cock, and she falls over the edge, screaming all the way down as I slam into her from behind. "That's it, baby!"

The slap of skin on skin mixes with her cries echoing through the locker room. Pleasure rushes through me, balls tightening as the first spurt of cum explodes into her. I let out a sharp, agonized groan before pinning her squirming body to the lockers, preventing her from moving as my cock throbs inside her.

I pant in her ear, coming down from my orgasm as her swollen clit still pulses beneath my finger.

My cock slides out of her, taking some of my cum with me before I smack her ass. It gives a satisfying jiggle, and she jumps, the slap echoing in the empty locker room.

I chuckle and take her hand, guiding her to the showers. She has no clue what she's in for. We're just getting started. "Come on, little flower. I need another."

AFTER PRACTICE, my mind is buzzing with thoughts of Violet. What I'll do to her tonight once I get my hands on her. I want to take her out on a real date. Get back to where we were before everything went to hell.

Chloe's chastising voice rings through my head. *At least wine and dine her before you sixty-nine her.*

I smile just as Luke claps me on the shoulder, still shirtless after his shower. "Hey, man. Can I talk to you for a sec?"

Luke used to be the golden retriever on the team. Always in

a good mood, cracking jokes, the comic relief when the locker room was tense after a loss.

He hasn't been the same since Chloe. A serious, thin line permanently etched across his mouth.

"Sure. What's up?"

"You're not with Violet Harris, are you?"

My spine stiffens. "What's it matter?"

If he has a problem with me and Violet, he can say that to my face. Maybe he can't find a way to forgive her, and I can't force him to, but that doesn't have to affect my relationship with her.

"I don't want to get in the middle of shit. I know you've been into her a long time. Just . . . you know she's screwing, like, half the guys on campus, right?"

An image of that smarmy tool from her writing class flashes in my mind, but I roll my eyes and force my shoulders to relax. She promised me there's nothing going on between them. "There's eight thousand students on this campus. You're telling me she's screwing two-thousand guys at once? No. If she's fucking me, my cock is the only one she's riding."

Luke steps closer, lowering his voice. "Seriously, man. Trey sent me some photos."

I slam my locker shut. "What photos?"

He opens up the app on his phone and shows me the screen. The background dark but the flash bright enough to clearly display the star in front of the camera.

Violet.

Down to her panties and bra, sticking her ass out for Trey.

On her knees in front of him.

Smiling.

My stomach churns so hard, I have to look away.

The buzzing in my head nearly drowns out my thudding

pulse. White-hot rage like I haven't felt since she first stepped foot on campus rockets through me.

Trey. Fucking *Trey*. She's been pretending like she's scared of him, like she actually told the dean about him, but this whole time, she's been fucking him behind my back. Blowing him in her underwear after her shift at the library on the nights she wasn't riding my cock.

That day in my apartment last semester, she lied to my face. She said she told him to stop, that she didn't want to kiss him.

How could I have been so fucking stupid? Trey warned me. He told me she was fucking with my head, playing mind games so I'd leave her alone. He was right.

I'll fucking end Trey when I see him, but he never promised to leave Violet alone. He's been wanting her for a long time now.

When I said no, he went behind my back and took what he wanted anyway.

He took her.

She chose *him*.

She spent all that time convincing me to trust her again only to do this.

Worse than walking in on my high school sweetheart riding some other guy's dick, because she didn't kill my sister first. I wasn't obsessed with her the way I was with Violet. Didn't vow to burn the world down if it meant keeping her safe. Didn't give her a second chance after she blew her shot.

I glance around the locker room. "Where the fuck is Trey?"

I'm going to beat his skull in.

Luke tucks his phone in his back pocket. "With Violet."

Chapter 31

After

Violet

I'M WRITING in the library with my back to the door when it squeaks open behind me. I spin around, smile already wide across my face knowing it's Wes.

But the footsteps aren't familiar. Not his combat boots and heavy gait.

No, the Devil who approaches has a lighter step. More stealth. More sinister.

Trey grins and sits beside me, hands clasped together on the table. My stomach drops like lead, the chill of panic enveloping me.

I start to stand, but he's too quick—his heavy hand comes down on my shoulder and forces me back into my seat, pain lancing down my arm and into my neck as my ass smacks back down. "Where you going, beautiful? I just got here."

A tight knot coils in my gut, but I keep my chin high. I won't let Trey get off on my fear anymore. "You need to leave me alone. Wes will kill you if he finds you here alone with me."

Trey's twisted smile makes bile rise to my throat. "I'd like to see him try."

When his palm lands on my leg, I throw it off. "Don't touch me," I hiss.

Trey tsks. "Remember, pretty girl? You're going to let me touch you. Anywhere I want. Or my knife will."

"Don't," I plead, the marks he left on my stomach still scabbed and healing.

But his hand is already back on my knee, traveling up my thigh.

His touch feels like slimy bugs crawling up my skin. All I want is to push him off, run out of the room, but I know he'll be too fast. He'll catch me then stab me or cut me.

Trey's hand drifts up my skirt and reaches my panties. Tears spring to my eyes.

"Stop." And even though it comes out in a whisper, I know he can hear me. But he ignores my plea.

He stands abruptly, his chair squealing against the floor, and shoves mine back. I yelp, and he pries my thighs apart, positioning himself between them from where he kneels in front of me.

The same position he was in the last time we were in the library together. Right before Wes grabbed me and pulled me away, preventing Trey from getting his mouth on me.

His tongue licks slowly up from my knee to the edge of my panties. I want to shove at him, kick him, but I don't dare with that knife in his pocket.

When his nose brushes against the apex of my thighs, he sniffs audibly. I cringe. "Mmm." His hot breath hits my panties, and I want to shrivel. "I hope you taste as good as you smell."

I nearly heave as he repeats the motion on my other leg, leaving a trail of saliva in his wake. Marking me.

His thumb drifts up between my legs, rubbing against my sensitive nub, and I cry out when his mouth latches on my thigh. Sucking like he intends to bruise my whole body.

"Trey, stop!" I yell.

"Not until I find out how wet you are for me."

That's when the door behind me swings open.

Wes

TREY'S GOT his head under Violet's skirt.

He's groping her, feeling her up. And she's letting him.

"See?" Luke mutters. "She's just fucking with your head."

Luke is right. Trey was right. This whole thing has just been a mind game to her. She got in my pants, weaseled her way into my heart, all so I'd call off the revenge plot.

Her head whips around, eyes wide when she spots me. Just like Britt, all over again. "Wes—"

I've got Trey off her and on the floor before either of them can say another word.

Rage blinds me, sending my fists flying into Trey's head and the floor beneath him before finally connecting with his nose. Bone crunches under my fist, and fuck, it hurts so good. No sweeter feeling than the snap of your enemy's bone and carti- lage. He roars in pain like the little bitch he is.

"I told you to fucking stay away from her!" My spit sprays his face.

Luke tugs at my shoulders. Little more than a fly. "Wes! Come on, man! Stop!"

My fists connect with Trey's chest, his eye. A maniacal laugh swells at the image of Trey with a black eye tomorrow to match his bruised nose, and maybe I'll gift him a limp too.

"Think about the team, Novak!"

Right. We need Trey alive for the team.

I let Luke pull me off him.

That's all that matters now. All that should've mattered to me after Violet killed my sister.

My priorities got fucked in this mess. What I need is to focus on hockey, getting drafted, and escaping this hellhole. Getting as far away from Violet fucking Harris as I can.

She hovers near the door, shaking and wide-eyed like I haven't seen her in weeks. Her hands clutched tight around her chest, skirt still askew. My teeth grind together.

This time, Luke doesn't hold me back. He crouches beside a groaning Trey while I stalk toward Violet.

When she cowers, I salivate. I've missed her fear. "You've been fucking around behind my back?"

She shakes her head quickly, eyes growing comically wider. "No! I swear. He threatened me—"

"Yeah? Did he threaten you when you blew him too?"

Her face falls. She's at a loss for words.

"Yeah. I fucking know," I snarl. "How many of my teammates did you blow behind the library? Or is Trey just special?"

Nausea churns in my gut like a tornado. This is fucking happening again. Wasn't enough when I caught my ex cheating on me. Wasn't enough when Violet killed my sister. I still convinced myself I could trust her. That she deserved a second chance.

Still haven't learned my fucking lesson.

"I didn't!" she wails.

More fucking lies.

I punch the wall beside her head, knuckles coming back bloody, but the pain doesn't register. Hard to feel more pain when you're already drowning in it. "I saw the pictures, Violet! You in your underwear, posing for him." I grit my teeth and hiss, "On your fucking knees in front of him."

Tears flood her eyes now. "He made me do that! He put a knife to my throat, Wes. He has a knife on him now!"

I whirl on Trey, still flat on the floor groaning and clutching his bloody nose.

"Fuck you, man!" he spits.

I ignore him and pat him down, searching his pockets for the knife. When I can't find anything, I instruct Luke to search him.

"I don't have a fucking knife," he snaps. "Your little bitch is a liar. She wanted my mouth on her pussy. She was begging for my cock."

Violet shakes her head vehemently, eyes wide. "He said he had one. He's threatened me with a knife before. I just assumed—"

"Explain the photos then. Why didn't you tell me after he took them? Why would you hide that from me?"

She steps toward me, face red and features scrunched up as she tries to reign in her tears. "He said if I told anyone, he'd kill you. Please, Wes. You know me. You can trust me."

That's exactly what Britt said after I found her riding some other guy's cock.

What would I have walked in on if Luke and I showed up a minute later? Trey's dick inside Violet while she moaned, begging him to choke her and call her a good girl? "Tell me, who's tongue feels better on your pussy? Mine or his?"

She's full-on sobbing now, reaching for me. I step back. The thought of her touch makes me want to set myself on fire. "Please, Wes. Please believe me. I didn't want to do any of those things. I would never hurt you like that."

I shake my head. A different sort of fury coiling in my stomach this time. Not the roaring, raging tiger but the hissing, poisonous viper. "I can't believe I let myself trust you again. You killed my fucking sister, and I *forgave* you for that. I forgave you for the worst thing anyone's ever done to me because I'm the biggest fucking moron on the planet. Why did I think putting trust in someone like you would work out?"

Disbelief and disappointment settle into her features, but she meets my gaze. "I will apologize every single day for what I did. A hundred times a day. But until you're ready to forgive me, you'll never believe it. You'll never trust me."

I loom over her, cupping her chin and forcing her to look up at me. One last time. That solid concrete wall I erected after she killed Chloe is back up. Slammed down between us, and impenetrable this time. "Don't let me see your fucking face again. Because I can promise you, you won't like what happens if I do. As far as I'm concerned, the Violet I knew died the same night as my sister." I release her, knowing I'll never touch her again. She knows it too. "You're dead to me."

Chapter 32

Before

Violet

TREY IS AT THIS PARTY. But so is Wes, so I'm not going anywhere.

In the living room, Chloe hands me a red plastic cup full of dark liquid. Her parents are out of town for the weekend, and Chloe and Wes are taking full advantage of their empty house to throw the first summer break party.

Wes is in the kitchen with the other Devils, challenging each other to drinking contests. I don't know when or how, but I'm planning on getting him alone tonight.

"Are my ears bleeding?" I shout to Chloe over the music.

"I'll go tell Luke to turn it down!"

"Are you two official yet?"

They've been practically glued at the hip since the carnival. She chugs from her cup. "I'm waiting until I bang him. Gotta try before I buy."

I laugh and lift my cup to my lips. "Pretty sure trying him would be dating, and buying would be marriage."

She shrugs. "What about you and Wes?"

Before I can swallow a drop, I sputter on my drink. "What do you mean?"

Neither of us has told Chloe about the kiss at the carnival yet. We've been waiting for the right time to break the news to her.

"Oh my god." She rolls her eyes. "How much longer do I have to keep pushing you two together before you finally come to your senses?"

"Wait. What?"

"Violet. I wasn't exactly being subtle. I've spent months trying to get you and Wes together. Leaving you alone together, ambushing you with a double date, dragging you to my parents' house for the weekend. I literally abandoned you with him at the carnival."

My mouth hangs open. "So . . . wait. This whole time, you've wanted me to date your brother?"

I can't believe it. For months, Wes and I have been worrying about upsetting Chloe by giving in to the attraction between us, and that's exactly what she wanted.

She shoves my shoulder. "Obviously! How awesome would that be? You could marry him, and we'd be real sisters! Plus, I wouldn't have to deal with Wes's mopey ass anymore."

"He's never seemed mopey to me." Wes has only ever been charming, smart, funny, dangerous, sexy—

"Because you were lucky enough not to grow up with him. He puts on this act like he's some tough guy who just wants to play hockey and hoe around, but getting cheated on really broke him. He's been so scared of getting hurt like that again, he hasn't let anyone else in. But I could tell the day he met you that you were the only girl who stood a chance at changing that."

My heart aches and warms at the same time. Aching for the pain and hurt Wes has gone through. Warming with hope that

Chloe's right—that Wes is letting me in. Breaking down those walls he built to keep his heart safe so he can finally trust someone with it. Trust *me* with it.

"What if we break up?" I ask. "You said you didn't want to be caught in the middle."

She scoffs. "Like I give a shit about that. I'll still be your best friend, and he'll still be my brother. Your relationship doesn't have anything to do with me."

I laugh, even as I give her arm a playful smack. "Then why did you tell Wes you didn't want us dating?"

"Because it'd make you forbidden fruit." She takes a long gulp from her drink. "If he knew he couldn't have you, he'd want you that much more. If he sensed I was conspiring to get you two together, he'd run for the hills. He needed to realize he was ready for a relationship again on his own, not because I pressured him into it."

"I knew you were up to something." I shake my head. Looking back, Chloe's scheming was obvious, but at the time, I let myself ignore all the signs, not wanting to get my hopes up that Wes could ever be interested in me if it meant I'd get my heart broken.

Though her lying and scheming might be questionable, her motives were pure. Chloe just wanted the best for Wes. And for me.

She finishes her cup before grabbing my arm. "Let's go s-swimming."

I laugh. "Are you already slurring? You're such a lightweight."

"*You're* such a lightweight." She elbows me before hiccuping.

"Did you pregame without me?" I gasp in mock horror as Chloe leads the way out to the patio.

"I would never." She trips on her way out the sliding glass door, but I manage to catch her before she goes down.

"Are you sure you want to go swimming?" I giggle. "Maybe you need to sit down for a minute. I'm pretty sure you're a danger to yourself right now. Possibly others."

"Swimming will help me sober up."

I'm pretty sure I've heard a shower helps sober someone up, so maybe she's right.

She leads me across the grass like she's ice-skating, sending me into another fit of giggles until we reach the pool's edge. Mr. Novak only opened the pool last week, and it's probably still cold this early in the season, especially now that night has fallen. But if Chloe's in, I'm in.

"We have to jump," she declares.

"With our clothes on?"

"No way, these are my best clothes."

I laugh. She's in denim shorts and a pink T-shirt with a hole in the hem.

We strip, giggling the entire time. "Are you sure you want to do this? The water's probably freezing still."

"Don't be a b-baby," she slurs.

But she continues hovering at the pool's edge, not jumping into the water or grabbing my hand to pull me with her.

I lean over and tell her, "I dare you."

For the first time, she hesitates, her face almost blank as she stares into the inky depths.

But we never back down from a dare.

I take a step away from the edge before shoving her with both hands into the pool.

I jump in right after her, the water colliding with my skin like ice. But I don't care, laughing when I come up for air.

For a few seconds, I can't see her as chlorinated water, wet hair, and darkness obstruct my vision. I fling water her way, waiting for a few good splashes in return.

Until I finally notice the silence.

Chloe isn't splashing me back. She's not laughing.

The night air around us is so quiet, so still, a chill rakes down my spine.

"Chloe?"

Nothing. Nothing but more silence. No movement.

I call out her name again, heart hammering now as I move in the direction of where she fell in. My hands find her hair first, floating on the water's surface. She's facedown.

My heart drops to the bottom of the pool.

"*Chloe!*" The scream rips from my throat. I try pushing her toward the edge, back to safety. Try to flip her so she can breathe again, but she's so heavy and the panic is making my head spin. "Chloe!"

Beneath the single light illuminating the patio, a figure emerges, rushing toward us. He's at the pool's edge in seconds, tall and looming over where I'm struggling to get Chloe out of the water.

Wes pulls her out in a second, water rushing as it flows off her.

I climb up the ladder and watch helplessly as Wes presses two fingers to Chloe's neck. Then flattens a hand against her chest. "*Fuck!*" he shouts. "Call 911!"

I scramble for our clothes, finally managing to dig out my phone with shaking hands and dial 911. But once Wes starts performing chest compressions, I lose it. Screaming and screaming, even as the operator answers.

"*Shut the fuck up!*" Wes's scream is like nothing I've ever heard. Every part of me freezes, including my lungs. Silencing me.

He rips the phone out of my hand, putting it on speaker so

the operator can instruct him on how to give Chloe CPR. Even as the sirens approach and the first responders swarm, Wes continues diligently giving her chest compressions, showing no signs of slowing even as he breaks out in a sweat, even as his hands shake.

I keep waiting for her to move. For her to gasp in a breath. To turn and heave up the water flooding her lungs.

But she doesn't.

She doesn't.

She doesn't move. Doesn't breathe.

She's not Chloe anymore.

Chapter 33

After

Violet

I STUPIDLY THOUGHT Wes had fallen in love with me. That he'd forgiven me, against all odds.

I was wrong.

Of course he hasn't forgiven me. I've known since that day outside the courthouse that Wes would never be able to forgive me for what I did to Chloe. To their family. To him.

Maybe he convinced himself he could, for a little while. Kissed me, fucked me, held me, protected me, opened up to me.

But no matter how hard he tried, forgiveness and trust remained out of reach.

Even with the evidence of my supposed infidelity staring him in the face, he should know I'd never betray him like that. He knows what kind of guy Trey is and what he's capable of doing to me. Wes shouldn't believe a sadistic psychopath like Trey over me, but his mind has been warped by what his ex did. He thinks what he witnessed between me and Trey was a repeat of the night he found his ex in bed with another guy, especially because he believes I lied about Trey threatening me with a knife.

I'm still in love with him, and I know I will be for a long time. Long after he's moved on and fallen in love with someone else. The reality of that future already makes my chest ache.

Aneesa storms into the room when she finds me still in bed. "It's been three days, Violet. You can't wallow over that asshole forever."

I've hardly left my bed. Haven't showered, haven't gone to class, and haven't written a word. I can't wrap my head around how I'll ever finish my book now. How can I write a love story when I've lost my muse?

Aneesa rips the blanket off me like that will convince me to get out of bed. All it does is make me curl into a tighter ball. At least my breakup with Wes has gotten Aneesa to talk to me again.

"I'm not bringing you food anymore. You'll need to actually get out of bed and go to the dining hall with me."

"I'm not hungry," I mumble. Since Chloe died, I can't remember the last time I had an appetite.

Aneesa sits on the edge of my mattress, features softer and voice gentler. "You need to keep living your life, Violet. Go to class and get your degree. You can't throw away everything you've worked for over Wes Novak."

I grab my pillow to stifle my sob. That's what Aneesa doesn't understand. None of this is just over Wes. Every night, I relive the same nightmare, waking with a gasp in a puddle of sweat. But it's not a nightmare—it's a memory. Of the night I would give anything to take back.

My words crack alongside my heart. "I miss her so much."

Chloe would have all the answers. She would know what to say to Wes to get him to see reason. Know what to say to me to pull me out from this pit I've fallen into that I'm not sure I'll ever claw my way out of.

But she's not here. My best friend drowned right in front of me. Because of me.

Being with Wes helped me forget, helped me gather the pieces of my shattered heart and start to put them back together. But that deep, raw wound has never healed.

Maybe it never will, and I'm still not sure how I can keep living when she isn't.

"Chloe would want you to take care of yourself." Aneesa's voice is low and soothing as she rubs my shoulder, shaking with a sob. "She wouldn't want to see you punishing yourself for the rest of your life, Violet. Chloe's already forgiven you. You need to forgive yourself now."

I hurt my best friend. I lost her.

The ache of her absence still weighs heavy on my chest every day. With every breath.

I've been expecting Wes to forgive me. But how can he when I can't even forgive myself?

Wes

COACH HAS BEEN RIDING my ass the entire practice. "Head in the game, Novak!"

Blades cut through ice and guys shout. Sounds that used to get my adrenaline pumping, but I can't get my mind off Violet. She's seeped into my brain like poison.

I can't trust her. I saw what she was doing with Trey with my own fucking eyes. Saw the pictures he took of her smiling on her knees before him. Forgiving her for Chloe was impossible enough. Every time I turn around, she stabs me in the back.

Coach blows his whistle when a tall girl steps onto the ice. He shouts at her that this is a closed practice, not that that's ever stopped any of the puck bunnies, but she completely ignores him and waves at me, a deep scowl on her face.

Behind her, the librarian hobbles up. *Oh fuck.* I'm in deep shit.

"Give me five minutes, Coach," I call.

He rolls his eyes but lets me go.

When I reach the wall, the librarian plants her hands on her brittle hips. "I thought I told you not to hurt her."

Before I can defend myself, Aneesa jumps in. "You have no right to treat her like this. I'm sorry you lost your sister, but it was an accident, and you're not justice incarnate. You need to leave Violet alone."

My nostrils flare. So she sent her only allies on campus after me. Like I'm the fucking problem here. Typical women protecting their own even when they're in the wrong. "Don't worry. I'm happy to leave her alone."

"She didn't cheat on you, and you know that. Why she was with you in the first place is a mystery to me, but Violet isn't that kind of person. She wouldn't do that, least of all with a guy as shitty as Trey. Even if she chose you, she does have some standards."

I cross my arms, just about done with their little intervention. "I know what I saw."

Before Luke showed me those photos, I would've thought the same. That Violet wouldn't be capable of betraying me like that. The same way I wouldn't be capable of doing that to her. Too in love with each other to think we could find somebody better. Too in love to want to hurt each other like that.

But I've seen the proof myself. Britt tried making excuses too, sent me dozens of messages begging to get back together, but I didn't fall for it with her and I'm not gonna fall for it with Violet.

She's already gotten her second chance. Not my fault she wasted it.

The librarian steps forward, pointing her finger in my face. Even though she's almost two feet shorter than me, the deep furrow to her brows is intimidating. "You listen to me, boy. That girl is sweet as pie and she doesn't deserve to be treated like dog shit." The curse leaving her mouth almost surprises me enough to laugh if I wasn't being scolded. She hits my chest. "You better grow up and be the man you're pretending to be if you want to deserve her."

I skate back over to the team, circling the center of the rink while Coach gives a "motivational" speech that's mostly a list of everything we're doing wrong. Luke nudges me. "What was that about?"

I snort. "Guilt-tripping me about Violet."

"Have you talked to her?"

"Hell no."

"Why not?"

I give him an incredulous look. "Why would I? You were there too. You saw exactly what I did. And the photos."

"Yeah." Luke drops his gaze, dragging his stick along the ice. "Maybe I had it out for Violet too. For Chloe. I didn't question those photos—I just believed Trey outright because I hated Violet so much for what she did. But . . ."

"But what?" I snap, not liking the direction this is headed.

"But the more I think about it, the more it doesn't sit right with me. We know what kind of girl Violet is. And the type of guy Trey is. You seriously think she'd strip in the middle of the night on campus and let him take photos of her?"

That doesn't sound like Violet at all. "I've got no idea what she's capable of anymore."

"Novak! Valentine! Listen up!"

We fall silent while we pretend to listen to Coach rattle on until Luke adds, "I've got your back no matter what. But if Chloe was here, we both know whose side she'd be on."

Violet

ANEESA IS STUDYING while I binge-watch Netflix when someone knocks on the door.

For a second, my stupid heart flutters. But the knock isn't heavy enough to belong to Wes.

Aneesa opens the door, and my mother barges in.

She's in her hotel manager uniform—dark slacks and vest over a blue button-up so pale it's almost white, complete with a cute little bowtie.

She beelines straight to my bedside and frowns. "So this is what you've been so busy doing?"

My eyes flash to Aneesa. "You called my mom?"

Her eyes are wide. "No, I swear I didn't."

The same way she swore she didn't report Wes to Dean Forrester.

Mom waves us off. "She didn't call me. After my daughter didn't answer dozens of texts or calls for three days, I decided to visit campus myself to make sure she was still alive."

"Well, now you know."

She perches on the edge of my bed, features softening with concern as she brushes my hair behind my ear. "Violet, what happened? What's wrong?"

My eyes burn as the tears build up anew. "I tried telling you. I told you I shouldn't stay on campus. Now Wes hates me more than he already did, and everywhere I look, everywhere I go, I'm reminded of Chloe. I know you blame me for killing her and ruining our lives. That's fine. You can punish me and treat me like shit forever. But my best friend is dead and if I want to lay in bed for three days and finally take time to mourn her, that's what I'm going to fucking do. And I'm not going to let you or Wes or anybody stop me."

I can't believe I just said all that. The words poured out of me unbidden. But I don't regret a single syllable. All of it what I've been longing to say to her for months.

Mom's face falls. I miss how close we used to be. Ending Chloe's life meant ending the relationship with my mother as I knew it too.

We sit in silence for a few moments until she turns to Aneesa. "Would you mind giving me and my daughter a few minutes?"

Aneesa nods quickly and scrambles out of the room, grateful for an excuse to escape. The door quietly clicks shut behind her.

Mom clasps her hands together tight in her lap. "I . . . I don't know what to say, Violet," she starts. "You're right. I've been punishing you for what you did. The legal fees, the judgment from colleagues and the community, the strain between us and the Novaks . . . I've been taking it all out on you. That was wrong of me." She reaches for my hand, a lump sticking in my throat. She used to hug me every time she saw me, but I can't remember the last time she touched me. "You were affected by losing your best friend too, and I'm sorry I didn't support you more through that."

"It's been awful," I whisper, my voice hoarse. "Especially having to mourn her alone."

For a little while, I had Wes. But just as soon as we'd found our way back to each other, I lost him again.

260

Mom scoots closer, running her fingers through my hair. "I am so sorry, sweetheart. I'm sorry I've let you carry this huge burden on your own."

Even though I assumed I was all cried out, more tears hit my pillow. "I thought I could finally talk to Wes about it. But he hates me again."

She shakes her head, somehow adamant. "He doesn't hate you, honey," Mom soothes. "He's hurting. And he's carrying his own guilt over that night."

I prop myself up on my elbow. "What guilt could he have?"

"He was her big brother. He was supposed to protect her and he couldn't."

I shake my head quickly. "That's not his fault. He couldn't have done anything."

"Exactly. But that's not how he feels. He only seems to hate you because he hates himself, and he's taking it out on you—the most obvious target. He was there, and he didn't get to her in time. I'm sure you can understand how heavy a burden that is to bear."

I'm not sure how to process Mom's words. I never considered that Wes may feel any amount of guilt about that night. "So you think Wes was just lashing out at me?"

She presses her lips together. "I'm sure he was very upset with you for your role. But he knows it was an accident. He knows there's a reason the judge gave you a not-guilty verdict. But Wes is certainly struggling with his own inner demons. A battle I would wager he's losing."

If she's right, I wish I'd heard the admission from Wes himself. Wish he'd been willing to open up to me about his darkest feelings eating away at him.

I would've told him it wasn't his fault. That he has no reason to feel guilty. Even if he never wants anything to do with me again, someday I'll tell him.

Mom squeezes my hand. "And Violet? The same is true for you. What happened was a horrible, tragic accident. But it wasn't your fault."

I throw my arms around Mom and sob into her shoulder. The words I've been needing to hear since that night.

Chapter 34

Before

Wes

> Make your move tonight.

THE RUM's already got me a little lightheaded, so the text from Chloe doesn't compute right away.

I text her back.

> Thought you didn't want us together.

> Quit playing dumb. We both know you two are perfect for each other.

I can't help it—I grin at my phone. Not sure how perfect I am for her, but Violet does seem pretty fucking perfect for me.

> Where are you?

No response. The two of them are probably up to their usual antics. Daring each other to do some stupid, immature shit like they're in seventh grade again. Maybe because neither of them really got a childhood. Between changing schools every time Dad was traded to another team and dedicating all her time to skating, Chloe barely had any friends. Violet spent most of her time alone too, finding her friends in the pages of books. Kindred spirits.

Ten minutes pass and Chloe still hasn't texted me back. When Luke challenges me to beer pong, I ask for a rain check and go looking for them. I stop a few of my teammates from breaking shit so my parents don't find out we threw a party and murder us. Trey shoves another plastic cup in my hand before I'm out the door.

Finally, I step out into the cool, summer air, a balm to my skin. A goddamn relief after being clustered in a hot house with a bunch of drunk, sweaty college students.

From the dim porch light, I can just barely make out the shadows of two skinny girls, hovering at the pool's edge. Their laughter floats through the night air, and my chest swells at Violet's. That musical, melodic laugh. I want to be the one responsible for that sound.

She's stripped down to her underwear. I itch to snatch her clothes while she's in the pool and make her parade around in the light so I can rake my gaze over every inch of her body. Pull her into my room and peel off the rest.

Before I can step off the porch, Violet leans over and says something in my sister's ear.

Chloe braces her arms out, like she's about to jump into the dark water. But she hesitates.

A few seconds pass. They both hover there, waiting.

Then Violet shoves her in.

Chloe hits with a loud splash, and I laugh alongside Violet. She jumps in after Chloe and resurfaces seconds later. I want to be in that pool with her. Want to be the one brushing her hair out of her face and yanking her mouth to mine.

I start to strip off my shirt, huge grin on my face, when Violet's giggles turn to blood-curdling screams.

Something's wrong. Chloe isn't moving.

My legs take off before my brain can catch up. When I finally reach the pool, Chloe's facedown in the water.

Violet's trying to grab her, trying to pull her out, but she's too weak and panicked.

I haul my sister's motionless body out of the water and press a frantic hand to her neck. Then her chest. Nothing. No pulse.

My own heart fucking stops.

"Call 911!" I scream to Violet. To anyone.

Violet manages to dig her phone out from their pile of clothes and calls 911. Eventually, her wailing is all I can hear until I snarl at her to shut the fuck up. The 911 operator talks me through giving my sister CPR while the sirens get closer and closer.

But I already know it's too late. My sister isn't moving. She isn't breathing. She's gone.

And Violet, her best friend, is the one who fucking pushed her.

Chapter 35

After

Wes

I CAN'T TAKE it anymore. I've been holding in the truth about that night for months, and it's finally splintered me.

My heart is in my throat the entire ride home. My parents are never going to forgive me for what I'm about to tell them.

I burst into the house while they're still in the middle of dinner, the kitchen filled with the aroma of melted cheese and baked noodles. Dad's famous lasagna. Chloe's favorite.

"Wes?" Mom stands. "What are you doing home, honey?"

"We've got plenty of lasagna," Dad offers.

"I'm not hungry." I swallow, but that lump in my throat doesn't go away. "Actually, can I talk to you?"

They exchange a glance, both of them silently asking if the other knows what this is about. They're both clueless.

"Everything all right, son?" Dad asks.

I take the closest empty chair. "I need to tell you guys something. About the night Chloe died."

Their frowns deepen. Mom sits again and reaches for my hand. "What is it, honey?"

"I didn't just find Chloe in the pool." I take a slow breath through my nose to calm my pounding heart. "I saw Violet push her in."

"Okay," Mom says slowly, brows pulled together in confusion and concern. "We know Violet pushed her."

I close my eyes. "You don't get it. I watched Violet push her in." I grind out the words, each one more difficult than the last. Heart breaking all over again. "I watched Violet jump in after her, and I was just standing there. Laughing. She and I were both laughing, like it was some funny joke. I didn't even realize anything was wrong until Violet started screaming. I should've run over the second she pushed her in." I try to swallow the lump in my throat, but it doesn't go down, and my final words come out hoarse. "I could've saved her."

Mom jumps up from her chair, the legs squealing across the floor before she wraps her arms around me. "Oh, honey. You didn't do anything wrong. You couldn't have saved her."

Words I've needed to hear for a long time but don't deserve.

Dad pats my shoulder. "It's not your fault, son."

I pinch my nose, trying to force the tears back. "Yes, it is. I saw it happen, and I just stood there. Violet pushed her, but she drowned because of me."

I can't hold back the sob anymore. I bury my face in my hands, trying to muffle the agonized sounds leaving my chest.

I could've saved her. I *should've* saved her. That's the thought that's been haunting me every single night since she died. I stood by and laughed while my sister drowned.

I let Violet take all the blame. She was the one who pushed her, after all. If she hadn't done that, my sister wouldn't need saving.

But no matter how many times I told myself that, no matter how much I hurt Violet and punished her for what she did, that ache in my chest never went away. The burden of guilt on my shoulders, threatening to snap me in two, growing heavier and heavier by the day.

I am cleaved in two now.

Mom holds me, rocks me like a small child again while I sob into her arms.

"What happened to Chloe was an accident." Mom's voice is watery now too, but she's trying to hold it together. For me. The only child she has left. "You can't blame yourself for what happened, Wes. You can't blame Violet either. It was an awful, horrible accident. I'm so sorry you lost your sister. But it isn't your fault. Don't think that for even a second."

Dad squeezes my hand, and I brush the tears out of my eyes long enough to see his own shimmering. In my whole life, I've only seen my dad cry twice—when he got the news about Chloe and when we attended her funeral. But his voice shakes again, just like it did when he delivered the eulogy for his only daughter. "You should be proud, Wes. You were such a great big brother to her."

That shatters me completely.

Chapter 36

After

Wes

DURING THE GAME, Trey knocks me off my feet.

"I'm on your team, asshole!" At least on the ice.

His lips are twisted up in a half-smirk, half-sneer. Stick raised high in the air like he's going to bring it crashing down on me.

"On your feet, Novak!" Coach shouts.

By the time I'm up again, Trey is back to chasing guys on the other team and defending the net.

Luke's right. I was an idiot for thinking Violet would actually pose for those photos willingly, that she'd let a guy like Trey kiss her or go down on her after he'd cut her up like a fucking cannibal about to dig into dessert.

I let my past blind me. Let another girl's behavior affect how I treated Violet. Constantly waiting for her to betray me too. So even when she didn't, even when her loyalty to me never wavered, I convinced myself she did.

I need to make things right with her. When she came back to campus, I thought tormenting her would make me feel better. Would bring me the peace that her not-guilty verdict didn't.

But it hasn't. Bullying her for what she did to Chloe has only made me feel worse. Another burden weighing on my soul.

If Chloe knew what I've done to Violet, she'd never forgive me. If she knew that I'm still punishing her—for something she didn't even do—she'd crucify me herself.

I hear her words in my ear, crystal clear like her ghost is right next to me on the ice. Hands on her hips, in her figure skating suit. *Move on, Wes. What's done is done. We only get this one life, and you're wasting it.*

I swallow, choking back tears while the guys dart past me, the crowd chants and jeers, and Coach hollers my name.

I'll never move forward if I'm always stuck in the past. My parents were right—I need to forgive Violet. Forgive myself. Because not forgiving her, not forgiving us, is only hurting me. Not helping.

And I'm fucking tired of the pain. Of feeling it, and causing it.

Violet and I fucked up that night. But it was an accident, and Chloe knows we're sorry.

We're in this together. Which is why I can't properly grieve my sister without Violet by my side.

I won't let Trey or any other asshole get between us again. Violet is the most loyal girl I've ever met. Loyal to her best friend to the grave. Loyal to me, even when I don't deserve it.

My little flower, strong enough to weather any storm. Blooming just for me.

The puck sails past my shoulder, and I snap into action, the buzzer about to blare any second. My blades slice through the ice, and all the sounds at my back are muffled to a dull drone.

With every echoing thud of my pulse in my ears, I brace for the buzzer to go off.

My stick smacks the puck so hard, my shoulder screams, but it whizzes toward the net and right past the goalie's waiting hands.

The buzzer isn't loud enough to drown out the cheers of the Devils, thudding into me and shouting, sticks hoisted in the air in victory.

I barely make it through the handshakes and team meeting in the locker room, every cell in my body buzzing, before I strip off my gear as fast as I can and fly out the door.

Violet

WHAT HAPPENED to Chloe was my fault. But it was also an accident.

I'll have to live with the guilt of what I did forever, but I can't keep punishing myself. Aneesa was right—Chloe would want me to be happy. She would want me to move forward. She knows how much I miss her. How what I did haunts me every day.

But there's no undoing what I did. And now I have to find a way to be okay with myself. To keep living, even if I have to do it without her.

I can't wait for Wes to forgive me, and I'm not putting up with the pranks or the torment from him and the Devils anymore. Wes may think he is judge, jury, and executioner, but he's wrong. The judge decided I'm not guilty. We'll all have to live with that.

I check the time on my phone. His game should be ending

—I still have enough time to make it across campus to confront him.

I need Wes to know that punishing me isn't going to bring Chloe back. This needs to stop. If we avoid each other, we can deal with the other being on campus until he graduates in the spring.

If he's not willing to do that, then I'll leave. Maybe Mom will let me come home, but even if she doesn't, I'll be fine. I'll rent an apartment and go to a community college. Or maybe I'll get a few jobs while I write my books and publish them.

The thought of Chloe never getting to read any of my books shatters my heart. But writing them, dedicating the first one to her, will help me start putting the pieces back together.

I take the long route to the ice rink, attempting to psych myself up and rehearse what I'm going to say to Wes. I don't expect forgiveness or friendship. But I do hope he'll listen.

By the time I make it to the rink, the parking lot is nearly empty, the game long over. Shit. Maybe I'm too late. Maybe he's already left.

I hurry inside and to the locker room. Silent on the other side of the door.

"Wes?" I call out.

Silence.

I knock on the door. "Wes?"

Nothing. I give a tug on the handle, but it doesn't budge.

I'm not letting him avoid me. Until he opens that door, I'm not leaving. I'll bang on this door all night, blow up his phone, whatever it takes to get him to listen to me.

"Wes!" I shout. Maybe he's not in there. Maybe I already missed him.

Just as I'm about to turn and head back, the door swings open.

A hand reaches out and grabs my arm, yanking me into the room and slamming the door shut.

Chapter 37

After

Wes

SHE'S NOT in her dorm or the dining hall. When I get to the library, the old librarian is the only one behind the desk, glasses drooping down her nose as her eyes dart across the page of the book open in front of her.

"Is Violet putting books away?"

The librarian scowls when she sees me. "She's not here. And I hope you have a grand gesture planned for her that's better than *hey, uh, my bad.*"

Jesus, I don't have time for another lecture. "Any idea where I can find her?"

The librarian shrugs and returns to her book.

Right. I grit my teeth, head back out of the library, and pull out my phone, sweeping past notifications to call Violet.

Her phone rings and rings. She's not answering.

This is why I didn't want to call or text in the first place. She doesn't want to talk to me, and the only way I can force her to is in person.

I check my texts when I notice one from Trey.

Don't worry. We're gonna take care of your girl for you, pussy.

Fuck.

Chapter 38

After

Violet

A DEVIL in a white hockey mask pins me against the door with his arm across my throat. Four of his teammates line up behind him, all of their faces masked.

But there's nothing Trey can do to disguise his eyes. I'd recognize them anywhere.

Terror pools low in my belly.

A swift glance across the Devils with sticks in their hands tells me Wes isn't among them. Two whose names I don't remember, juniors. Then a familiar pair of brown eyes—Brody. The final player shorter and ganglier than the others—Mason, the freshman who needs to prove himself.

"Wes!" I shout, praying he's just outside the locker room or stepping out of the showers.

Trey snickers, his arm digging harder against my throat. A clear warning. "He's not here."

"Let me go. I came to talk to him."

Last time Trey had me cornered, I didn't dare fight back. But this time, I'll go down swinging.

He's not going to intimidate me or terrorize me anymore.

That chapter is over. I don't deserve any of this, and I'm not putting up with it for another second.

I know I can't take down five huge hockey players single-handedly, especially not without a weapon, but I'll be damned if I go down without a fight.

"Wes doesn't want to see you," Trey snarls, the mask distorting his words even as he leans closer so we're eye level. "When are you gonna get that through your thick head?"

I claw at Trey's arms, but he doesn't budge. "Let me go, Trey."

He snorts, and the guys behind him chuckle. "We don't follow your orders," he tells me. "You follow ours, sweetheart."

"No, I *don't*." I spit at him and it splatters across his mask.

A horrifying smile crawls across his face through the cluster of holes in his mask. "So she finally wants to play." His finger travels down my cheek, every cell in my body recoiling. "We have plans for you, pretty girl. You're coming with us."

"I'm not going anywhere with you."

He drops his arm from my throat, and my hands instinctively fly to my neck. "You will if you want to save your friend."

My stomach turns to lead.

Aneesa. Trey did something to Aneesa. "What are you talking about?"

"Don't want another roommate's blood on your hands, do you?" He slaps his palms above my head and leans in, hot breath curling across my cheeks from the tiny holes in his mask. "The first one might not look like an accident anymore."

"You're lying." But the words tremble. I wouldn't put it past Trey to do something to Aneesa to get to me.

I haven't seen Aneesa since this morning. Who knows where they took her.

He can do whatever he wants to me. But I can't let him lay a finger on her.

Trey laughs. "Would I lie to you, sweetheart?" His hand slithers around my hip. "Wasn't exactly hard to find her."

I can't let anything bad happen to her because of me. I won't.

"So what's it going to be? You coming with us willingly? Explain to your friend why she's there." He leans in, mouth curdled like rotten milk. "Or are we dragging you?"

Fear like I've never felt grips my throat and crushes my windpipe. But I lift my chin and meet Trey's malevolent stare through the holes in his mask. "Let's go."

IN THE CAR, they hold me in place and blindfold me. Once we lurch to a halt, three different pairs of hands drag me out of the car so hard, my shoulder nearly pops out of its socket. Too many to fight them off or tear at my blindfold.

I scream and someone claps a hand over my mouth while the rest of them tug me into a building, our shoes echoing, dust filling my nose. I have no idea where we are.

I manage to shake off the hand. "Aneesa!"

But her voice doesn't come. Did they gag her? Put her in another room?

Is it already too late to save her?

"Where is she?"

Someone pulls my blindfold off right before they shove me to the ground.

Trey looms over me, a hideous smile beneath his mask. The other Devils hold their hockey sticks like bats. "You're just as stupid as your little boyfriend."

She's not here. He manipulated me into coming here of my own free will. He's the worst monster I've ever met, but at least she's safe. He would've brought me here either way—quietly or kicking and screaming.

But at least I don't need to worry about Aneesa.

Only myself.

"Why are you doing this? Wes told you to leave me alone."

"Wes was the mastermind. He planned all of this. He's just too much of a little bitch to follow through." Trey bends, twisting his fingers in my hair and nearly ripping it from my scalp. I cry out. "An idiot who fell in love with a little pussy."

My guts turn watery. Wes planned this ambush back when he was still plotting his revenge against me. If it's anything like the night of manhunt, I need to start running.

But I'm too late.

Trey is already aiming a kick at my stomach.

His foot collides with my abdomen so hard, I think my intestines explode. I scream, the pain the only thing I can feel, consuming my entire mind.

He circles me, letting the pain settle deep while he figures out where to land his next blow.

"Tried getting him kicked off campus so we could have a little more fun with you, but you spoiled that, didn't you?"

My mouth falls open. "You?" I gasp, amazed blood isn't pooling from my mouth. "You were the one who reported Wes to Dean Forrester?"

I can't believe I blamed Aneesa, even after she swore to me that she didn't say anything.

"Yep. But thanks to you, Novak's still here," he snarls. "Even after everything he did to you, you didn't send his ass packing. All because you liked riding his cock."

"Why would you try to get your own captain kicked off campus?"

"Novak never deserved to be captain. And you never deserved his protection. With him gone, guess who would be captain?" I can practically feel Trey's sneer as he leans down and whispers into my ear. "Guess who would have you all to himself?"

He stops in front of me, and I don't even have time to flinch before his foot rushes at me, finding its mark between my ribs.

I scream, the sharp pain ripping through every fiber. My vision flashes once, twice.

I try to scramble back but don't get far before I bump against someone's shoe. They kick me forward, nearly splintering my spine in two. My scream echoes in the empty building.

"Shame you didn't get to ride my cock at the party," Trey croons. "We would've had so much fun. You never would've thought about Novak again."

My head is spinning, but I still manage to taunt him. "I was already having plenty of fun with Wes before the frat party."

Trey crouches in front of my face. "I wasn't talking about that party." He reaches out and sweeps a strand of hair behind my ear. How he can kick me one second and touch me tenderly the next sickens me. "The one at Novak's. The one where you drowned your little friend."

My eyes scramble to find his face, still masked and lips twisted in wicked amusement. "Did you roofie my drink at that party too?"

I never actually drank a drop that night. I started to, but Chloe made me sputter before I could.

"Yep. Amazed you two stayed upright."

You two.

The blood in my veins hardens to ice.

You two.

The way Chloe was slurring and stumbling shortly after she started drinking. I called her a lightweight, accused her of pregaming without me, when really—

"You spiked Chloe's drink?"

He pats my cheek before hooking a finger in my mouth. "I told you. That threesome would've been mind-blowing."

Trey roofied Chloe's drink. That's why she looked so out of it while we stood by the edge of the pool, after I dared her to jump in.

I'm the one who pushed her. But maybe she wasn't able to swim because of the drug Trey gave her.

Even if it didn't cause her death, he still drugged my best friend. He planned to take advantage of her that night. Of both of us.

I wrap my lips around the finger he still has in my mouth, his eyes lighting up before I bring my teeth down as hard as I can.

He howls, lurching back. "Fucking *bitch!*"

I scramble up and try to keep my feet under me, aim for the tiny opening out of the empty warehouse, but someone strikes me down from behind.

I tumble to the concrete, scraping my hands and elbows and just narrowly missing a strike to the chin.

A hockey stick comes down on my head, the pain nearly splitting my skull open.

I curl up in the fetal position as all five of them surround me. Brody lands a kick to my back. Someone else strikes my legs with a stick.

Snot dribbles out of my nose, mixing with my tears. When Trey aims a punishing kick at my stomach again, blood sputters from my mouth.

His venomous words rattle in my head. "You're fucking *dead.*"

Chapter 39

After

Wes

THE TEAM HAS ALREADY LEFT the locker room by the time I get there.

Thank god I took her phone that day I ditched her in the middle of nowhere. Programmed her phone's location into my GPS.

She never did figure out how I always knew exactly where to find her.

"I'm coming, little flower," I whisper.

I know exactly what they have planned for her. Because I planned out every step of it. But I called it off weeks ago.

I guess they decided to take matters into their own hands. Under Trey's fucking leadership.

They picked a new location, thinking I'd go where we originally planned. So I wouldn't be able to save her.

But that's not happening again. I couldn't save Chloe, but I will save Violet.

I'm doing seventy and praying I don't get pulled over when the abandoned warehouse comes into view. Secluded, where no one would think to look for her.

The second I'm out of the car, Violet's screams rip through my eardrums.

Just like that night she was screaming over my sister's dead body.

But this time, it's Violet I need to save. And she's still alive. There's still hope.

If I can get to her in time.

In the warehouse, it's five of them on one of her. Every one of those motherfuckers landing blows on a defenseless girl. All of them wearing those fucking masks.

I'll skin each of them alive before I burn them from the toes up.

"Get the fuck away from her!" I bellow, charging right for them like I'm not outnumbered five to one.

The other guys jump back as I aim right for their leader.

Trey braces when he spots me coming and swings his stick at my head.

He misses. That's why he didn't get captain.

I grab the stick and we grapple over it, the other guys hovering nearby, torn between us. Their captain and the traitor they made the mistake of following. They'll each get their turn after I've handled him. "I fucking told you not to do this! You're all dead!"

Trey swings a kick for my balls but connects with my leg. Still hard enough for me to lose my grip on the stick. He swings it down, but I grab it again and pull it so hard, it slips out of both our hands, landing on the concrete with a clatter.

None of our teammates move to grab it. Neither does Violet, who's motionless now, still curled up on the ground.

My heart's going to explode if I can't check her pulse. Make sure she's still with me. I need to get her to safety *now*.

I throw a punch at Trey, connecting with his jaw and

making him spit out a curse. Delaying him long enough to give me time to spin and reach her.

I feel for a pulse, her neck still warm, heart still hammering hard beneath her skin.

So fucking strong. My resilient little flower.

"You're okay, baby." I grab her hand to let her know I'm here, I'm not going fucking anywhere without her, and her perfect hazel eyes flutter open. I let out a sound that's somewhere between a gasp of relief and a sob. "I love you, Violet. I love you so fucking much. I'm sorry I wasn't here to protect you, but I'm here now. You're going to be all right. I'm getting you out of here."

"The hell you are." Cold, sharp metal presses against my neck. Violet's eyes widen in horror, and she would scream again if she could. I freeze, my team's eyes round behind their masks. "Stand."

The last thing I want to do is obey a command from the devil himself, but with a knife pressed to my throat, it's my only chance at getting Violet out of here alive.

With every ounce of willpower in me, I release her hand. "I'm not leaving you," I murmur.

I stand slowly as Trey grips my shoulder and keeps the blade biting into my neck.

"Sorry it had to end this way, buddy," he says.

Maybe if I can swing back with my elbow, I can get him to drop the knife—

"Say goodbye to your girl." He leans closer, squeezing my shoulder. "She's mine now."

Before I can make another move, Trey swipes the blade across my neck.

Chapter 40

After

Violet

I DIDN'T THINK I could scream anymore, my throat ragged and raw, but I scream for him.

I scream for Wes as his knees hit the concrete and blood pours from his neck.

Too fast.

Too fucking fast.

The agony is tearing me apart at the seams. Every inch of my body has been ripped through by a tornado. With every kick they landed to my stomach, back, legs, arms, head, all I've been able to think about is the pain. Unending. Unyielding.

But none of it holds a candle to watching the man I love try to staunch the flow of blood from his own throat.

If Trey managed to cut his windpipe, Wes won't be able to breathe. If he sliced through a major artery, Wes has only minutes before he succumbs to the blood loss.

Maybe seconds.

Seconds left to tell him everything I need to. To tell him how much I love him. How much I ache for him when he's not around. How being with him helps me remember my best friend and grieve her. How his laugh makes me smile even when I've forgotten how. How getting wrapped in his arms makes me feel like I'm home.

I came here to save Aneesa. But I've only endangered Wes.

"Wes!"

But it's not my voice calling out to him.

Still, he doesn't glance their way. "Violet," he breathes. Tears well. He can still talk. He can still breathe.

With a bloody hand, he reaches for me, grasping mine like I'm his lifeline, the only thing tethering him to this world.

Footsteps charge into the warehouse, echoing around us.

Nineteen hockey players stampede across the concrete with sticks in hand, and somehow, miraculously, Wes manages a tiny smile. "I called for backup."

Luke is at the helm, and once he spots me and Wes covered in blood, he sets his sights on Trey, still clutching the knife. "Fucking *drop* it, dude!"

Shouts before a meaty slap against the concrete wall. Behind Wes, the rest of the team has Trey pinned and disarmed.

Relief manages to rush through me, even as every inch of me remains motionless in agony.

"You three, help me get these two to the hospital," Luke instructs. The first time I've ever seen him like this—giving orders, taking charge. I'm reminded again of why Chloe liked him so much. "The rest of you, get those assholes back to Coach. Let him figure out what to do with them."

Wes

ALL THE NURSES and doctors in this fucking hospital are incompetent. The cut across my throat is a superficial one. Didn't slash my windpipe or hit any major arteries. For someone who loves cutting people with knives so much, Trey sure is shit at it. A few stitches to the neck and I'm practically good as new, yet they keep fucking worrying about me when they should be worrying about *her*.

"Why the fuck is no one in here with her?" I roar out her open door. "My girl just got fucking assaulted! This is your last warning. If someone doesn't get their ass in this room and take care of her *now*, I'm dragging you all down to hell with me!"

A pissy nurse and a dead-eyed doctor hustle into the room. I don't really give a fuck what kind of attitude they want to give me as long as they do their fucking jobs and take care of her.

Despite the pain she's in, she manages to smile every time I bark an order.

Her mom arrives about an hour after I made the call, and I'm about to step out of the room to give them some privacy when she grabs my arm. "Thank you for protecting my daughter, Wes." Her eyes are shiny. "And for forgiving her."

I just hope she's forgiven me too. For not believing her. For letting that scumbag Trey get anywhere fucking near her.

As soon as she can speak, she tells me what Trey confessed to her while he and the rest of those scumbags were beating the shit out of her: He drugged Chloe's drink the night she died. He drugged Violet's too, but she never drank any of it.

Who knows. Maybe I could've lost them both that night.

Apparently, a routine toxicology report doesn't detect GHB, so the report only showed alcohol in Chloe's system during her autopsy. Maybe if we'd known to look for it, the medical examiner would've been able to determine whether she would've survived the push into the pool if she hadn't been drugged.

Even if Violet hadn't pushed her, maybe Chloe still would've jumped. Maybe I still wouldn't have been able to save her.

Trey will never be held responsible for what he did to my sister. Even if we could somehow prove that the GHB is what ultimately led to Chloe's death, we can't prove he was the one who put it in her drink.

But we can hold him responsible for what he did to Violet.

I take her hand and kneel at her bedside. Her head tilts, puzzled. "I'm so fucking sorry, Violet. I put all the blame on you. I put you through hell and back to pay for a crime that wasn't even yours."

"I pushed her," Violet whispers, voice hoarse and eyes shiny.

I blink back my own tears, shaking my head. "Yeah, and look how many other people push their friends into pools. They're not criminals, and neither are you. You and I both know Chloe wouldn't have died if Trey hadn't spiked her drink."

She swipes at her tears and sniffles, squeezing my hand tighter. "I know that's supposed to make me feel better, but it doesn't."

I swallow, breath shuddering. "That night, I was watching you and Chloe from the patio. I saw the whole thing. I watched her hit the water, but I didn't run over until I heard you screaming. If I'd gotten there sooner—"

"No." Her voice is hard, adamant. "Nothing that happened that night is your fault. None of it, Wes."

Her words make my bottom lip wobble until I bite down on it. "Then I want you to listen to me, Violet. I don't want you to go another day feeling guilty either. It wasn't your fault." I stand when she buries her face in her hands and starts to cry. I wrap my arms around her and pull her into me. "None of it."

She's able to leave the hospital after a few days, and I take her right back to my apartment. The only time I leave her side is to meet with Dean Forrester in his office to tell him everything that happened. He's already got the gist of it from the police, but he wants my perspective so he can make his determination about the punishment my five teammates deserve.

I point at my neck before showing him a picture of Violet, bruised and battered in her hospital bed. "Whatever punishment you think this deserves."

The news comes in an email from Coach first.

Five of our players have been suspended from campus. All of them are facing criminal charges.

Finally some fucking justice.

After a couple weeks, Violet's weaned off the painkillers and her bruises have nearly faded. The doctor said she's lucky she only sustained bruised ribs and no concussion.

I say Trey's lucky to be standing. All five of those guys are fucking lucky to be alive.

Aneesa's been visiting Violet almost daily, bringing her meals and snacks. Like I don't know how to feed my fucking girlfriend.

I snap at her whenever she knocks and wakes Violet up or overstays her welcome. She snaps right back. I can't help but respect her for it, and Violet seems to find our bickering amusing.

Aneesa might never forgive me for how I treated Violet. But I'm glad. That means my girl has a good friend looking out for her.

Without Chloe, she needs a friend.

I know it would make my sister happy.

Chapter 41

After

Violet

"So you're officially dating Wes now?" Aneesa sits with me on Wes's couch, Netflix on the TV in front of us and a bowl of popcorn between us. He's supposedly at the library to give us a girls' night, but I have a feeling he's waiting right outside the door in case I need anything.

Beside us sits a tower of library books. Edith has been bringing me a stack every week to keep me busy. Wes told me that she and Aneesa showed up at the rink to scold him for breaking my heart, and when I thanked her for talking sense into him, she told me she's happy to yell at him anytime.

A grin spreads so wide across my face, it hurts. "He started calling me his girlfriend in the hospital."

Though I felt like his girl long before that. Maybe since the moment his eyes landed on me.

Aneesa crunches on a handful of popcorn. "I guess he's demonstrated his worth in the past few weeks by how well he's been taking care of you. I miss sharing the dorm with you, though."

"I miss it too. I'm sure I'll be back next semester. Wes is worried they're going to stick him with another roommate."

"He's Wes Novak. I'm sure if he tells the administration he doesn't want a roommate for his final semester, they'll agree to it. Especially given everything you two have been through."

As much as I love living with Aneesa, I hope she's right. Staying here with Wes has been heaven, even through recovery. The bad pain days, the nightmares that have me screaming awake in the middle of the night, he's always right there to wrap his arms around me, pull me against him, and remind me that no one is ever going to lay a finger on me with him around.

"Listen." Aneesa clasps her hands together on her lap. "I'm sorry I pushed you so much to stay away from Wes. I thought I was protecting you, but that wasn't my decision to make. I should've—"

I hold up my hand to stop her. "If I've learned anything, it's that there's no point dwelling on what-ifs. You're an amazing friend, Aneesa. I couldn't ask for a better one."

The best friend I've had since Chloe. I have a feeling that if they'd ever gotten a chance to meet, the three of us would be inseparable.

Aneesa wraps me in a sudden hug, nearly knocking over the bowl of popcorn.

If there's anything I've learned this semester, it's that you can't undo what's already been done. You just have to learn from it and do better from now on.

I'll always regret pushing Chloe in that pool. But I also know there's a chance she would've jumped in all on her own. There's a good chance she would've survived if Trey hadn't drugged her.

I know Chloe forgave me long ago for what I did that night, and I'm finally forgiving myself.

"So now that you've nursed me back to health, I can finally tell you what I went to the locker room to say to you that day."

Wes pauses his delicious massage of my foot and I nearly groan in protest. "What's that?"

"I was going to offer to leave campus if that would make you happy."

Wes tips his head back and laughs. "Good one, baby. You're not going fucking anywhere."

I beam at him. "Then I'm pretty sure I've recovered enough for a proper reunion."

"Yeah?" He grins and scoops me onto his lap like an eager puppy, making me giggle.

Despite his impatience, his kiss is tender and slow. His lips parting mine gently, the perfect fit.

When his tongue sweeps into my mouth, I moan. I grind against his cock, already hard for me, and now I'm the impatient one.

But Wes continues taking his time with me. His hands stay soft on my neck until they sweep into my hair and massage my scalp. I groan. "I could get used to this."

A smirk plays across his lips, still pressed against my own. "Good. Because this is the rest of your life, little flower."

I lift a teasing brow, even as my heart stutters. "The rest of my life, huh? Isn't it a little soon to be talking about marriage?"

His playful smirk turns serious. "I told you, Violet. You're mine. You're not getting rid of me now."

I crash my lips against his and thread my fingers through his hair. Exactly the words I wanted to hear. Needed to hear.

Wes lays me on the couch with heartbreaking tenderness. "Is this okay?" Concern in those startling blue eyes.

Maybe when I'm further in my recovery—physically and mentally—he'll be able to wrap his belt around my throat again. Or his hand. Make me crawl to him. Beg. Maybe even chase me through the woods again. Someday, I'll admit to him I liked it a lot more than I let on.

But for now, this is exactly what I want.

"Perfect," I whisper.

His mouth is on mine again until he kisses from my chin up my jaw and down my neck. Every kiss, every brush of his hands against my skin, sends shivers down my spine.

I've had him so many times before, but this time is different. Because I know I have every part of Wes now. Not just his tongue and fingers and cock, but his heart too.

The warmth from his mouth on my neck vanishes when he peers down at me. "You're everything to me, Violet. No one else will touch you, and no one will even think about hurting you with me around." He grabs my hand and sets it against his chest, over his heart. "You have me. All of me. As long as you want me, I'm yours. I'd burn down every inch of this world if you asked me to."

I grin at him. "That's a very kind offer, but I'd like to continue living in this world with you for a long, long time if that's all right with you."

"Couldn't ask for anything better," he murmurs.

I pull him down to me in another kiss. We stay like that for a while until his hand starts inching up my shirt.

He slips it tenderly over my head and unclasps my bra, taking it off slowly.

When my torso is bare before him, he admires me for a few moments. Not touching yet, just staring. "I am so fucking lucky," he breathes, enunciating every word.

I'm about to tell him I'm the lucky one when he steals my breath, sucking my nipple into his mouth. He's gentle at first, still uncertain about what will hurt me, until I grind my pussy against his leg and tug his hair. His hands come around my back, pulling my body closer to him as he sucks on me harder.

I'm already drenched, so ready for him. Every part.

When he releases me, he lets out a groan that makes my toes tingle before sucking on my other nipple. I arch into him.

"Wes," I gasp. "I can't wait any longer."

He chuckles and slides his way down my body. "I've missed hearing you beg, baby."

He slides my shorts down, taking my panties with them. I am fully bare below him now, and he takes in every inch of me. "You are so fucking gorgeous."

He settles himself down between my thighs, hot breath hitting the wetness between my legs. I hiss just as his lips press a tender kiss to my clit.

The contact makes me jolt. "Oh my god!"

"Just you wait, baby." His tongue glides up my slit, and I writhe beneath him. "Good girl," he murmurs. "Come on my tongue."

His tongue works me in big, sweeping strokes, taking his time building up that pleasure between my legs. When my clit starts throbbing, he pulls it between his lips, sucking me hard.

I cry out, arching off the couch. "Wes," I breathe. "I'm going to come."

"I know, baby. I want your clit throbbing in my mouth." With that, he sinks a finger inside me.

The stretch makes tears of pleasure spring to my eyes. He thrusts his finger inside me, sucking on my clit as hard as he can, and pleasure mounts so high, it sets me on fire.

When my pussy starts to clench around his finger, he pumps inside me. "Yes, baby. Come for me."

I do. Crying out his name first before I scream, orgasm

ripping through me like I've never felt before. My mind shrapnel.

His jeans are unzipped in a second and he slides his cock inside me while my pussy is still throbbing. He takes his time, rocking into me slowly. Like I'm made of glass.

Until I pull him closer and tell him, "I want you to fuck me so hard, my nails leave scars on your back."

That's all he needs to hear.

He slams in to the hilt, making me scream in ecstasy. He rubs at my clit with his thumb, continuing to drive overwhelming pleasure through me. It's been so long since we've come together, my clit already aching for another release.

I don't think I'll ever be able to go that long without Wes Novak inside me again.

"You're so fucking tight around my cock." His thumb swirls around my clit, pulling a moan from the depths of my chest. "This is mine." His hand travels to my ass and squeezes. "This is mine." To my breast. "This is mine." Then to my chest, my heart pounding rhythmically beneath his palm. "And most importantly, *this* is mine. All of you, every inch. I'll remind you every day. I'll never let you forget."

My nails dig into his back, scraping down. "Remind me harder."

He rams into me, my tits bouncing wildly as he drives pleasure through me, the orgasm rising until it finally crests.

I throw my legs around his hips to bury him as deep inside me as he can get as every wave of my orgasm crashes.

"I love you so fucking much, Violet." With a loud, long groan, he thrusts hard once, twice, three times before he collapses on top of me. His cock pulsates as he shoots his cum deep inside me, my pussy clenching with every throb.

We lay there together, catching our breaths, Wes crushing me into the couch until he brushes a kiss against my lips. "I don't know if I've said this yet . . . I know you don't need my forgiveness, but you have it. And I hope you can forgive me too."

This time when his words make me cry, they're happy tears. "You don't need mine either, but I do." I stroke my fingers down his cheek, soft and hard at the same time. Just like the rest of him. "Thank you."

Epilogue

Violet

WES IS TRYING to teach me how to skate again and it's going terribly.

His loud, musical laugh carries across the rink every time he tries to release me only for my arms to pinwheel right before he catches me.

He guides us to the edge of the rink, fully supporting me, the only way I'm able to stay upright on my skates. He spins me, pushing me up against the wall, cupping the back of my head, and bringing my mouth to his.

When his hand slides up my shirt, he groans. "What do you say to fooling around on the ice?" he murmurs against my lips.

My thighs clench.

"I've got a surprise for you first," I tell him.

I pull off my skates and rush to my bag, pulling out a huge stack of pages bound together.

He beams when I hand it to him. "Holy shit. Did you finish your book?"

I grin and nod, the excitement and pride on his face making

the accomplishment even sweeter. Making all the blood, sweat, and tears worth it.

"I can't wait to find out how filthy it is."

"Extremely," I tell him. "Read the dedication."

He flips the page, already knowing I've dedicated it to his sister.

"To Chloe," he reads. "You are a sister in the truest sense of the word. Without you, I never would've written this. Thank you."

His throat bobs as he swallows. He's already swiping at a tear.

And he hasn't even gotten to his dedication yet.

So I read it to him. "To Wes, you are the reason I could write a happy ending."

Acknowledgments

To Alex, thank you for your endless support of me and my career. You've never doubted me for a second, and it's your unfailing belief in me that keeps me believing in myself. I say it a hundred times a day, but I need to immortalize it in ink: I love you.

To my betas, Lauren, Jenni, Kelsey, and Kira, thank you so much for your incredible feedback and cheerleading! Your early reads gave me the confidence I needed when I had my doubts about this book. To Lauren and Kelsey, thank you for always making my books better. I truly never want to publish a book without you two.

To my readers, thank you, thank you, *thank you* for taking a chance on my books. I wake up every day amazed that this is my career and that I get to share my dark, twisted love stories with all of you. I'm honored by your enthusiasm and support, and I hope I can continue giving you book boyfriends to add to your collection. I couldn't do this without you. *Thank you.*

About the Author

Harmony West writes dark forbidden romance. She enjoys her love stories with a side of mystery, twists, and spice.

For updates on Harmony West's latest releases, subscribe to her newsletter at www.harmonywestbooks.com/subscribe or follow her on social media @authorharmonywest.

Printed in Great Britain
by Amazon

43936679R10179